Midnight Peril

by Vicki L. Andrews

Genesis Press Inc.
Columbus, Mississippi

Indigo Love Stories are published by
Genesis Press, Inc.
406A 3rd Avenue North
Columbus, MS 39701

Copyright © 1998 by *Vicki L. Andrews*

MIDNIGHT PERIL

ISBN: 1-885478-27-5

Manufactured in the United States of America

First Edition

To My Best Girlfriends:
Lesa, Sharon, and Nancy
and to my daughter
Adrionna and son Seth.

Indigo Love Stories

Indigo Love Stories are available from Genesis Press:

Everlastin' Love by Gay G. Gunn
1-885478-02-X   10.95
Nowhere to Run by Gay G. Gunn
1-885478-13-5   10.95
Pride And Joi by Gay G. Gunn
1-885478-34-8   15.95
Dark Storm Rising by Chinelu Moore
1-885478-05-4   10.95
Shades of Desire by Monica White
1-885478-06-2   8.95
Reckless Surrender by Rochelle Alers
1-885478-17-8   6.95
Careless Whispers by Rochelle Alers
1-885478-00-3   8.95
Gentle Yearning by Rochelle Alers
1-885478-24-0   10.95
Breeze by Robin Lynette Hampton
1-885478-07-0   10.95
Whispers in the Sand by LaFlorya Gauthier
1-885478-09-7   10.95
Love Unveiled by Gloria Greene
1-885478-08-9   10.95
Love's Deceptions by Charlene A. Berry
1-885478-10-0   10.95
Yesterday Is Gone by Beverly Clark
1-885478-12-7   10.95
A Love to Cherish by Beverly Clark
1-885478-35-6   10.9
Love Always by Mildred E. Riley
1-885478-15-1   10.95
Passion by T.T. Henderson
1-885478-21-6   10.95
Glory of Love by Sinclair LeBeau
1-885478-19-4   10.95
Again, My Love by Kayla Perrin
1-885478-23-2   10.95
Midnight Peril by Vicki Andrews
1-885478-27-5   10.95
Quiet Storm by Donna Hill
1-885478-29-1   10.95
Rooms of the Heart by Donna Hill
1-885478-41-0   4.99
Dark Embrace by Crystal W. Harris
1-885478-47-X   4.99
No Regrets by Mildred E. Riley
1-885478-33-X   15.95
Naked Soul by Gwynne Forster
1-885478-32-1   15.95

CHAPTER I

Leslie Hughes and her client, Horace Brown, stood as requested, impatient and nervous, awaiting the announcement that could adversely change Horace's life forever. She felt her heart stop; her blood seemed to cease to flow as the hushed tone of the courtroom smothered them.

"We the jury find the defendant, Horace Brown, guilty of involuntary manslaughter."

Leslie's heart sank as she saw the heartbroken man slump low beside her. Leslie struggled to maintain her professional dignity as she stood beside an innocent man. Clearly in shock, Horace's face turned an ashen gray, and Leslie feared he might faint. She gently touched his shoulder and applied mild pressure, urging him to sit.

"Does the defendant wish to waive time for sentencing?" Judge Sherman said.

"Yes, Your Honor." Leslie replied, forcing herself to turn her attention back to the judge. She continued to lightly stroke her client's back.

"Thank you, jurors, for your participation in this matter. The attorneys may want to speak to you regarding your decision, and you are free to do so once the courtroom has been cleared," Judge Sherman advised.

"All rise," the bailiff called, as Judge Sherman left his lofty position and quickly disappeared.

Turning to face her client whose face was hidden in his dark, large, calloused hands, the hands of a hard-working man, she angrily swiped at a tear, clearly unable to withhold her disappointment at the outcome of this case. Tears were not for lawyers. There was no place for sympathy either. She knew the rules of the game, and she always tried to play them the way it was expected, but this case—this case—caused butterflies to launch in her stomach. An angry swoop and dive of emotions ran through her like a freight train, especially once she scanned the courtroom and noted that Jeffrey Brown wasn't even there to witness the fall his father had just taken.

⁂

Horace blocked out the remainder of the technical language between his lawyer and the judge as he reflected back on that horrible day almost ten months ago. In his mind, it replayed like something that just happened yesterday.

Jeff came running into the house screaming, "Dad! Dad!"

Horace awoke with a start, mouth dry, his mind not fully engaged yet. His heart beat fast as he was startled from a dream.

"What? What's wrong?" he remembered asking, his voice thick and heavy with the grogginess of sleep.

"I'm in trouble. It wasn't my fault! It wasn't my fault!"

"What wasn't your fault? What are you talking about?"

"That stupid fool jumped out at the car. I swear he did!"

"Who? Slow down, Son, what are you talking about? Who jumped out? What car?"

2

"Dad, I was just taking a spin to the store. You were asleep and there wasn't anything good to eat. So I was just going to get a Coke and some chips."

"In the car?" Horace screamed.

"Yeah! I do it all the time. This fool he just . . . he just appeared out of nowhere."

"Hold up! Are you telling me you hit somebody?"

"He threw himself at the car! It's not my fault."

As the reality of the situation hit Horace, he grabbed Jeff and shook him.

"Where did this happen?" he screamed into Jeff's face, holding both his arms in a tight grip, trying to control his feelings of rage and fear.

"Around the corner. I—I left the car there," he said, his voice dropping, wincing from the pain his father was unknowingly inflicting.

"Let's go!"

Surprisingly, when they returned, the car was as Jeff had left it, the door open, the dome light on and the engine running. Right away Horace noticed that only one headlight was on.

"Where's the person?" Horace asked, and as soon as the question left his lips he saw a huddled mass on the side of the street. Horace heard the distant wail of a police siren. He remembered that in that instant, as if in a dream, he made a decision that changed his life forever.

"Go home right now! Run and don't tell anybody anything. Do you hear me? I'll handle this. Go!"

And for the first time Horace could remember, Jeff did exactly as he was told. He turned and ran. Horace still couldn't recall if he even looked back.

Once Jeff was safely out of sight, Horace sprinted to the

3

person who was injured, fearing that he or she might be dead. He carefully turned the body over and was surprised that there didn't appear to be much physical damage, and just a trickle of blood from his mouth. Then an onslaught of unpleasant smells assaulted his nostrils. He reeked of urine and bile and body odor. His full beard had flecks and crumbs of food in it; his clothes were tattered and dirty. Horace cautiously leaned forward, afraid to touch him, but knowing he must. He knew CPR and after listening for a heartbeat but finding none, he began to pump his chest. Just when he was about to place his mouth over the man's, hoping he wouldn't heave from the smell, a hand landed on his shoulder and a rough voice said, "We've got it now."

Horace's problems did not begin on this day—with this accident. The complete awareness of this fact hit him while he sat and watched his lawyer, the judge and the other attorney, speak excitedly in language he did not understand. He had to take responsibility for his own actions, as well as that of his son. He had always been quick to attempt to balance the actions of his rebellious, reckless son with endless excuses, and reasons why. He always had an answer to get Jeff out of trouble, forever defending him against "mean" teachers or "strict" daycare providers or "stupid" coaches who made him sit out of games. Even when it was clear that Jeff had done wrong, he'd protected him with the fierceness of a female. His inability to clearly see his son's faults had kept him on a roller-coaster ride full of disappointment, cover-ups and constantly blaming the wrong person. He felt a sense of responsibility for his son that went beyond that which would be reasonable. It was his goal that his son would have a father, a protector, and a friend—always. Something he never had and desperately wanted. From the time he was nine-years-old and watched his father walk out on him and his mother, then witnessed her struggle to keep a roof over their heads, he vowed he'd never abandon any child of his if he were ever blessed to have one. And he took that vow very seriously.

Another black man bites the dust, falling like a weather-worn leaf to the ground; he would dissipate into nothingness, his whole life over, Leslie thought, gone like a whisper. Adding the fact that he was innocent made this whole mess that much harder a pill to swallow. She knew he had covered up for his teenage son who had been driving the car that struck a pedestrian. She knew Jeff was an unlicensed driver—a minor—taking a spin in the car he'd stolen from his sleeping father. She knew the entire story, but she was a lawyer. She could never tell anybody the truth. The attorney-client relationship was strictly confidential, and this fact kept her from saying anything. Although she had urged her client to tell the truth, necessarily having to implicate his son, he'd refused. She remembered how he, in a low, humble voice, explained his reasoning to her.

"At fifty years old," he'd explained, "my life is over; but Jeff, well, Jeff is just beginning to live." Yes, Leslie thought, he's beginning to live a life as a fifteen-year-old, wanna-be gang banger, a troublemaker, and a liar. But his father thought he walked on water. There was nothing she could do about that. He had made another critical mistake when he urged her to conduct a jury trial, where he pleaded innocent, confidently doubting that a jury would find him guilty. The accident wasn't a hit and run—to the jury's knowledge—so Horace doubted that a jury of his peers would see it as anything other than an accident. He was wrong. The victim had no family, apparently was an indigent who had wandered into the neighborhood. No one had claimed his body or knew his identity. But the State of California had a responsibility for all its residents; thus the prosecution of Horace began. A life was gone; now he would have to pay.

Leslie pondered how she had come to be a part of this scenario. She had been assigned this case as a *pro bono* matter. When she'd received the notice from the overworked city attorney's office, she remembered how she wanted to scream "No!" But it was her civic responsibility to help those who needed legal representation even if they couldn't afford it. She was slightly agitated that she would again be throwing herself into the all-too-personal, intricate fibers of another person's life. But she humbly accepted the assignment, wondering, not for the first time, how she could enter someone's life at the most gut-wrenching stage of personal tragedy and stay objective—dispassionate—as lawyers are taught to be. Unless you had a heart of stone, which Leslie did not, it was simply beyond her ability not to feel their pain, thus making it her own, beginning the slow process of sinking deeper and deeper, drowning in someone else's despair. She was expected to perform miracles, always mindful not to ever get personally involved—a feat Leslie found more and more to be impossible—knowing how firmly entrenched into the delicate fabric of another human's problems she would become.

Mr. Brown and Jeff were prime examples of why she no longer practiced law at the D.A.'s office. The outcome could sometimes be too painful to accept, clouding her usual ability to be objective, leaving scars and tracks of agony behind.

She waved a solemn goodbye to Horace as he was led back to his cell to await the sentencing hearing.

"You hang in there, Horace. I'll be back tomorrow and we'll talk."

❦

"I'm home!" Leslie yelled, as she walked through the door and threw her raincoat over the sofa. As usual, there was no response. Leslie felt the walls and floor vibrate to the rhythmic beat of the rap music coming from her daughter's bedroom. She sighed heavily while scanning the mail that Anastasia had placed on the sofa table, trying to prepare herself to deal rationally with her own rebellious teen. Placing her briefcase on the kitchen counter, Leslie gingerly approached the door, chanting a quick prayer: Oh Lord, give me the strength to deal with this chil' today. Amen. She knocked softly at first, then began to pound the door when Anastasia still had not answered.

The door flew open and her daughter stood before her chewing gum like it would somehow get away if she didn't chomp on it fast and hard. Her face was beginning to lose its look of innocence. Black eyeliner and thick mascara lined her eyes; her mouth, which so much resembled that of her father— small and shapely—was smeared with black lipstick, and she had started twisting her hair to form little snake-like braids, her version of dreadlocks. She and Leslie were about the same height, but Anastasia towered over her now wearing thick platform shoes, the 70s style of hip-hugging jeans and a small crop top.

"Hi," Leslie yelled over the loud repetitive lyrics of the rapper named Tupac.

"Hey," came the very bland reply.

"How was school today? And turn that music down while

we're talking!" Leslie shouted, losing grip of her patience, while the room continued to shake and vibrate from too much bass.

Anastasia's favorite thing to do now to completely irritate her mother was to roll her eyes heavenward while blowing heavy puffs of air from puffed-up cheeks. She turned the knob on the stereo ever so slightly, barely reducing the noise level.

"Some more, please," Leslie demanded.

"Dag, Mom, why you sweatin' me? Just got in the door and already you sweatin' me."

"I know two things for sure: One, you better watch your tone of voice when you speak to me and two, you better turn that stereo down before I take it away," Leslie said with deliberate emphasis on each word.

Noting her mother's tone, Anastasia muted the stereo.

"What's up, Mom?" Anastasia said, attempting to act and sound innocent.

"How was school today?" Leslie again asked.

"Okay," came the only reply she ever got to any question she asked these days. How's school? Okay. How was the movie? Okay. How did you like dinner? Okay. Nothing more, nothing less. Always.

"For a pretty good student, you sure have a limited vocabulary," Leslie teased.

"Yeah, well, whatever."

"Yeah, well, whatever," Leslie repeated, losing control of her anger now. "You know what, Anastasia? I've had a really bad day. An important case of mine blew up in my face and I'm pretty upset about it. My client loves his son so much that he's willing to go to jail for him and here I come home and can't even get you to respect me enough to turn the stereo down!"

"Here we go again," Anastasia replied, again raising her eyes heavenward as if she wished the Lord would strike her mother speechless.

Tears of frustration that Leslie had averted shedding earlier today came back with a surprising rush, catching both of them off guard.

Leslie could see that Anastasia instantly regretted her tone because she put her arm around her mother and crooned, "I'm sorry, Mom. I'm sorry." But her apologetic words didn't stop the flow of tears now that they had started. Leslie left the room, slamming the door behind her, leaving a bewildered Anastasia to stare at the door as if an alien had just rushed out.

Leslie fled to the sanctity and quiet of her bedroom, completely unable to understand the actions of her beautiful daughter. Her behavior was beyond Leslie's reasoning powers. Anastasia had become insensitive and horribly disrespectful. Leslie thought about what her client had done today and wondered if she would ever be able to do anything half as brave and self-sacrificing. Anastasia was becoming a difficult teenager, seeming to always challenge Leslie's authority and lately she even tested Leslie's right to love her. How could she defend her if she were ever caught doing something wrong? Leslie grabbed her head, instantly felt nauseous as the ever-present headache began to throb. Not another headache, she thought, as she stumbled to the medicine cabinet. She cupped her hands and gulped the cold tap water, washing down three aspirins. She stared at her reflection in the mirror, noting her eyes were red, as was her nose; tear streaks had left tracks in her previously flawless Fashion Fair make-up. She grabbed a tissue and blotted away the streaks, then blew her nose.

"You're letting all this stuff get to you, girl," she said aloud to her anguished reflection.

She sat down on her bed, resisting the urge to be inside the comfortable folds of soft cotton and warmth. She realized that Anastasia was literally pushing her away whenever she praised her or even tried to hug her. Leslie attempted to understand her mood swings, knowing they both had suffered a loss–one neither of them ever expected to happen so soon. Darryl, loving father and devoted husband, as his headstone accurately read, had died suddenly five years ago in his sleep. This tragedy had happened right at the beginning of Anastasia's puberty, the most difficult time in a child's life anyway. Leslie knew that many emotions surged through her daughter at every turn and making them more intense was the fact that she had to add accepting that her father was gone forever.

Leslie began to feel sorry for herself, wondering why Anastasia didn't realize that she missed Darryl, too. So much so that she literally ached in places she never thought she could; her nerve endings tingled, coupled with painful throbs, especially at night. She missed his touch, warm hugs and long talks, whispering dreams to each other, sharing a love that was complete. She felt lethargic and her head ached. She was no longer able to resist the urge to lie down. She slipped off her pumps, pulled the comforter protectively around her like a shield and fell asleep, completely clothed.

CHAPTER II

Bright, warm light shined on Leslie's face, awakening her from her deep sleep. The morning came much too quickly, crashing into Leslie, rudely awakening her from the delicious warmth of her bed, the deep coma-like sleep that was free of any physical, emotional, or mental pain. If she could, she would stay right where she was, comatose and free of the anxieties of yesterday. After all, it was Saturday. She lazily stretched, snuggling deeper under the sheets. She was mentally turning the pages of her schedule in her mind when suddenly she jumped up, panicked when she finally remembered what she had to do today. Glancing at the clock she realized, on top of everything else, she would be late. "Damn," she muttered, as she stretched, yawned and headed, half-asleep, to the bathroom.

As she glimpsed her face in the mirror, she remembered how Darryl used to tell her how beautiful she was, even in the morning. He'd tease her about the way her hair would stand around her head, calling it a radical halo, frequently running his fingers through the lush fullness of her mane. She smiled as she thought about how when the first traces of gray had prematurely begun to appear, he had talked her into trying a new hair color—dark brown with highlights that turned her gray hair into streaks of gold. As she continued to examine her face, she noted that her lips were puffy and still held a hint of yesterday's lipstick. Her clothes were wrinkled beyond what any ironing board could straighten, and as she remembered all the details of last night, she was disgusted that she had allowed Anastasia to upset her so much that she'd not only cried in front of her, but then allowed herself to fall asleep in her clothes.

Her eyes were bloodshot, she noticed, and wondered if that was a result of the headache she went to bed with. She hated to see those fine, squiggly lines of red streaking the whites of her eyes, taking away from the beauty of their pretty shade of brown. Darryl had always told her how much he was mesmerized by her eyes, the way they changed when she was in a particular mood; dark and stormy when anger seized her or hazel and light when she was in a darkened smoke-filled room.

She cleansed her face. Her complexion was smooth and she was blessed, as are most people of African-American descent, with skin free of lines or wrinkles. Her coloring closely resembled that of peanut butter. It radiated richness, had a definite warm glow. She rushed through her morning routine, again disgusted that she'd almost allowed herself to sleep through the entire event.

Quickly she stepped into the shower, donning a shower cap so as not to get her hair wet. The last thing she needed was to have to blow dry it. That took too long. Her hair was too thick and full and every hairdresser she'd ever been to loved it, until they realized what a pain it was to relax, not to mention the hours of struggling with its thickness during the press and curl days.

At her massive walk-in closet, stuffed with clothes in all colors of the rainbow with dozens of shoes to match, she tried to find something quickly that fit today's occasion. Something that wouldn't look too casual or anything that looked like she was just coming from her law office. After much consideration, she chose a purple dress with large pearl buttons. It flattered her figure, and the shoes matched perfectly.

As she finished dressing, she remembered that not only was she expected at the high school's open house, she was also supposed to help set up. She wondered now if she'd be too late. She thought about Anastasia then and wondered if she'd gotten herself up and to the school already this morning. She also worried if she'd eaten any dinner last night, regretting, again, her emotional outburst. Leslie quietly walked from her bedroom to Anastasia's, gently knocked on her door, unaware that she cocked her head to the side listening, then waited to feel reverberating floorboards. After no answer, she knocked again as she turned the knob. Anastasia's room was in a state of complete chaos, something she had noticed last night but had not had the chance to tell her to clean it up. There was a half-eaten sandwich and chips on the headboard, and an empty Pepsi can that had fallen on top of the comforter, spilling remnants of dark brown soda on the beautiful, expensive fabric. Leslie sighed. It was times like last night that made her really miss her husband. She wasn't good at being a single mother. She realized she needed help, and for the millionth time she ached for Darryl's guidance, his touch and words of understanding.

While she missed her husband terribly, she was grateful to have a good friend and confidante in Bryan. He tried to help her. He attempted to understand, but he and Anastasia did not get along. In fact, Anastasia hated him and her resentment of him being with Leslie was evident in the snide way she spoke to him—or didn't speak to him—constantly forcing Leslie to step in and remind her to use her manners. Bryan was always willing to hear Leslie's tales of woe but he did appear uncomfortable in Anastasia's presence. He'd joke with her or tell her how pretty she looked, but Anastasia would accept none of it, and then Bryan would begin to squirm, nervously urging Leslie that it was time to go. She almost laughed aloud when she thought about the time Anastasia had told him he really should stop trying to be funny, that he looked stupid. His face had gone through a slow metamorphosis going from puzzled to struck to angry, then swiftly back to a fake smile when his eyes landed on Leslie's face. She had stifled a laugh and quickly admonished Anastasia that what she had said was not nice, to apologize, then go to her room.

Leslie remembered then that she and Bryan were going out this evening. She welcomed the chance to get away from her anxieties about Anastasia. Bryan would temporarily make them flutter away.

She quietly closed the door to Anastasia's room and returned to her own. She critically examined herself once she was fully dressed and wondered, not for the first time lately, if she looked like a woman of forty with a sixteen-year-old daughter. She only had the opportunity to entertain that thought for a moment before she realized that she was still running late and didn't have time for such triviality. She grabbed her purse and flew out the door, glancing at her watch. "Maybe I won't be too late after all."

Pulling into the school's parking lot in her honey–colored Mercedes, Leslie stepped from the car and entered the school's amphitheater. She spotted Anastasia immediately. A feeling of profound relief swept unexpectedly over her. The pride a mother has for her child gripped her as she watched Anastasia serving coffee and donuts to parents and teachers who had already arrived. Anastasia saw her mother coming and smiled, obviously in a good mood today.

"Hi, Mom. You're late."

"I know, I know. Don't make me feel any worse about it than I already do."

"Okay, then I forgive you. Want some coffee and a donut? The money goes toward the school girls' club."

Leslie scanned the auditorium. It was very crowded; lots of parents had turned out today. That was a good sign.

"Just coffee, honey," she replied and began digging around in her Dooney bag, one of several she owned, and slipped a five dollar bill in her daughter's palm. "Keep the change—a little something extra for you and the girls."

"Mom . . ."

"Hmm?"

"Sorry about last night," Anastasia whispered.

"I am too, baby. But we've got to talk about that and some other things, okay?"

"Do we have to?" Anastasia whined.

"Yes, we do," Leslie said with a definite termination-of-conversation tone of voice.

"It doesn't look like they need me to help set up. Did Mrs. Franks say anything to you?"

"Yeah, I told her you were running late, and she said to tell you everything was taken care of so just enjoy the program," Anastasia said. She looked over her mother's shoulder and said, "May I help you?"

Leslie backed away. For a moment she watched Anastasia pour coffee and chat easily with her customer. She felt so proud watching her, realizing she was growing into a beautiful young woman.

The typically chilly October morning caused Leslie to want to cross her arms in an attempt to ward off the cold that had slowly started to creep clear through to her bones. Young girls were placed strategically throughout the area, handing out programs and a large green sheet of paper. Leslie stopped for a moment and surveyed the crowd, trying to juggle her purse while attempting to sip the pungent, hot coffee, hold the program and the green piece of construction paper. She wanted to glance at her watch to see if the program was about to start, but couldn't manage that. She decided to head down the steep stairs, looking for a spot that was close and centered before the stage below. She sat down and immediately the moisture on the aluminum bleacher—wet from last night's dew—seeped through her dress. That's when she realized what the green mat was for. She laughed at herself, shaking her head and made a remark to the person beside her.

Unbeknownst to Leslie, all her actions were being closely monitored. All her gestures and the look in her eyes had caught the attention of another parent who watched her. The smile on her face, the way she tilted her head to one side when she laughed, the animated way she talked made her admirer think of a quiet beauty. A smile crept over his lips. He had never seen her before, but for some strange reason—one even he couldn't readily identify—he felt a compelling need to know who she was.

He actually had noticed her earlier, when she first arrived. There was a definite sparkle in her eyes when they had

16

alighted upon the young girl serving coffee. She didn't see anyone else in that moment, only the girl. Unaware of his perusal, Leslie unintentionally had turned her body slightly, so that she faced him, giving him a better view of her face from where he stood. She spoke conspiratorially to the young girl. He assumed the girl was her daughter and once he really looked at the younger woman, there were definite physical similarities between them. Their smiles were the same, and the kidding manner in which they spoke to one another told him a lot. Yes, he surmised, they must be mother and daughter.

He continued to watch her even after the program had started.

"Ladies and gentlemen, moms and dads. Please take your seats and let's begin our program. Thank you all for coming today, for taking time out of your collective busy schedules to be here on a Saturday morning to show much-needed support for your children. We at George Washington High are very proud of our students and our school . . ."

⚜

The speeches droned on and on, one teacher after another singing the praises of George Washington High, allowing Leslie's mind to wander. She began to think again about Horace and Jeff, trying to strategize on how to get a reduced sentence for him. She was so deep in thought that she hadn't realized the speaker had left the podium until Anastasia began to frantically shake her.

"Mom! Mom!" Anastasia said. "Come on! What are you doing still sitting here? Or haven't you noticed the program's over?"

"Oh . . . uh . . . I guess I was daydreaming. Where did

everybody go?" she asked, looking around at the nearly deserted area.

"To visit the classrooms and meet teachers—you know, what parents come to open house for," her daughter said, exaggerating. "Come on, we only have a little time to go to each classroom, and I really want you to meet my first period teacher. She gets on my last nerve!"

"Okay, okay. Let's go."

Together they walked around the beautiful campus, where green lush grass and bushes were plentiful. Shade from huge trees shielded the picturesque campus from the midday sun that had finally arrived to grace another beautiful San Diego day. Flowers of various types sprinkled the earth, giving the area a pleasant atmosphere.

The first teacher Leslie met was not particularly friendly. She spoke with clipped sentences and gave the impression of being irritated, even though Leslie doubted she was. She immediately could see why Anastasia didn't like her. If Leslie hadn't been used to dealing with clients and lawyers whose personalities were just like hers, she'd also be a little put off by her mannerism and her tone of voice.

The next two teachers were not particularly interesting as far as Leslie was concerned, making her feel even more restless than before. Couldn't they think of anything unique to say? They both seemed so hurried, as if they really couldn't be bothered with expressing specific interest or details about her child. However, the fourth teacher confidentially spoke about Anastasia's attitude, completely surprising Leslie who thought she was the only one experiencing her daughter's wrath. Leslie assured the teacher that she was working with Anastasia on this problem and to let her know if it got worse. Thanking her for her honesty, Leslie left.

"Mom, I gotta go to the bathroom. Wait for me here. I'll be right back, okay?"

"Sure, go ahead. I need to rest anyway."

As Leslie watched the activity around her—students and parents trying to find classrooms—a man came toward her from across the lawn, smiling and waving. She looked around, thinking, Is he waving at me? I don't think so. But he was. As he advanced upon her, she noticed his full lips, dark eyes, incredibly deep dimples, an enticing smile which was slightly lopsided that gave him a seductive look. His closely cropped, wavy hair was shiny in the sunlight. Not bad, Leslie thought. He walked toward her with a gait only a brotha could have. Extending his hand in greeting, he whispered in her ear, "I've been watching you."

Flattered but cautious, she stepped back, looked him in the eye, and replied, "Oh, really? Why is that?"

He laughed a deep, hearty laugh, displaying his dimpled smile. He had a devilish manner about him, she noticed.

"I'm sorry. Let me start over by introducing myself. My name is Robert. My son attends this school. And, just so you know, I always notice beautiful women. In fact, I saw when you sat down on that wet bleacher, you shot up like something bit you!" Again he laughed, sending ripples of unexpected pleasure through her. Then, she laughed with him.

"Well," she blushed, "I'm glad you're having a good time at my expense. I was wondering why the girls were handing out those green mats. As soon as I sat down I knew!" She paused and looked at him, "Pleasure to meet you, Robert. My name is Leslie—Leslie Hughes. Have we met before?"

"No. Today was the first time I ever laid eyes on you."

"And . . . ," she remarked, enjoying the flirtation, "what did I do to catch your attention besides put a big wet stain on the

19

back of my dress and nearly spill coffee on the front?"

"Ahh, beautiful and funny."

"Thank you."

"Trust me, it was an enduring incident that left me wanting more. So, Leslie, are you married?"

"No," she paused awkwardly, "not anymore."

"Good. I'm glad you're not. I wouldn't want to be standing here flirting with a married woman. Not good for my reputation. I was wondering if you'd be interested in joining me later for a cup of coffee or something?"

Anastasia appeared out of nowhere, startling Leslie. Suddenly she felt a little embarrassed. Rather than answer him, she did the perfunctory introductions. "Robert, this is my daughter, Anastasia. Anastasia, this is Robert. His son is a student here too."

Leslie could see that Anastasia immediately took a defensive posture. "Who's your son? What grade is he in?" was all she could manage to reply. She glanced at her mother and rolled her eyes.

"Well, my son is in the ninth grade, and his name is Malcolm. He's in ROTC and they have him escorting people and standing guard somewhere on the campus. I'll have to catch up with him later. Maybe I can introduce you to him."

"No thanks. I don't deal with freshmen," Anastasia said. Leslie, although she shouldn't have been, was completely surprised at her daughter's rudeness. She gaped at Anastasia, rapidly blinking as if slapped. She glanced at Robert. He smiled.

Mercifully, a bell rang, signalling that it was time to be in the next classroom. Leslie took one last look at Robert, knowing she had not gotten the chance to answer his question about having coffee, but decided to let it pass for now. What she really wanted to do was apologize for Anastasia's behavior.

"Well, Robert, we must move on. They don't give us much time in each classroom. It was a pleasure meeting you." She said this as she and her daughter started walking away. To her surprise he walked with her. Her daughter marched ahead of her, angrily hurrying to the next class.

"I would still very much like to meet you for coffee," he said in a low tone. His deep voice sent delicious chills and shock waves through her. "Don't worry about your daughter's tone," he conspiratorially whispered. "I understand perfectly well the teenage attitude, 'cause I got one myself. I don't usually do this, but I'd really be pleased if you'd consider meeting me later—after this is over—for coffee, or whatever you'd like. Perhaps even grab some lunch."

She looked at him and he was so handsome and seemed to be sincere. Then he smiled as he stared into her eyes as if he were trying to read her soul. Suddenly, her heart began to flutter in her chest and for a brief moment, she was slightly excited by the prospect. What is going on here? she wondered about her own reaction to him. She tried to gather herself together; she knew she had to say no but she didn't want to hurt his feelings. Yet, for some reason, she felt she would only be hurting herself if she declined.

"I appreciate the offer but I'm seeing someone right now."

"Oh. Well, can't blame a man for trying, right?"

"Guess not."

"It was nice talking to you. Maybe I'll see you around another time," he said, unable to mask a regretful tone.

Leslie noticed his look of extreme disappointment as he turned to walk away. She stood nailed to the spot, staring at him, wondering who he was and what she might be missing by not seeing him again. An uncharacteristic longing came over her. At that moment a feeling deep inside her stirred and her instincts nudged her. She instantly felt that she should not let this opportunity pass.

"Excuse me," she called, waving her hand. When he turned around he had a broad smile on his face as if he knew she'd change her mind. She smiled back. "If the offer stands, I'll meet you for coffee."

"Great!"

Leslie wondered what in the world she was doing, but for some reason it felt good—this flirtation she was engaging in with him. She quickly scribbled her number on a business card and hastily scurried to catch up with Anastasia, who graced her with one of her nasty expressions that could have been interpreted as "drop-dead, Mom." Leslie chose to ignore her and, for the first time today, she had a genuine smile on her face.

CHAPTER III

Leslie and Anastasia arrived at home exhausted and ready for lunch. Leslie started to prepare sandwiches, grabbing lunch meat, cheese, lettuce and tomatoes from the fridge. She decided to brew coffee, too. She noticed that Anastasia still looked upset with her for agreeing to meet Robert for coffee. She readied herself for much attitude and said, "What's on your mind?"

"I thought you were seeing Bryan, Mom. What are you, a two-timer?"

"No, I'm not a two-timer," Leslie tersely said. "But I think the better question is, why were you so rude to him?"

"'Cause, it's embarrassing."

"What's embarrassing?"

"Men are always checkin' you out, everywhere we go."

"That's not true."

"Yes it is and I get tired of it. Sometimes I wish you didn't look the way you do."

"What would you prefer, an old hag, a witch ridin' a broom and wearin' a funny hat. Is that what you'd like? I thought you were proud of me."

"I am, but—well, it's irritating that you get so much

23

attention. Sometimes you don't even notice it."

"That's because when we're together I'm more interested in you and what you're saying or doing rather than people around us. Besides, I've noticed you getting quite a few stares yourself."

Her face brightened and Anastasia replied, "Really!"

"Yes, really. What is this? You only see what happens to me, but not you?"

"It doesn't really matter. This is a dumb discussion anyway," Anastasia said, beginning to pout.

"Anastasia, you are a beautiful, smart young lady. Never forget that."

"Yeah, right, Mom," Anastasia replied, as her shoulders slumped and her head hung low.

"What's wrong, honey?"

"I'm not hungry anymore," Anastasia said, abruptly ending their conversation as she left the room.

Leslie heard the door slam, knowing next would be that hard core, irritating thump and bump of rap music, and she wondered if things were ever going to change back to the way they used to be. I want my little girl back. She closed her eyes, holding her head in her hands, wishing she had the strength to pray about it. Instead of talking to God, she mumbled, "What am I going to do about our daughter, Darryl?"

Anastasia slumped against her bedroom door while silent tears washed over her face. Angrily, she swiped at them with the back of her hand. She missed her father so much and her mom just did not understand. Sometimes Anastasia thought her mother was too busy working, trying to save a bunch of sorry-ass people who weren't worth her mother's precious time or energy. She realized that she resented everything now. Even the fact that she had a beautiful, smart mother annoyed her. She marched across the room to stare at her own face and could not see her own youthful beauty reflected there. Daddy used to tell me what a pretty girl I was. Nobody tells me that anymore. I hate living in this house. I hate school. I hate that stupid boyfriend Mom has. And now she's flirting with somebody new. God, I can't take this. Even my own boyfriend likes her! It seems like my mom's gettin' all the play. What's up with that? she wondered. Is something wrong with me, Daddy? she whispered. Ever since you left, nothing has been the same. We had to move; Mom said there were too many memories in our old house. I liked that house. I miss my friends. I miss you, Daddy.

She knew she was acting like a big baby. What would the few friends she did have think of her if they could see her acting like this—crying and blubbering to herself—talking to her dead father. She blew her nose, wiped her face and snapped on the stereo. She boogied and shimmied around the room, her sorry attempt to forget.

The telephone rang, interrupting Leslie's thoughts. The bread on her sandwich was already getting hard and her coffee now cold.

"Hello."

"Hi there. This is Robert. We met earlier today up at the school."

She sat up straighter as butterflies assaulted her empty stomach.

"Hi. How did the rest of your day go?"

"Pretty good. I learned some interesting things about my son. Seems he's a bit of a class clown, talking too much and generally getting in the teacher's way."

"Hmmm, typical teenage boy, I guess. At least you know he's got a personality. I was a bit of a class clown in my day, too, so I completely understand."

"Really? You don't seem the type. I picture you as being very studious and reserved. A teacher's pet even. Am I right?"

"No, you are not right." She said this with laughter in her voice, feigning righteous indignation. "Well, actually you've got me pegged correctly. I was studious, I had to be. My parents had high hopes for me, and I couldn't let them down."

"Where are you from, Leslie?" Robert asked, and she could tell that he wanted to know as much about her as she did him.

"Here. I was born and raised right in beautiful, always sunny San Diego. It's my home and I love it. My parents are deceased, so I have fond memories of them wherever I go in the city. For that reason alone I think I'll never leave."

"Sounds like you had a good relationship with them."

"Yes, I did."

"You seem too young to have parents that are gone."

"They died young."

"What happened to them? Or do you mind talking about it?"

"No, I'm past the flood of tears that used to accompany any conversation regarding my parents and their deaths. They died in India on a bus tour."

"What were they doing in India, of all places?"

"They both dreamed of seeing the Taj Mahal. Unfortunately, they never made it. Apparently, the bus driver was driving entirely too fast for a road as uneven and dangerous as that one was. The bus tipped over, taking the lives of almost everyone on board."

"I'm sorry, Leslie."

"You know the worst thing about it was I heard about it on the news. I still remember this strange, tingling sensation that ran through my body as I listened to the newscast. As soon as they said there were several American tourists on that bus, somehow, I knew my parents were among them."

"Sounds like some kind of psychic force nudged you."

"Maybe. Anyway, to make a long story short, their deaths were a horrible blow for me, but I've learned to accept it. My parents are buried together in the same plot, side by side, not far from here."

Robert listened and said quietly, "They're still together, Leslie. Never forget that."

"You think so—"

"Yes, I do. In fact, I'd like to tell you more about my philosophy on life and death when we meet for coffee."

Hesitantly Leslie said, "Sure, where would you like to go?"

"Hmmm, let's meet at a coffee house downtown called The Gathering. You know where it is?"

"Sure do, my office isn't far from there. No problem—we'll meet—when?"

"How about in an hour? Is that okay for you?"

Leslie laughed, finding his nervous need-to-please attitude an endearing quality.

"An hour is fine."

"Good. And Leslie—I'm looking forward to it."

Leslie surprised herself when she responded, "Me too."

CHAPTER IV

Leslie's pace slowed as she approached the entrance to The Gathering. A patron leaving graciously held the door for her. The aroma that wafted out instantly transported her back to her college days, struggling over an assignment, sipping hot, freshly brewed coffee, knowing she was probably in for a long night holed up in one of the neighborhood coffeehouses. She shielded her eyes, squinting from the glare of the sun reflecting off the display case filled with rich desserts dripping vanilla or chocolate icing, eclairs oozing creamy fillings and pastries topped with luscious cherries or strawberries. The air was slightly tinged with the distinctive scent of cinnamon or vanilla, along with freshly baked bread, blueberry and banana-nut muffins and the warm, unique scent of yeast. Her stomach growled as the heavenly scents seemed to swirl about her head, reminding her that she hadn't eaten her sandwich.

She saw Robert sitting at a table in the corner. He was staring at her with an expectant expression on his face. She smiled and waved, noting an anxious flutter deep in her belly. God, what am I doing? Her mind's eye briefly flashed on Bryan's face, which made her feel suddenly very uncomfortable.

She could see that Robert intended to watch her every move. She glided into the room, her head held high, shoulders back, a slight yet noticeable swing to her hips that she knew would not escape his scrutiny of her.

"Hi," he greeted her, standing.

"Hi."

"Thanks for coming," Robert said, graciously extending the chair for her. His hand briefly touched hers; his warmth electrified her. Startled, she clumsily plopped into the chair, blinking furiously, trying to regain control of herself.

"No problem," she stuttered.

"Are you all right?" he said, realizing that she, too, was fighting an irresistible attraction to him.

"Actually, I'm a little flustered."

"Why?"

"As I told you at the school, I'm dating someone. This feels—well—it feels strange." She peered intently at his face. A smile lurked around the corners of his mouth, mischief written all over his face.

"Well, Leslie, let me assure you that I don't bite."

"That's good to know," she replied.

"Well—not hard, anyway."

They exchanged a look, then both burst out laughing. A waitress appeared to take their orders. He asked her what she'd like, but she couldn't think of anything, so he ordered a cappuccino for both of them.

"Are you hungry? Would you like to order sandwiches? They have delicious smoked turkey with cranberries on the side and chunky potato salad."

"Hmm, that sounds good."

"Great. Please bring two orders. Thanks."

"You know, it seems like I'm always laughing when I'm

29

around you." Leslie remarked. "Why is that?"

"Because I'm a funny guy, and I'm also probably the man of your dreams. Do you believe in destiny, Leslie?"

"I believe in the here and now," Leslie said. Her voice sounded sensual and husky to her ears.

"What would you say if I told you I think we were supposed to meet today?"

"I'd say you've got an active imagination."

"Skeptical, huh."

"Very."

"I was supposed to be on a plane this morning heading for San Francisco, but my flight was cancelled due to heavy fog in the Bay Area. So . . ."

"So, you ended up coming to your son's open house and lo and behold, there I stood, right?" she said sarcastically.

"Well, something like that. I could have just waited for another flight, but I got to feeling guilty about letting business get in the way of my parental responsibilities, so I cancelled the entire meeting and headed for the school." He paused. "Destiny."

"You have to understand something about me, okay. First of all, I'm an attorney, so I deal strictly in facts—in what's concrete. Now, you may be able to fantasize about destiny and premonitions, ghosts, etc., but, in my business, I can't."

"It might surprise you to know that my business is mergers and acquisitions. I buy and sell companies all the time on my gut feelings, on spiritual guidance, and, of course, concrete facts and figures," he said, chuckling.

"Very interesting. I'm glad you cleared up that business about gut feelings; otherwise I'd think you were a broke man, huh?"

Laughing, he responded, "I do my homework."

"I'm sure you do," Leslie responded. She crossed her legs and settled more comfortably in her chair as she toyed with her left earring.

"Leslie, I've got a confession to make."

"Okay." Leslie said, eyeing him suspiciously.

"I broke a few speed limits on my way over here. I couldn't wait to see your beautiful face again."

"You're going to make me blush and that's not easy to do. Thank you for such a nice compliment. Beautiful is an adjective I don't hear very often."

"Well, you should, because you are." He paused then, giving her a sultry look. "I appreciate you meeting me on the spur of the moment like this. I'm usually not this impulsive, but today for some reason I really wanted to talk to you—to get to know you. So, tell me more about yourself, Leslie."

"Well, I've shared a lot already; there really isn't much more to tell. I'm a partner in a medium-size law firm. My practice is limited to corporate litigation. I have a teenage daughter, whom you met today."

"Right; she didn't seem very happy that I was talking to you."

"No, she wasn't. I guess I should mention that I'm also a widow. Anastasia still misses her father very much. And, she's—well—going through some things. It's been difficult for both of us."

"I'm so sorry to hear about all your losses. Your parents and your husband. You seem very strong in spite of it all. I admire that kind of strength."

"Well, you do what ya gotta do," she said, attempting to lighten up their conversation.

"My teenager is a handful too. Got much attitude and those raging hormones—whew—that in and of itself can make you

31

crazy. And sometimes the disrespectful way he talks to me. He often forgets who he's dealing with."

"You too, huh," Leslie said, softly chuckling, happy that he did understand parenting.

"Oh believe me, we have our rounds from time to time. But, getting back to you, you're a partner, hmm, impressive. Quite an accomplishment for somebody who seems to be so young."

"I'm not that young and believe me it was very hard to get where I am, and I definitely paid some serious dues. I earned that partnership, and the position I hold now with the firm is solid. I have their attention and their respect, and that's very important to me." She noticed he was staring at her mouth, listening intently to her words and she felt her face heat up. She quickly grabbed a napkin and blotted her upper lip which she was afraid was probably damp with sweat.

"Now—it's your turn. Tell me about yourself," Leslie managed to say.

"I own my own business, involving mergers and acquisitions, as I already mentioned. My son and I take care of each other, with the help of my live-in housekeeper."

"Must be nice. I have a cleaning lady who comes in once a week."

"It is nice, but it can't replace the intimate touch that a woman who loves you gives."

"Meaning your wife?"

"Nope. I've never been married, close a time or two. Haven't found the right woman for our lives."

"Then, I guess I'm confused. Your son is from a previous relationship?"

"No."

"No?" Leslie said incredulously.

"No. Let me stop the suspense and just tell you that I

adopted Malcolm."

"You adopted him, that's great! Not many single men do such a thing."

"I'm special, just in case you hadn't noticed."

Smiling, Leslie said, "I guess you are special. I mean to give up the bachelor's life to be a single father, that's pretty incredible."

"I wanted to be a father, and since it seemed to be taking too long to find a woman, I went the unconventional route. Voila, adoption was the answer."

"Was it hard for a single man to adopt a child?"

"Not if you've got good references, money, determination, a guardian angel, much faith, and, did I mention, money," he said laughing.

"Yes, you did. I'm impressed."

"Don't be. It was probably a selfish thing to do, but I've created a good life for a child that otherwise might not have any life outside of an institution. I'm very proud of Malcolm. Had him since he was two."

"Two! Oh, the terrible twos. How'd you handle that?"

"Very carefully. It was hard, but my mother helped me through the rough spots. I swear I was on the phone with her constantly. God bless her."

"He's fifteen now, right?"

"Yep, I'll be growing more gray hairs in a few short months—he's going to be driving soon."

"You're right about that. I remember how scared I was when Anastasia wanted me to start teaching her how to drive. I always had a look of pure terror on my face. But we survived it and she's actually a very good driver."

"You strike me as a very patient woman, kind and loving. I sensed that about you when I watched you today."

"Flattery will get you everywhere," Leslie said, "But seriously, even though I try, Lord knows I lose my patience plenty of times."

"Don't we all. Something about you has totally intrigued me. Actually, watching you took my breath away. So, with a reaction like that I had to find out more about you. It's strange."

"It must be those guardian angels of yours, guiding you to me, huh," Leslie said, suddenly feeling self-conscious. She toyed with her spoon, tipping it back and forth with one manicured nail. The electricity between them was obvious. She felt it deep in the dark corners of her feminine senses.

Placing his hand on top of hers, Robert stopped her fidgeting fingers by threading his long fingers through hers; he gently stroked the side of her thumb. This intimate rhythmic stroke caused Leslie's stomach to tumble. She blinked rapidly several times and attempted to pull her hand away.

"Please don't pull away, Leslie. I don't mean to make you uncomfortable. I just wanted to touch you. There's a lot to be learned from a person's touch." He continued to stroke her hand. "Did you know that?"

"Here you go." The waitress had returned, forcing him to release her hand. "Two turkey sandwiches on whole wheat, with a side of potato salad. The bread's fresh—still warm in fact—just made it this morning. Enjoy!" the waitress said, placing huge sandwiches before them, along with steamy hot cups of cappuccinos with a frothy foam on top, sprinkled lightly with cinnamon.

Leslie ate with more gusto than usual; hunger from missing dinner and breakfast overwhelmed her sense of ladylike daintiness. They talked between bites of food, Robert disclosing funny stories about Malcolm as they ate and she sharing childhood memories of Anastasia. She easily mentioned Darryl's name more than one time, noticing that knowledge of her deceased husband did not fluster Robert. His discussion turned again to the power of touch and Leslie was uncertain about how to deal with a man who she had just met wanting to touch her in such a suggestive manner.

"Ummm, Robert, can we take a walk or something? I'd like to walk off the food we just ate and I could use some fresh air." Before I faint, she thought.

"Sure, we can do that. Let me pay the check and we're on our way."

He left the table and Leslie breathed a heavy sigh of relief. The tension was getting next to her. What am I doing? She felt a mixture of awe, desire, and cautiousness. She wondered if this guy was for real.

"Leslie, are you ready to go?" Robert said, startling her out of her introspection.

"Yes, let's go."

CHAPTER V

Leslie and Robert walked around Seaport Village, looking out over the harbor filled with various sizes and kinds of yachts and boats. Seaport Village was a tourist attraction built right on the harbor. It was a quaint, beautiful location. Its uneven cobblestone walkways and two-story structures of salmon or beige stucco, some with bright colored flags and bell towers, were wonderful. A unique restaurant resembling a log cabin was situated right on the pier. It extended over the water, perched on high stilts, with waves crashing into its bottom. Breathtaking views of the ocean and the city were plentiful from every corner of Seaport Village, along with spectacular views of Coronado Island and the Coronado Bay Bridge, huge navy ships and colorful sailboats. Numerous unique stores and specialty shops sprinkled the courtyard. Robert and Leslie easily talked about everything their eyes lighted upon. They whispered about the famous Hotel Del on Coronado. They shared stories about the making of the movie *Some Like It Hot* with Marilyn Monroe that had been filmed there. They had similar taste and interest in movies: the classics and almost anything with an African American actor or cast.

They continued their stroll, ending up at the tip of The Village where they teased each other about catching a water taxi, wondering where it would take them; from the tip of La Jolla Shores, to Point Loma or even into Mexico.

The clear day allowed them to see twinkling sparks of light which was evidence of the homes along the shore around Tijuana, Mexico. The warmth of the sea breezes stroked their faces and tickled their ears, where it seemed to whisper to them, making them somewhat winded from gulping the continuous breeze that whisked around them. While they stood admiring the view, Robert reached for her hand. The minute they touched, it seemed an electric current passed through her. He must have felt it too because a knowing smile passed his lips. A smile Leslie did not miss. She remembered his comment about learning a lot about a person from their touch. She wondered then what he'd just detected from hers.

They stopped at an ice cream vendor where Robert purchased cones for them both. Leslie tried to decline, feigning fullness from their lunch, but he insisted that a small scoop wouldn't hurt her. She selected French vanilla. She greedily licked the creamy yellow mixture, which slipped past her teeth to settle coolly upon her tongue, where she played with it for a moment until she decided to allow it to slide, ever so slowly and deliciously down her throat, creating a sensation of utter satisfaction. She closed her eyes to enjoy every sensation it created and she sensed Robert's gaze on her. When she opened her eyes, he watched her with fascination, focusing on her tongue as she lapped up the cream beginning to melt and drip in the hot sun.

Leslie also took this opportunity to really look at him. His eyes seemed to dance whenever they gazed upon her. His smile created a slow transformation of his face to one of animation, friendliness, almost childlike when his cheeks puffed ever-so-slightly to reveal deep dimples. She caught him staring at her while she ate her cone, and the look he gave her sent butterfly-type flutters in her stomach. She shivered in response to the image that flashed in her mind of him smiling that same way during the act of love. Embarrassed at where her mind had wandered, she quickly looked away.

"Are you cold, Leslie?"

"No. Just got a little chill. The ice cream's very good. Thank you."

"You're welcome. Are you always this easy to please?"

"Who said I was easy to please?" Leslie said, teasingly. She put her hands on her hips and rolled her head in a sister-girl stance.

"Well, excuse me."

"You're excused," she replied, softly chuckling.

"Leslie, let's sit for a minute, watch the people go by and talk. Is that okay with you?"

"That's fine." As they were getting settled, Leslie thought again about what she was doing and what it could all possibly mean.

Although she was enjoying herself immensely, she was nudged with guilt as thoughts of sharing ice cream and Seaport Village—her and Darryl's favorite spot—with Robert. As a family they came here often to fly kites, have picnic lunches and watch Anastasia run around, happy and carefree. Anastasia, she knew, would definitely not be gracious about accepting any new man into her life. She barely tolerated Bryan. And as good as talking with Robert felt, she tried to deny herself full enjoyment, telling herself it could go no farther than this. She had responsibilities and obligations and priorities, a full, busy life which she did not think could or should include a new love interest. She had to find a way to tell Robert this before he got too comfortable.

"Leslie I'm curious about something. What are you looking for in a man? I mean, what could a man, like me, bring to the table that would interest you—make you happy?"

"Before we go too far, Robert, please remember that I already have a wonderful man in my life, someone who's been my friend for many, many years. This conversation is premature."

"You've mentioned this man a couple of times, so let me rephrase the question. What does he do that makes you happy?"

Brushing a piece of hair out of her eyes, she sighed again, wondering if she should answer this question. Quickly deciding it was okay, she said, "Friendship, for one."

"And, what else?"

"He really listens to me and gives me positive feedback. We're both attorneys so we have our respective professions in common."

"And—"

"And, well, he's—he's—"

"If you can't answer that question, Leslie, perhaps you need to reevaluate your relationship. I mean, don't get me wrong, I'm not trying to get in your business, but if anyone asked me that about you, and you were my woman, I'd know right away what our relationship would be about, what it is that I do to make you happy."

"Well, it's not really that I don't know, it's just that I think the question is extremely personal and inappropriate."

Ignoring her comment, Robert boldly plunged ahead.

"If I were involved with you, I hope I could say that you bring joy to my life, laughter to my world, and that having you in it completes my circle. We would be each other's rock, strongly committed to each other—to having a good relationship." A determined look crossed his face and Leslie looked away. At that moment her emotions were suddenly raw; she felt uncertain—exposed.

"Oh," he continued, "and the sex would have to be incredible!"

"You would have to go there, huh. Well, Robert, there are many facets to who I am and not everyone can deal with it."

"Like what? You seem easy to get along with."

"It's not about how easy I am to get along with. Not all men deal effectively with a woman who's strong and independent. Bryan does. He accepts that about me; actually he's glad I'm that way."

"Ain't nothing wrong with being strong and independent," Robert said.

"There's also my lifestyle, being a single parent, and my work can be very hard sometimes and Bryan understands all of that. I never have to explain myself, and that's important to me. And I guess I don't have to mention that having a temperamental teen is also trying, but we've managed to work around it."

Robert watched Leslie's gestures and facial expressions closely. He must know that I feel uncomfortable, she thought, but still he pressed on.

"I understand that, but what about sex, passion and laughter and adventure—what about fun?"

"We have fun together," Leslie said a bit defensively.

"And passion? What about that?"

He mentioned sex and passion again. This time she couldn't stand sitting there any longer. How come I feel claustrophobic and I'm outside? she thought. Suddenly she jumped when a clump of melting ice cream hit her thigh. Then she noticed it was also running down her hand.

"I'll be back," she said, practically running to the restroom. Yeah, Leslie, what about passion? her mind inquired, as she dashed away from Robert and his penetrating stare and unwanted questions.

He struck a cord of longing deep inside her, she realized, one she rarely allowed herself to think about. The only person in her life that would make her face her loneliness was her best friend, Michelle. Michelle was no stranger to relationships; she had had plenty. As attractive and outgoing as she was, she made Leslie look like a wallflower. But Michelle had a depth of warmth that no other woman friend of Leslie had. She'd make her laugh when all Leslie wanted to do was cry and together they would go through the miseries of Leslie's life. She understood Anastasia and often paved the way for the two of them to talk when anger got in the way.

Michelle was always probing and wondering about Bryan, frequently asking Leslie if he "had it going on," she'd say without any tact. Leslie could not even explain to herself why their relationship wasn't sexually passionate. For her, it just was not there. It was an emotion she had thus far not allowed to grip her. Besides, she was just fine with things as they were. She had a man, she had companionship when she wanted it. She had a fulfilling career and a child to round out her life. Who needed passion? I do, she answered her own question as she exited the bathroom to rejoin Robert.

As she approached him she felt completely silly at running away like that. Leslie tried hard not to appear to him as if she was flustered. She hoped her plea of needing to clean up diverted him so he wouldn't know the real reason she had chosen to run. Unfortunately, he was too smart. He read her face like a book.

"Leslie, I'm sorry. I really didn't mean to upset you."

"I'm okay. It's just that—"

"You don't have to explain anything to me. Okay."

"Look, I really need to be getting back now."

"Leslie, please let me say one more thing, and then I'll keep my big mouth shut." He reached for her hand, which was embarrassingly cold and damp, no longer firm with determination and purpose. Reluctantly she allowed the contact, which still made her uncomfortable even though the firm pressure of his large hand was warmly pleasant. "I think you're a very special woman. I knew it the second I laid eyes on you. Spending this time talking to you has confirmed everything I thought. Thank you."

"Thank you—for what?"

"For being you, for allowing me to spend this wonderful afternoon with you, getting to know you. I appreciate it. I really do." His voice was genuine.

"You're welcome." She fought to hold back the emotions that were tumbling through her from every angle it seemed. "I've really got to be going now. I have plans this evening." She gently pulled her hand out of his, realizing that the contact was lasting longer than it should.

He stared at her face, his eyes slowly taking in every inch of her face. He sighed, shook his head and led her back to the safety of her car. He hoped she wasn't going to run out of his life. He wanted very badly to see her again. Somehow he knew he could take away the hint of sadness he saw in her eyes.

CHAPTER VI

Leslie drove distractedly, weaving in and out of lanes as her mind continued to creep back to her encounter with Robert. The word *passion* continued to bounce around, Leslie's head. She remembered passion—innocent passion—showered upon her by her first love, Darryl. From the moment they met at a church function, there was a spark—an electricity—that seemed to draw them to each other. The crowded room seemed to recede as they communicated their attraction for each other across the room. His smile was beautiful, revealing white teeth that weren't perfect but enhanced his mouth, lips that were small but sensuously shaped; the beginnings of facial hair—fine and smooth—graced his upper lip. He approached her, and with a simple hello they began a whirlwind courtship that led to marriage less than six months later.

Their wedding night began with nervous laughter and awkward moments. She was definitely a virgin, and this fact was evident in the way she recalled being afraid to take off her wedding gown. She softly chuckled as she remembered walking around their new apartment with reams of white silk and lace flowing behind her, knocking over a vase of flowers

43

on the coffee table.

"Why don't you take that dress off before you completely destroy the apartment?" he laughingly teased.

"Oh, no. I'm fine," she quickly replied.

She remembered trying to sit down on the sofa which sat very low to the floor in their furnished apartment. Her gown did not cooperate as she tugged and pulled, scooping up the fabric in great handfuls.

Darryl laughed again, then said, "Here let me help you."

He made a wide circle around her, exaggerating his movements with grand gestures, giving her wide berth. He stopped behind her and spoke softly in her ear.

"You are the most beautiful woman I've ever seen in a wedding gown. To know you are my wife makes me so proud . . . and scared."

"Scared? Why?"

"Because I want to do everything right for you. I'm afraid that somehow I'll disappoint you."

"That's exactly my fear. What if I'm not a good wife?"

He simply kissed the back of her neck, very tenderly, then he began to slowly unzip the dress.

"I love you, Leslie," he repeated over and over as he placed kisses all over her neck, her back. He caressed her arms as he freed them from the lacy material and stayed behind her as she finally stepped out of the dress. She wore a satin bra and matching panties, a garter and stockings. She shyly turned around, fighting the urge to cross her arms over her chest to hide herself.

"Can I touch you?" he asked.

"Yes," she replied in a small, timid voice.

He stroked her shoulder blades, softly caressing her collar bone. Goosebumps crept up her arms and he gently touched her there.

"Can I kiss you here?" he asked as he pointed to the spot on her chest where her pulsating heart could be seen rapidly beating beneath her skin.

"Yes," she whispered.

He planted tiny, butterfly kisses in a circle all around her heart, letting his lips linger there as her heart's beat became one, in unison with his.

"Baby, don't be scared. I've got you and I'll never let you go. All my love I will forever give to you."

She remembered the tears of joy. She remembered her innocence and the fact that he kept his promise to her. He loved her totally—passionately—from that day forward.

They made love softly as he continued to ask her permission to touch her here or there. She finally gave in to her desire as the incessant urge to have him inside of her overwhelmed her feminine instincts. She aggressively said, "Now, Darryl, now!" as she searched his face for understanding.

And with that he helped her cross the sweet line between pleasure and pain as her virginity was given to him with the most powerful essence of her—her love, trust and commitment—all wrapped tightly inside his embrace.

She loved him still and she missed him. She realized she had fled the scrutiny of Robert because she still held on to that love. She wasn't even able to give herself intimately to Bryan. Suddenly she felt as if she was betraying everyone—Darryl, Bryan, Anastasia, and even in a limited way, Robert. She began to second-guess herself now, thinking she never should have agreed to meet Robert. How can I hide my feelings of uncertainty about everything—even our relationship—from Bryan tonight? Bryan, she knew, was pretty good at reading her emotions; instinctively he knew when she was upset. Unashamed, she usually shared with him her concerns and fears. But not this time. No way could she tell him about Robert, about passion, about missing Darryl so very, very much. All these things she'd have to keep to herself for now.

The only thing she could do was think about something else and maybe—just maybe—by the time she saw him tonight, all traces of her talk with Robert would be gone from her mind, and she hoped her face and voice wouldn't betray her.

She mentally pictured her closet to select what she would wear tonight. She never had to worry about her attire as she shopped carefully and somewhat constantly. She had dozens of formal outfits, and because she was very picky about which events she attended, she was never seen in the same thing twice. She loved dressing up. Childlike in her enthusiasm for dressing to the nines, she prided herself that she was always one of the most elegant Black women at these affairs.

Her thoughts shifted from her wardrobe to Bryan again. Bryan McKay, a brilliant attorney and long-time friend and confidante, would be escorting her tonight to a firm-sponsored benefit. She'd known him since law school and almost immediately had formed a bond—a kinship—with him. Despite the fact that she was married, they had formed a bond of mutual respect and acquired a comfortable friendship. He was very attractive in many ways. His modesty was genuine, his mind quick, and his reasoning powers were impeccable, an excellent quality for a litigator.

Whenever they had a chance to visit, she'd openly ask him why he didn't have a girlfriend and he'd complain that he couldn't juggle women and school. To Leslie he seemed like an excellent catch, but so far no one had caught him. Leslie knew perfectly well his position on singleness for they had debated it on more than one occasion over the years. He loved his solidarity, time alone to think his thoughts and dream his dreams. He was fully aware of how picky he could be about the appearance of his home, having been taught from a very young boy to be neat and clean. He often stated that chaos in his home or office caused him to feel unsettled, unable to think clearly. While Leslie completely understood how he felt, she had come to realize that compromise is the key to a good relationship. The ability to compromise, she told Bryan, would help make him a more rounded individual, not quite so self-centered. He'd always laugh at her, shake his head in agreement and still concede that he knew his faults and that was why he chose to remain single. Besides, he felt women could really complicate a man's life with all their demands and needs.

Now he was managing his own practice, not affording them many opportunities to get together, but whenever they did, they easily fell into their familiar, comfortable routine of being companionably together. In the beginning of their budding friendship, they would discuss world events, the ever-changing judicial system, the weather—topics that weren't necessarily too personal or intimate. He respected the fact that she was married but once she suffered the tragic loss of Darryl, he became more than a friend, helping her through this crisis, even handling some legal matters concerning his estate and their assets when she could no longer manage to think rationally, grief overwhelming her ability to be rational.

Even though Bryan practiced criminal law, he also handled various other legal situations. He worked long hours and he worked alone. It was his belief that working by himself was the best way for him to be a good attorney and accomplish his own goals, not someone else's. He had recently been involved in a number of newsworthy, controversial cases which put his face in the news and on the television.

On top of his impeccable work habits, he was classically handsome. Definitely the kind of man that made women turn around and take notice. He was tall, with one of those bodies that no matter what he wore, jeans and a t-shirt or an Armani suit, he always looked good.

On one occasion she remembered he actually had hurt her feelings by stating that one of the reasons he loved being with her was because she was a "low maintenance" woman. Which in Leslie's mind translated to "no maintenance" and that was a completely wrong assumption about who she was and what she needed. Although she argued with him in a quiet way, she realized then how much he didn't really know about her and she didn't take the time to really share her feelings, fearing that she'd alienate him, causing a rift in their friendship. He wanted someone special in his life; thus Leslie was there and somehow the terms and level of their companionship had developed in such a way that now she was comfortable with the terms they had unwittingly established.

As aggressive as Bryan was with his cases, he never was quite so aggressive with her and up until now, that suited her just fine. After all, she didn't need any further complications in her life either.

As she thought about Bryan she couldn't help also thinking about Robert, causing her to wonder about what kind of man he was too. Black men, she mused, were a treasure. A good one was hard to find, but if you got lucky enough to snag one, he would be as fine and delicate as a piece of gold; as strong, pungent, and flavorful as an excellent glass of wine; with strength and power like that of a diamond—a precious jewel. She'd had been blessed with her very own jewel once. Maybe that was all she ever needed.

Her thoughts were beginning to stray far from the night ahead, she realized as she pulled into her garage. Well, it really didn't matter. She knew that upstairs in her closet she would find exactly the right dress to set the mood for her evening with Bryan at the Atlantic City Casino Night fund raising event.

⟡

Leslie was just splashing Coco Chanel behind her ears when Bryan rang the doorbell. He was as prompt as ever. She loved that about him. Up to this point, they rarely ever kept each other waiting. He looked extremely handsome in his midnight blue tuxedo with a paisley vest, stark-white banded collar shirt with a bold stone of cobalt blue—a button holder—at his throat. My, my, my, he is so fine!

"Hey lady, don't you look beautiful tonight," Bryan said.

"I was just about to say the same thing to you. But fine was the term I was going to use."

"Oh well, you know, what can I say?" he said while twirling around, primping and acting like a stuck-on-himself soul brother. She laughed at him, suddenly wanting a hug really badly as her mind thought of Robert and the laughter they had shared today.

"Would you like something to drink before we leave? I've got an excellent Chardonnay chilling," she said.

"Actually, I was wondering if you're on the menu of things to drink, because, oooh, girl, I'd like to take a sip of you!" Bryan said mischievously.

"Watch out, now, I just might take you up on that offer later. Now, do you want some wine or not?"

"No, not really. I'm going to wait till we get there, and then I'll have something. But I don't mind if you do."

"Nope, I'll pass too. Well then, I guess we're ready to go. Let me get my coat."

As she walked in front of him she could feel his admiring eyes on her. The dress she wore was cut low in the back, revealing her smooth, caramel skin. Her gold-sequined dress fit every curve of her body like a glove. Luckily, the dress looked as if it was designed just for her.

"Let's go."

"I'm with you." Just then he grabbed her and tenderly placed a kiss on her cheek and then a quick peck on her neck.

"Umm, you smell good. You sure you want to go to this thing? I mean, we could stay here and make a little magic of our own," Bryan teased.

Leslie's eyebrow shot up in a questioning way at his aggressive moves and his undertones tonight. While this certainly was not the first time they had taken a simple compliment of each other to another level, it surprised her because she was not thinking of him in this way. Certainly not tonight. Her confused state of mind came back suddenly as she teetered on the edge of uncertainty about how things had been going with Bryan. And nothing brought that confusion to the surface more quickly than her day with Robert. His easygoing manner and clear interest in her caused stirrings of longing deep within her that she could no longer deny. It was unfortunate that these feelings did not extend to Bryan, and she was sad and somewhat ashamed that the passion she and Robert talked about today did not apply to her relationship with Bryan.

"While the thought of staying here sounds nice, I've got to go. You know my firm is sponsoring this event because I practically forced them into it. It wouldn't look too good if I didn't show up, now would it?" He was still holding her close, looking into her eyes as she said this. He released her then. Leslie noticed a brief flicker of something cross his face, but she could not interpret it. While she really wanted to be kissed—passionately—the question was, by whom?

"You're right. I was just testing you anyway, girl. Let's go do dis," he said, using his favorite slang.

Every now and then he showed a playful side, dropped the conservative lawyer act, and was just another Black man sweet-talking a woman. The down-to-earth Bryan didn't emerge as often as Leslie would have liked, but when he did, Leslie found that Bryan very intriguing, kind of dangerous, worldly and very exciting.

They drove in his car, which was immaculate as always. The smooth leather seats in his Cadillac Seville hugged her body, and the smell of new leather surrounded her senses. She loved that new-car smell—it was mixed with the sweet scent of his masculine cologne. She closed her eyes and took deep breaths while her mind took her back to Darryl and their numerous adventures on car trips. He too had been a careful, courteous driver. Smooth and in control just like Bryan was. That was definitely one of the things she liked about him. He often reminded her of Darryl, his mannerisms, his conversation and his ability to listen intently to her when she spoke. All those elements were important to her, and as she weighed all the things she wanted in a man, Bryan met most of them. She did not think she would ever love him in the same intense way she had loved Darryl. Her heart had become one with Darryl's long ago and deep inside she thought it would always belong to him and him alone. Death might have parted them, but only in a physical sense; spiritually he would always be there.

Bryan interrupted her introspection as he continued to chat about his newest client—a criminal—or "gangsta," as he put it, chuckling about how unconvincing this guy's arguments had been. Even to Bryan's ears it was all bull, pure and simple.

"But you're still going to take the case, aren't you?" Leslie asked.

"Damn straight. He may be a criminal, but he's a criminal who can pay my fees!"

"Bryan, I'm shocked! Is everything all about money to you nowadays?"

"No, but everyone deserves good representation. All I'm saying is, if he can pay for it, well, then, he's got it."

Leslie stared at his profile and for a moment wondered about where his ethics and morality were going. While she agreed that everyone deserved a good lawyer, she didn't think she could represent someone whom she didn't believe in, someone who she doubted was telling her the truth. She wondered how Bryan could do it.

They continued to talk easily and comfortably on the way to the event. She decided to put aside her judgments and instead focused on listening to the deep baritone of his voice as a comfortable, relaxed feeling came over her. Concentrating on the words he used and the way he used them helped her to see how and why he was such a good attorney, realizing that on more than one occasion she had found herself telling him things she would never tell any other man, except her late husband. Bryan was easygoing, and he never made her feel that she had to be on the defensive. The dialogue they shared was amicable and so easy.

"Good evening, madam." The valet attendant had opened her door, extended his hand to help her from the car. They had arrived and she had barely noticed.

"Good evening. Thank you," she replied.

They entered the elegant hotel lobby. Leslie knew exactly where to go. The ballroom was up the escalator. As they rode the escalator she started whispering to Bryan.

"I'm so nervous! I put my heart and soul into this project. It better be a success!"

"Don't worry. If I know you, it will be more than a success."

"Well, all I know is I practically beat the managing partners down trying to get them to lend their support and their money to this project."

"Don't forget you beat me up too! I haven't forgotten the check I wrote to help your cause. I was glad to do it. It's about time we started giving back to our community."

"You got that right."

As they arrived on the top floor, she grabbed Bryan's hand and led the way, bypassing the table that was strategically placed to check people in, give them name tags and a schedule of the evening's program. She waved at her secretary, who immediately saw her once she stepped off the escalator. Leslie and Bryan began talking with some of the other lawyers who had already arrived, sharing mindless niceties with them while in the back of her mind Leslie again silently prayed that this evening would be a success.

The grand ballroom had been set up to resemble a casino. She recalled how hectic the planning had been, remembering how difficult it was to convince the retailers who rented the gambling tables that her event would not include real gambling, that her guests would be provided fake chips to play the games. No one was going to lose money tonight, at least not from gambling.

The majority of the proceeds would go to various African-American agencies that badly needed operating capital. She and her committee had chosen several non-profit organizations; one helped educate teenagers about sex and preventing teen pregnancy. Another agency they'd selected had facilities that boys and girls could go to after school located in neighborhoods where minorities lived; the only African-American adoption agency in the city would also receive some of the proceeds, and so would a newly-formed shelter which housed approximately sixty homeless families.

She walked around the ballroom inspecting the various displays of items for auction, the card tables and the crap tables. She became mesmerized by the spinning roulette wheel and talked with a blackjack dealer. The dealers she'd hired were actually from Las Vegas, completing the authenticity of their make-believe casino. Each table had a small plaque displaying the name of the law firm which had graciously contributed funds for that table. Almost all of the major law firms had participated, gladly attaching their names to this most generous fund raising event. Leslie critically looked around the room, making sure everything was as she and her committee wanted it to be.

The food tables were beautifully decorated with fresh flowers and a delicious array of fruits and cheeses, succulent shrimp, hot wings, potato salad, dinner rolls, and pasta in silver-domed dishes with various sauces to choose from, marinara, alfredo, and pesto. She was pleased that everything looked great.

Throughout the evening there would be a silent auction. The items that were being auctioned were generously donated from a number of successful businesses in San Diego. When she first came up with the idea to hold an auction and a casino evening, she had decided to approach various business owners with her concept, making it clear that the purpose was to help fund minorities, their education and their community. She realized that being that straightforward and bold might backfire, but she believed in her project. She felt strongly that it was about time the city of San Diego took a special interest in these communities. She made a personal commitment to pave the way for others to take the same care and interest she had, to try to make things better for her people.

"Everything looks great, Leslie. You did yourself proud, girl," Bryan said as he came up behind her and spoke gently in her ear.

"Yeah, it does, doesn't it?" she said proudly. "I'm so excited! I want to jump up and down and scream, 'Isn't this great! Isn't this wonderful!' Look at this —" she said, extending her hands wide.

"You look like you're about to jump right out of your skin. You need a drink. Girl, calm yourself down," he said as he grabbed her hand, laughing at the exuberance she was displaying.

"Okay. Let's go get one right now."

The large ballroom was set up with bartenders in the four corners of the room, making easy access for the patrons. The proceeds collected from the sale of cocktails would also go to the charities. Drink up, my friends, she thought. She had even had the foresight to arrange for a block of rooms to be used in case anyone was too drunk to drive home. She had tried to think of everything to ensure all the guests had a good time, without risk to themselves or others. Always the lawyer!

In no time the party was in full swing, and it appeared that people were having a great time. Upon their arrival guests had been provided with play money and chips to wager, so the blackjack and crap tables were full of people learning how to gamble. It turned out to be a wonderful way to learn to play the games without real financial risk. They had left plenty of room for a dance floor. As the music changed from smooth, mellow jazz to more soulful music, top 40s, R&B, and occasional slow jams, people began to dance. Gambling, drinking, laughing, talking and bidding were happening simultaneously. It was a whirlwind of activity, and Leslie felt proud that everyone had supported the effort and seemed to be genuinely enjoying themselves.

She had stopped to talk to one of the managing partners at her firm and Bryan excused himself. Later, she scanned the room looking for him. He was standing at the crap table, talking with a gentleman she didn't immediately recognize. He was very handsome, tall and slim, with generous lips and a thick mustache. They seemed to be speaking in hushed tones, standing very close to each other, heads bowed almost touching, as if they were whispering. She walked over to them, very curious and anxious to get a better look and, of course, to introduce herself. She thought it might be one of Bryan's clients.

"Hello, gentlemen. You having a good time?"

"Oh, Leslie," Bryan jumped. "Uh, this is a good friend of mine—uh, Walter—Walter Brody." Bryan seemed to be nervous and stumbled over his words. Leslie was taken by surprise at his reaction; she didn't know what it meant or how to take it.

"Hello, Leslie." He extended his hand for Leslie to shake. "I've heard so much about you. Bryan and I have been friends for quite some time, and he told me about this Casino Night affair. I decided to drop by and see it for myself. I didn't receive an invitation. Perhaps because I'm not a member of the elite legal community." He said this looking directly at Bryan with contempt in his eyes.

There definitely was friction in the air, and Leslie was even more puzzled than before. This man was definitely not a client.

"Well, Mr. Brody, I'm delighted you could attend," Leslie greeted him pleasantly. "This event certainly was not meant to exclude other members of our community. In fact, you'll find a variety of business people here tonight. If I had known you were a friend of Bryan, I would have sent you an invitation myself."

"That would have been nice. But, anyway, I'm enjoying myself. Whoever set this up did a really good job. It's really authentic. I almost feel like I'm in Atlantic City, minus the lights and noise." He paused and then added, "And real winnings." He smiled then and Leslie laughed.

"Well, there is a flip side to that. There will be no losses either. Not tonight."

She noticed that Bryan hadn't said a word. He was quiet, seemed preoccupied, and although Leslie made it a point to include him in their conversation by glancing periodically at him, he seemed distant. Then, abruptly, he just walked away.

Leslie was surprised, then felt oddly as if she had been intruding. Worried that somehow she had just offended Bryan, she decided to leave. She extended her hand to Walter. "I've really enjoyed talking to you, Walter, but I think I'd better start mingling around the room, make sure all my other guests are enjoying themselves too." They shook hands as Leslie excused herself to join some of her co-workers at the blackjack table. Walking away, Leslie suppressed a shudder. His hand was as smooth and soft as a baby's behind; his handshake limp, dowdy, unimpressive. Oooh, she did not like a man with soft hands; a callous here and there was a sign of an honest, hard-working man as far as she was concerned. She whispered, "Yuck," and plastered a smile on her face as she quickly rejoined the others.

❧

Outside, Bryan furiously paced the lobby, taking large strides, stomping, causing small clouds of dust to sprinkle the air around him. He was clearly agitated. Walter watched him for a time, wondering whether it was safe to approach him. He looked as if he could kill somebody, Walter decided. What the hell, if he's pissed, he's pissed. He'll get over it. He always does.

"Hey, man. You out here pacing like something done pissed you off. What's up?" Walter tried to sound funny, but Bryan obviously missed his humor, because he glared at him as if he'd like to kick his behind.

"What the hell you mean? 'What's up?' Man, what was you tryin' to do in there—give me away? Why'd you show up here anyway? I told you not to come." He tried to keep his voice low; but when he got mad, he also got loud.

"Look, from where I sit, if anybody's going to give you away, it's going to be you. Why you tripping? You know I just wanted to meet the lady. She kinda fine, if you like that sort of woman." Walter smirked.

"You know why I'm tripping. I told you before, it's not necessary for you to show up at stuff like this. I've tried to tell you repeatedly that I know what I'm doing and why. You've just got to trust me, okay? I'm runnin' out of patience. I swear if you do this again, our deal is off! You got that?"

"Yeah, I got it. I just wonder how long you think I'm going

to play this game with you. How long you think I'm going to wait?" Walter stormed off, not expecting an answer.

❦

Leslie stood back witnessing this exchange from across the room. Puzzled, she gingerly approached Bryan.

"Bryan, what's going on? Why is your friend leaving? Why is he so angry?"

"Oh, baby, it's nothing, really. Just a—uh—business dispute, that's all. Hey, how's it going inside? We haven't had a chance to dance yet. I think I hear Luther playing. Come on, girl, let's dance."

He smoothly maneuvered Leslie onto the dance floor, and Leslie could tell he wanted to avoid answering any more of her questions. She allowed him to think she had been sidetracked, knowing full well they would have to discuss those questions later. Something just wasn't quite right about all this. There was no way she was going to let this slide—not without an explanation more concrete than "a business dispute." What kind of dispute could elicit that kind of exchange? What "deal" had Bryan been referring to?

They danced, talked, ate, gambled, and genuinely had a wonderful evening together. She wished it didn't have to end. The silent auction was a success. Everyone seemed pleased at the things they successfully had bid on and taken home. The ample proceeds would provide a generous contribution to all the charities selected to receive the funds. Leslie left the closing up to her colleagues, and she and Bryan decided to head home. She was exhausted.

In the car, she unconsciously took more deep breaths, inhaling his fragrance mingled with the leather interior again.

She thought about Darryl; she could almost hear his voice telling her she'd done a good job. Smiling at the thought of him, she reached down to slip off her shoes and closed her eyes. She ended up dozing on the way home, and she didn't rouse until Bryan gave her a peck on the cheek to awaken her. Her eyes were still closed but she smiled at him.

"Oh, Bryan, I'm so sorry I fell asleep. I guess it really has been a long day."

"Don't even worry about it. I knew you were tired. You did a good job, Leslie," he said, his voice softening. "It looked like everybody had a good time. Even I bid on some items. I ended up with one thing. Well—actually—I got something for you."

"What, Bryan? What did you get for me?" Surprised, Leslie stared at his perfect silhouette, illuminated by the light of the full moon.

"Flowers."

"Flowers?"

"Yep, a six-month supply of flowers to be sent to you on a weekly basis. A different bouquet every week. I thought you'd like that. Beautiful flowers for a beautiful lady." He leaned over to affectionately kiss her again.

"That is so sweet, Bryan. Thank you. You know I love fresh flowers. I meant to bid on that myself, but I got so preoccupied that by the time I remembered it, the bidding was closed. Hmmm, so you got them, huh, just for me. You are something else."

"That I am!"

"Bryan . . . what was really going on between you and that guy, Walter?"

"Nothing. Don't worry about it. It really was nothing. Okay?"

"If you say so, but it didn't feel like nothing."

Suddenly she felt shut out of something she did not understand. And it hurt her feelings. So much so that even though she knew she should invite him in once they got to her house—she wished she could be excited about it—about him—but hearing Bryan talk about representing people simply for money and thoughts of Robert kept her from being the least bit enthusiastic about extending such an invitation. But, she chided herself, he had just purchased a six-month supply of flowers for her. She turned to him, realizing she had to ask him in at least for coffee, if only for the sake of manners and continuing their routine. Though she felt guilty about it, tonight she prayed that he'd refuse.

"Would you like to come in?" Leslie asked, holding her breath, afraid he'd say yes.

"Can't. Sorry, Leslie, I've got some research to do tomorrow. I'd better call it a night."

She exhaled with relief. "Maybe next time." She paused. "Well, then, I guess this is goodnight. Thank you for being there for me tonight."

"No prob. You know I'm always there for you."

He quickly exited the car to open her door. They walked together to her front door. Leslie was exhausted but happy. Bryan gave her a big hug and was quickly gone. Today was a good day, Leslie thought.

As she slowly climbed the stairs, visions of Darryl danced through her head. She remembered their nights of passionate, blissful lovemaking, but now only the bitter taste of loneliness assaulted her thoughts. She trudged to her bedroom where she was forced to undress and get into bed alone. Before she fell asleep the word *passion*, *passion*, *passion*, kept repeatedly running through her head, as if trying to cast a spell, and surprisingly Robert's face floated in and out of her dreams.

CHAPTER VII

Monday morning came much too fast, but Leslie was up bright and early. She felt euphoric, eagerly anticipating the day. She knew her good mood had a lot to do with the success of her fund raiser, Atlantic City Casino Night, and she had to give some credit to having met Robert. The easy rapport they had with each other left her feeling as if she'd found an old friend. Puzzled about her weekend, Leslie couldn't wait to call her girlfriend, Michelle, to get her opinion about everything that had happened. Glad she was free for lunch today, Leslie's morning flew by as she rushed to meet her friend, confidante, and adviser in all matters of the heart.

"Hey, girl, waz up?" Michelle cried excitedly as she saw Leslie approach.

The two women warmly hugged each other; then giddy with pleasure they sat, anxious to begin telling each other all about the latest happenings in their respective lives.

"Too much, girl, too much."

"Oh, oh, now give me the scoop. What happened while I was away this weekend?"

"I met a man."

"Who?"

"His name is Robert. I met him at George Washington High at a school thing for Anastasia. Anyway, he saw me and— struck by my beauty," she giggled, "he started talking to me— asked me to join him for coffee."

"And . . ."

"Well . . . we had coffee, then we walked around Seaport Village, and had a wonderful conversation. I really liked him, until—"

"What! What happened?"

"He started talking about passion and if I had any in my life, and my relationship with Bryan came up."

"You told him about Bryan!"

"Well indirectly, but anyway, he got all personal and wanted to know what Bryan did that made me happy. And—I couldn't answer the question."

"You know I've always said your relationship with him is beyond strange. I mean, you've known the guy for years and you've never slept with him. That's got to be some kind of record, or something."

"It's not a sexual relationship; our friendship is so much more than that. We have been intimate in a way. Know what I mean?"

"I wish I didn't, but yes, I definitely do."

"Anyway, we both know how sex can sometimes ruin everything you have that's good."

"Only in your world, Leslie. In mine, it solidifies the relationship, especially when I get through rockin' his world, okay!" she said, snapping her finger in her unique, sassy way. "Seriously, Leslie, don't you want that kind of intimacy with Bryan?"

She sighed loudly before she answered, "You don't understand. I guess it's more complicated than even I can explain. The bottom line is, I am happy with Bryan."

"So happy that you spent an entire afternoon with a guy you just met, having the time of your life, getting all horny and shit."

"Who said I was horny? Damn, Michelle, you can be so crude sometimes."

"You should try it, girlfriend, it's good for your soul."

"Let's order. I'm starved."

"You got that right. You're starving for some serious lovin', and don't front about it, Leslie. Remember, I know you."

"How could I forget?"

Over lunch, their conversation turned to less passionate subjects and Leslie tried to push the Bryan/Robert subject out of her mind. Once she returned to her office, Leslie's mind drifted to that embarrassing night with Bryan many years ago.

Warm summer breezes lifted the soft folds of her skirt as she and Bryan headed to the outdoor concert at Humphrey's By the Bay. Bryan had decided to treat her to a special concert featuring the soulful vocalist, Peabo Bryson, knowing that one of her greatest pleasures was music, especially slow jams, where provocative lyrics, coupled with the sexy moans of a saxophone could cause her to feel weak. That's exactly what happened the night she listened to Peabo sing some of his greatest hits. His voice penetrated her soul, particularly when he sang "Feel the Fire." These lyrics roused an emotional, deep yearning within her, pulling at her strings of desire to an extent that she actually felt dizzy with the need to give in—to thoroughly enjoy a night of sensual pleasure. Each time she glanced at Bryan's profile, a burning sensation would begin to build from the bottom of her toes, spreading to her tummy, where a tumble and rolling sensation caused a warmth to settle nicely between her legs, like heated embers of passionate yearning waiting for sweet release.

They left the concert walking hand-in-hand, both on the edge of sinful desire. Bryan held her hand gently at first, then applied firm pressure to her sweaty palm. She squeezed his hand back and looked into his eyes, hoping he would see the power of her physical need for him there. He stopped in the middle of the parking lot to give her a deep, penetrating kiss. He whispered something in her ear; she didn't really hear what he had uttered; it really did not matter because his intentions were clear, for she knew tonight would be the night they'd make love for the first time.

Hungrily and eagerly anticipating their union, Leslie quickly unlocked her front door, hoping Anastasia would not hear her enter and, like two children doing something naughty, Leslie and Bryan headed for the staircase, whispering and giggling, to her room. Bryan stopped her from turning on the light by grabbing her hand and gently placing it on top of his rising manhood. She groaned out loud. He covered her mouth with sensual kisses, covering her face with butterfly kisses, tracing wet paths down her throat where he settled for a few minutes, enjoying the feel of her quickening pulse against his lips. Again, Leslie moaned. Leslie's excitement grew with every touch and stroke of his expertly guided hands. She missed this so much, she realized.

She began to fumble for his zipper and ended up slamming her head into his chin. They both yelped and then collapsed, giggling helplessly, onto her bed. She apologized over and over again, muttering, "I'm sorry," through hiccuped laughter.

She remembered how she decided to straddle him and that seemed to be when everything went wrong. The erection he had earlier been so eager to have her touch was now gone. She wasn't worried at first; she just began to kiss him and glide her soft hands over his muscled arms and chest. She realized after some time that he was still not responding, not only in terms of no longer being excited, but there were no moans of ecstasy spilling from his lips. He didn't even respond by gyrating and moving his limbs against hers. Leslie stopped her attempts at seduction and stared into his face. His eyes were open, his lips slightly parted, and he was staring at the ceiling. Leslie rolled off him.

"What's wrong, Bryan?"

"I'm not sure."

"What do you mean 'you're not sure'? I thought you wanted this."

Suddenly, he jumped from the bed, quickly rearranging his clothing. His face was a mask of confusion and embarrassment. Leslie read it wrong. She thought he realized he didn't really desire her at all, that the ambience of the evening had caused him to feel—temporarily—something unreal. She jumped from the bed suddenly angry. She felt like a woman scorned.

"Bryan, I think you'd better go."

"Uh, yeah, I think so too," was all he said as he quickly left her room, leaving Leslie startled, angry and ashamed.

The question "Why doesn't he want me?" reverberated in her head all night long, as Leslie fell into a troubled, tearful sleep.

"Excuse me, Leslie."

Startled from her musing, Leslie looked up into the face of her assistant.

"Yes, Jessica," she replied while absentmindedly rearranging the papers on her desk.

"It's almost six and I was wondering if you mind if I leave now. Do you need anything else from me tonight?"

"No, that's fine. You can go."

"Are you all right, Leslie? You seem a little shaken. Everything okay?"

"Oh, everything's fine. I was just thinking about something that happened a long time ago. I'm fine. You go ahead, enjoy your evening and I'll see you tomorrow."

She left Leslie alone with her thoughts and her doubts about Bryan. Leslie realized that she was wasting precious time thinking about the past when there was so much going on in the present. She grabbed her purse and decided to head to the jail before visiting hours were up. She'd promised Horace she'd come see him and that's exactly what she was going to do.

CHAPTER VIII

Anastasia came rushing into the kitchen, opened the refrigerator, snatched an apple and turned, looking wildly anxious at her mother.

"Hey, Mom. I'm late. I was supposed to be at school early today to do more research before my first class. I've got that special research project in science and I don't have enough material yet."

"Well, you go ahead, but slow down—you've got plenty of time. What time did you want to be there?"

"At least forty-five minutes before the first bell rings. Now I'm only going to have thirty minutes even if I hurry."

Anastasia gave her mother a quick kiss and ran out the door. Startled at her uncustomary sign of affection, Leslie watched her go and prayed she'd drive carefully. That girl is so much like me when I was younger, a flurry of motion and activity, she thought. Maybe she's getting back to her old self; she did ask me to help her finish up her science project tonight. I hope so, Leslie thought.

Later that morning, Leslie entered her office and began to dig in. She should have done some research over the weekend but had been too busy having fun. Now she had to pay the piper. Leslie was concentrating on the document in front of her when the telephone rang, startling her.

"Leslie Hughes."

"Hey, girl! This is Bryan."

"Bryan, hi. How are you?"

"Great. Listen, I've got some free time this afternoon and wanted to know if I can steal you for a while—a little afternoon delight. Can you meet me for lunch?"

"An afternoon delight, hmm? Sounds kinky." Leslie laughed at his suggestion.

"Well, you never know where it could lead. Can you meet me, let's say, at one?"

"Sure. Wait. Let me check my calendar. Okay, no problem. I'll see you at one."

Leslie hung up thinking, now what's really going on? It was getting harder and harder for her to play this game of sexual hide-and-seek with Bryan, especially right after meeting Robert. Already she felt a difference coming over her. Now she began to realize how over the years he had constantly kept her off guard, and suddenly she didn't like it. The fact that she was never really sure what his intentions were or what she meant to him other than being really good friends—buddies— now left a sour taste in her mouth. While she loved Bryan, something was definitely missing. Passion? she questioned. She thought about herself and all she had to offer a man. She was without question sexy, smart, and interesting. Maybe today, at lunch, she'd bring up their relationship and actually talk about what her concerns were. Not really wanting to rock the boat, but feeling that there was no other choice, Leslie made the decision to plunge in and ask him if he was sexually attracted to her. Then she'd decide what to do.

Promptly at one o'clock, while Leslie was still buried in

books, trying to weed through the many cases regarding appealing the involuntary manslaughter conviction for Horace Brown, her secretary, Jessica, buzzed her.

"Yes, Jessica."

"Ms. Hughes, Mr. McKay is here to see you."

"Oh, he's right on time," Leslie said glancing at her watch, "Send him in, please."

Bryan walked into her office, grinning from ear to ear. She could tell that the sight of her buried in books was comical. The precarious way she had the books surrounding her looked as if they would topple over at the slightest breeze. She hadn't realized how many California Reporters and Federal Reports volumes from the library were now surrounding her, and her computer buzzed with even more cases from her LEXIS search.

"I know, I know. I got a little carried away," Leslie said.

"A little carried away—I think a lot carried away would be more accurate. Doing a 'little' research, huh?"

"Yes, smarty pants, I am. I know you're not making fun of me, when I know your office must look the same way when you're involved in some serious research."

"I have to admit it used to. Now I just take over one of my empty offices and it looks like a cyclone hit it. In my own office I appear at all times to be completely in control. It works for me." Bryan strutted around the room, bragging.

"Well, I don't have that luxury. I'm starved, so if you're through harassing me about my office, can we go?" Leslie stood next to him, smelling his oh-so-familiar cologne, instantly feeling the warmth, security and comfortableness between them. This feeling between true friends, she realized, could not easily be replaced.

"Harassing you? Leslie, I would never do that." He reached

for her then and slowly encircled her waist, pulled her close, and tenderly kissed her lips. She was surprised but tentatively welcomed his embrace. He smelled so good. He began to caress her back, his hands firm and solid stroking her, traveling up and down, even sliding to her buttocks, and she involuntarily sighed. The feeling that he could never be more than a friend tugged at her. Pulling away, she searched his face. Finally able to speak, she said, "This is so unlike you. Don't get me wrong, it's not that I dislike it—really—it's just—well, inappropriate behavior for my office." He released her then, looking sheepish, even embarrassed.

"I'm sorry, Leslie. I don't know what got into me. It will never happen again, okay?"

Warring with herself, trying to identify and understand her conflicting feelings—they were changing so very rapidly—she simply said, "Okay. No harm done. Shall we go?"

Bryan sensed that something had changed between himself and Leslie. His fear of losing her had caused him to show the kind of affection that he had always withheld from her. He didn't know why he had kissed her and fondled her derriere, but it felt good. It felt right.

For the first time that he could remember, there was a definite tension in the air—a sexual tension—that was almost palpable. He thought Leslie looked uncomfortable. Perhaps she was remembering the time they had tried to be intimate. His failure still haunted him. He wondered how she felt about it. They never spoke about it, pushing it aside like a bad dream—something you just don't really want to remember the details of. He realized that they had never really been together and he had to admit that he was more than a little curious. She felt right in his arms, releasing a soft, sensitive, comforting touch, and there was no denying how attractive she was. Her feminine softness was like a mystery—something to be distantly admired.

He remembered how when he first met her he had acted like such a school boy, wanting her to see him at work. It was important to him that she know that in the courtroom, he was a force to be dealt with. He wanted to show her how his good looks, charismatic manner and style could oftentimes manipulate a jury. So he invited her once to observe his closing arguments on a high profile trial, and as she watched him, he could feel her respect for him grow. He mesmerized that jury with his smooth voice, expressive gestures and eloquent speeches. The women watched him with open, hungry looks; and men seemed to openly admire his strong persona and ability to articulate his thoughts in such a way that one completely understood and sided with him, no matter what the other attorney might have said.

I need to set things right with Leslie, he thought. I do not want to lose her because I acted impulsively today.

"Leslie, can I see you later?" Bryan said as he nervously picked up his wine glass and gulped the ruby liquid. "There's something I want to talk to you about, and I don't want to do it here."

"Well, tonight might be a problem. I've got to help Anastasia with a school science project and it might take a while." Bryan felt his face fall, but Leslie quickly added, "But let me call you. If you don't mind getting together late, we could probably still work something out."

"Okay. Call me when you're through." Bryan was amazed at how panicked he sounded, even to himself. His anxiety was growing by the second. It was then he realized that his new client and all its implications were making him act in ways he was totally unfamiliar with. His personal life was a mess. He needed Leslie, more than ever before.

❦

Back at the office Leslie took one look at the pile of books and she just couldn't take it. Legal research was not on her mind. Bryan was. But somehow she managed to roll up her sleeves and dig in, and the afternoon actually went by quickly. Before she knew it, it was six o'clock and time to go home. Anastasia needed her help on that science project.

Anastasia and Leslie worked until very late and Leslie was simply too exhausted to call Bryan. The room was a mess; remnants of colored construction paper, cardboard, glue and typed material were everywhere. Leslie had sent Anastasia to bed, promising to put the finishing touches on her project, and it took longer than Leslie anticipated. Anastasia wasn't a very good typist, which forced Leslie to type her paper. Even though it was Leslie's usual policy not to do projects for Anastasia, she felt okay about finishing this one because Anastasia had done all the research herself. She had even attempted to type it, but the end result was not very good.

Several times during the evening Leslie had thought about Bryan, but promised herself not to call until they were finished. Unfortunately, they weren't finished soon enough, and any thoughts of getting together with Bryan were long gone as Leslie fell into an exhausted sleep right there on the sofa; waking around three a.m., she stumbled to her room.

CHAPTER IX

Several weeks later, Leslie again found herself analyzing her relationship with Bryan, but she felt her heart and mind succumbing to Robert's charms. The weather in San Diego started to cool as the rainy season began and, as they rapidly approached the holidays, Leslie felt herself heading for trouble. She had it bad for Robert, and Bryan began to pale in comparison.

Leslie and Robert began their friendship with a bang despite the fact that he knew of her 'relationship' with Bryan. He pursued her with intense abandon. They intensely explored each other's minds, relishing in their easy communication—spending almost all their lunch hours together. He'd pick her up and off they would go to secret places to share precious time with one another. She shared with him the intricacies of the law, while he taught her about investments and mergers, happy that she was extremely intelligent; already she knew all about the process of buying and selling companies. He helped her resolve issues with herself, regarding Anastasia, and he listened while she explained her fears about marrying again, about her late husband and everything else they could possibly think to discuss.

These days it wasn't uncommon for Leslie's girlish laughter to echo through her house in response to a corny joke Robert had just told her. She would clutch the telephone, giggling, her eyes tearing from laughing so hard. Robert had a talent for mimicking voices of cartoon characters, his favorites being Daffy Duck and Bugs Bunny, and he used these voices to playfully tell his jokes. In addition to everything else, Leslie loved his sense of humor. Robert could make her laugh even when she felt like crying, frustrated over the limitations of the law, or her daughter, or even herself. He always helped her see a brighter, lighter side, using laughter as the best medicine. Even when she had serious issues to deal with and wanted to discuss those with him, he listened intently, often gave her sound advice and then, when he was satisfied that she felt better, having come to a resolution, he'd make her smile. It seemed he knew what she needed, when she needed it, and even how much to give. His instincts were uncanny. Stark memories of Darryl began to appear less frequently. It happened so subtly Leslie hadn't noticed.

She does not know how much she means to me, Robert thought, as he listened to the beautiful sound of her voice or the sensuous tone in her laughter. He felt a kind of freedom with her—an unpretentiousness—that made his heart swell with pride just because he knew her. His occupation was such a serious business—mergers and acquisitions—which involved so many risky decisions involving other people's money. He loved that he could break away from all that and be himself whenever he was with her. He was a very sensitive, kind man. One too many times, other females had taken his kindness for weakness. He'd sense potential for betrayal long before the women he'd been involved with even knew they would at some point betray him. From the moment he'd laid eyes on Leslie weeks ago at George Washington High, he knew instinctively that she was the one and only woman he ever wanted in his life.

"Leslie, let's take the kids to a movie this weekend."

"Okay. Which one?"

"I really don't care; let's let Malcolm and Anastasia decide."

"Robert . . . you know Anastasia is a little standoffish these days. I'm reluctant to even ask her."

"Leslie—"

"Hmm?"

"Don't ask her. Tell her we're going. Trust me, she'll have a good time. I'll stuff her with enough popcorn, hot dogs, candy, soda and junk food to make her my friend for life!"

Leslie laughed, "That may just do it. Gorge my child with decadent treats. Good idea!"

Having just come from the movies, Leslie, Robert, Anastasia and Malcolm shared a laugh as they enjoyed a pizza. True to his word, Robert had indulged both Anastasia and Malcolm with popcorn, soda and candy at the movies. Malcolm, a young man who seemed to be forever hungry, requested more food, claiming to actually be starving, so they continued their evening at a nearby pizza parlor, where noise, video games and mediocre pizza were plentiful.

In the car on the way home, they each shared their opinion about how the movie made them feel. The mistreatment of the heroine that ensued disgusted all of them. Leslie's heart ached for that character. It was refreshing that neither Anastasia nor Malcolm liked the way the women were regarded throughout the movie. Malcolm expressed anger that a man could be so cold to his wife, and he openly praised his own father for teaching him to never beat on or disrespect a woman. Leslie was so proud of the man sitting beside her and the young man in the back seat. They continued to discuss the movie, and actually all of them had rejoiced when at the end, all the women had become strong enough to free themselves from such abusive lives. Anastasia, of course, had very strong opinions about the movie, and she was not shy at all about voicing them.

"Well, I think anytime a woman is in a situation like that, she should get out right away. What took her so long?" Anastasia asked.

"Back then things were different and women weren't regarded with much respect," Leslie explained. "That was evident in the way her own stepfather used her and then sold her to this man he didn't even know!"

"But to be fair," Robert joined in, "he was probably just following in the footsteps of his own father, mimicking what he did with his mother. Things always have a way of going full circle."

"Yeah, but Dad, where was their common sense?" Malcolm wondered. "I mean it doesn't take a genius to figure out that you don't treat people like dirt, especially not your family."

"I can't explain it, Son. I'm just grateful that we're not that way. We respect our women, don't we?" Robert glanced at Leslie, and then winked at Malcolm in the rearview mirror. Leslie smiled.

Anastasia said, sounding disgusted, "Oh, God, do you guys

have to make goo-goo eyes at each other all the time?"

"Sounds like you're jealous," Malcolm said.

"Oh, please!" Anastasia hotly replied.

Robert jumped in before they could start arguing. "I can't help it. She makes me feel good," Robert said as he covertly slipped his hand into hers.

"I hope I don't act all sappy like that when I'm in love," Malcolm said. "I mean, Dad, you look kinda goofy."

"Goofy!" Robert said, releasing Leslie's hand to begin twirling his fist in the air as if boxing. Using his best Goofy imitation he said, "Who you calling goofy? Boy, I'll knock you out for calling me goofy." They all laughed at him, even Anastasia.

Suddenly there was a far-away look in Anastasia's eyes. Even as Malcolm continued the mirth by playfully teasing his dad in return, Leslie noticed that Anastasia had lost interest. She had obviously tuned out the others. Leslie hoped she wasn't about to spoil everything by being rude. Until that moment, they had enjoyed laughter and easy companionship. Their entire evening together felt so right. Please don't spoil it, Leslie prayed, silently begging Anastasia.

Watching Anastasia made Leslie think more closely about her relationship with Robert. For weeks she and Robert had shared so much together; until now they had not included their children in the development of their relationship. But in Leslie's mind, they fit together like a hand in a smooth kidskin glove. Tender and supple were their touches, and their intimate conversations were always magic. They easily opened up to each other. It often seemed as if they read each other's mind. Although Leslie knew these kinds of relationships were possible, it surprised her that she was experiencing it so early on. Her marriage to Darryl and her sound relationship with him was wonderful for a lot of reasons. One of which definitely was because of years of togetherness, knowing each other over time, being sensitive and aware. They had built a solid marriage and a great friendship, but it took time. Robert, on the other hand, easily penetrated her heart, mind, body and soul. Her body ached to be touched by Robert. She wanted to make love to Robert. She seemed to be craving his strong, ebony hands; she wanted him to caress her body in the most intimate way. She blushed at her own thoughts. She instinctively knew he would be gentle, kind and patient as he guided her to ecstasy. She was as certain of this as she was her very own name. And she refused to let all these wonderful emotions be marred by Anastasia. She knew Anastasia tried to make her feel guilty, especially to the memory of Darryl, but Leslie knew Darryl would have wanted her to be happy and she was, she really, really was.

Early in the evening Robert had asked both the kids for their permission to continue the evening with Leslie—alone—after the movies. Anastasia, for the first time, actually giggled and said, "No problem; I'm just going to get on the telephone anyway."

Leslie knew that was true and laughed out loud.

"Go ahead, Dad, have a good time," Malcolm added.

Robert dropped Leslie and Anastasia off, promising to return in a few minutes, once Malcolm was safely at a friend's house.

Anastasia, true to her word, immediately went to her room. Leslie heard the music begin and then she heard Anastasia's telephone ring. How'd her friends know she was home? Leslie thought, shaking her head at how quickly she'd lost Anastasia's attention. They hadn't even had a chance to talk themselves; then off she went to her own little world. Leslie felt slighted. She wanted to know what she thought of Robert and Malcolm. She felt cheated out of having a conversation with her. Fortunately for her, Robert would be returning soon and she wouldn't have any more time to dwell on what she felt she'd lost, precious, intimate conversation with her daughter.

⚜

"Leslie, let's go down to the beach. It's a warm evening and nothing relaxes me quite like listening to the ocean. You game?" Robert asked, hoping she'd say yes.

"That sounds nice. Yeah, let's go to the beach. Let me just grab a jacket in case it's really cold down there."

"You don't need a jacket, Leslie; I'll keep you warm. Don't you worry about that," Robert said, gracing her with one of his dimpled, sexy smiles. Leslie returned the smile but grabbed a jacket anyway.

As they headed out the door, Leslie was excited for some reason, so much so that her heart started to race, butterflies fluttered in her stomach and she felt a fine line of sweat form on her nose. The ocean was not exactly what she had been thinking about earlier; she had been wishing they could figure out a way to head to her bedroom, but the beach would be nice too. Besides, she hadn't quite worked out the logistics of lovemaking in either her house or his, not with the kids around. That would take special planning.

The drive to the beach was pleasant. Conversation was minimal; they had reached the point in their relationship where quiet companionship was fulfilling. Leslie felt particularly calm and at peace.

As they rounded a corner, Leslie said, "Oh, Robert, this is beautiful!" They had arrived in Del Mar. It seemed as if they were at the top of the world, teetering on its edge, looking down on the expansive wonder of the Pacific Ocean. Even though it was twilight, the view was clear due to the light of early moon. She watched as powerful waves crashed, ebbed and flowed. "I love this. I love the ocean," Leslie sighed. "I'm glad you suggested we come here." Leslie hugged herself with pleasure. Her eyes sparkled and she looked very young sitting there as excited as a child.

"Well, can you wait till I park the car before you jump out?" Robert teased.

"Barely," Leslie said, never taking her eyes off the splendid wonder of the ocean.

They walked hand-in-hand down the sparkling moonlit sand, to get closer to the water. Robert had remembered to bring a blanket and together they spread it out. Just as they were settling in, Robert said he forgot something and ran back to the car. Leslie had no idea what he could be going to get, but she relaxed, closed her eyes and let the ocean breeze gently caress her face. She breathed deeply, taking in the salt air and sea smells. Yes, this was just what she needed, Leslie thought; how did Robert know?

"You're looking extremely comfortable and let me also add—beautiful—sitting there in the moonlight. You better keep those eyes open; you never know who might sneak up on you." He dropped to one knee and gently brushed her lips with his own. Leslie opened her eyes, willing him to kiss her deeper and longer. That's when she noticed he had a picnic basket in his hand.

"What's that you've got there? You are full of surprises tonight."

"Well, I don't think I should be predictable, do you?"

"No, I like your way of thinking," she said as she rolled

over and got on her knees, excited to view the contents. "Umm, my favorite wine, cheese, crackers, grapes," Leslie said as she continued to rummage through the wicker basket. "I'm beginning to think you had this all planned," she teased as she also removed several scented votive candles in small clear glass holders. She watched him as he strategically placed them around the corners of the blanket, lighting each one as he went.

"Do you know what the lighting of a votive candle means?" Robert asked.

"No, what does it mean?"

"As I light each one, it is in honor to you and your beauty. They are lit to show my devotion and gratitude to you."

Sudden tears began to sting her eyes as she glimpsed a look of adoration come across his face, the face of the man she was coming to love and cherish so much. The flames from the candles flickered and danced, which distorted and hid some of his emotions, but she could feel how much he cared about her. A feeling of joy filled her and the tears that hung on the tips of her lashes threatened to spill down her cheeks. This precious chocolate man kneeling before her was full of sensual surprises, and each thing he did confirmed for Leslie how special and wonderful he was.

"Leslie, I pay attention to you. I think I know your moods and I definitely notice what you like. That's why I just happen to have your favorite wine," he said with relish as he brandished the bottle in a theatrical manner, uncorking it. "Now, take this glass and let me toast you."

"Toast me? Why?" Leslie gingerly took the glass from his hand, gazing at him with an open, raw expression of love on her face.

"Because you are rapidly becoming a special force in my

life and there is no other person I'd like to be with right now, or any other time for that matter." Robert stopped to catch his breath; his voice was low, husky and tinged with emotion. "And that gives me cause to want to celebrate knowing you and . . . " He paused, the words obviously getting stuck.

"And what? Don't stop now."

"Okay, I'll just say it then." Robert blew out a deep, long breath of air. "I want to celebrate knowing you. I think it would be easy to love you 'cause I'm falling hard." He paused, shaking his head as if to wake up from a dream.

"Leslie, you mean so much to me. Woman, you've stolen my heart and I'm so glad you did. You're everything I've been missing in my life for a long, long time. Whenever I see your face or hear your voice, it's like the feeling I get whenever I go home and walk into my mama's kitchen, and she's baking a cake or some bread."

"Sounds to me like you're hungry," Leslie teased, attempting to lighten the intensity of the moment.

He just looked her up and down and in a voice full of emotion he said, "I am."

He reached for her then, taking the wine glass from her hand. He closed the space between them, leaning into her, and in a slow, deliberate motion, he kissed her. Her mouth was cool; it tasted bittersweet, coated with the flavor of fermented grapes, remnants of the wine she'd just sipped. He caressed the roof of her mouth, enjoying its smooth silkiness with each stroke. Lost in the essence of her cologne and her warm embrace, he began to swirl his tongue with hers in a romantic dance. He gently sucked her bottom lip, slipped his tongue in and out of her mouth in a provocative, slow rhythm until he felt Leslie heat up with passion and desire. His large hands surrounded her back to gently lay her down. He wanted to lie beside her but she urged him to stay within her embrace, obviously desiring to feel the full weight of him upon her. Her moans reminded him of the purrs of an adored cat being lovingly petted and stroked.

He fit perfectly in her arms, and she thought, into her life. His hands, big and strong, began trailing her sides, caressing her bare, silky smooth legs, roaming up her thighs. She gasped, delighted with the feel of him, his masculine scent powerful with the aura of desire, sending waves of emotion through her as her stomach dived, as if on a roller coaster, at every place his hands touched her. She arched in a natural response to this intimate touching. He started to unbutton her shirt, one button after the other, slowly and deliberately, until her breasts were exposed. She could see he was surprised that she hadn't worn a bra, and her breasts, firm and glorious, sprang up to meet him. Her nipples were hard, as if straining to be caressed. His breath caught in his throat and a lustful groan escaped his lips. Gently he began to suckle her breasts, flicking one nubile tip with his tongue. Leslie sighed with delight and pleasure. Her eyes were closed and she forgot all about where she was. All she wanted was for his mouth to never stop pleasing her, teasing her. He moved to the other nipple and played the same game with it. Arching, wiggling and rotating her hips, Leslie unashamedly responded to every heated stroke. She felt his hand surround her breasts and gently knead them, while he kissed her tummy, flicking his tongue in and out of her navel. She opened her eyes then, wondering how far down he planned to go. She didn't have to wonder long before she felt her skirt being lifted up and his hands slowly caressing her inner thighs. The sight of the moon slipped away as she again closed her eyes once he had finally reached and touched the center of her. She heard him moan aloud when he felt her moistness. That told him how much she wanted him. She couldn't wait for him to taste her. Slowly he began to tease her womanhood with soft licks with the tip of his tongue. She uttered a startled cry and began to rock and buck, inching closer and closer to his mouth. Flicking, licking, sucking, blowing and teasing her, he'd bring her to the brink of orgasmic release, then pull back and start all over again. Building and building the intensity until she exploded, quivering with euphoric delight.

Her cries of ecstasy sounded muffled and Robert didn't understand why, until he looked at her. She had placed her hand over her mouth. He smiled at her then. He realized then, without question, he loved this woman. He was happy he had pleased her; he wanted to give her the world. He continued to place kisses all over her body and her face, as he waited for her breathing to return to normal and her heart to slow its rapid pace. She opened her eyes. They seemed to be hazel in color, a beautiful effect he thought came about because of the reflection of the moon.

"Robert, I can't believe you did that—here!" Her mouth was open in an expression of awe. She giggled nervously. He joined her and soon they were both howling like school kids, laughing and holding each other. It all seemed so young and innocent and wonderful.

"Robert, you make me so happy. You just don't know how much—" Leslie hesitated and then added, "Now, did I embarrass you with how loud I can get?" She was clearly teasing him; he saw that in her eyes.

"No, baby. I likes my women loud!" he said looking down at her, propped up on his elbow.

"You're something else. Now are we going to finish what we started?" she said as she pulled him close to her and wiggled her hips, "or was this just a test run?" Leslie's voice took on that husky tone he loved.

"Oh most definitely, we are going to finish it, but not here. I thought we'd enjoy the rest of this wine," he said as he poured more into her glass, "and admire our up-close and personal view of the Pacific together. That okay with you?"

"Um, hmm. It's definitely okay with me."

Leslie quickly rearranged her clothes, buttoned her blouse and bashfully accepted the glass of wine Robert was handing her. What is this man doing to me? she thought. Her senses were on overload; she felt sexy and shy, desirable and virginal, all somewhat simultaneously. She was not used to feeling confusion, not now that she was a 40-year-old woman. This feeling was so foreign to her that she felt uncomfortable, but not so much that she wanted anything to stop.

They talked companionably, watching and listening to each other and the continuous, soothing waves of the ocean. This romantic setting was perfect. Leslie stared at the fluttering, quivering light of the candles and felt the same stirrings of emotion within her. Everything that had happened this evening—from the movie and pizza with the kids, to this romantic interlude, had all helped to form a bond, a union between them. This was indeed a special, almost perfect love they shared. Robert knew just what buttons to push and Leslie felt just fine about it.

"It really is starting to get chilly out here. I can tell you're cold." She noticed Robert's eyes roaming up and down the front of her blouse as she felt her nipples become taut again.

Leslie said quickly, "Oh, that's not just because I'm cold. It's also called desire. That also makes the nipples stand up."

"Desire, huh. Leslie, do you really desire me?"

"I can't believe you asked me that question. Of course I

desire you. In fact, I—I—"

"You what? Cat got your tongue? Now that's a first. Tell me what you were going to say; finish your sentence." She could tell that Robert desperately wanted to hear her voice her feelings.

"I was going to say that desiring the man I love comes with the territory." She looked at him squarely then. She didn't flinch at her own words; even though she hadn't meant to say them, now that they were out, she realized she didn't regret them because she actually meant it.

Reaching up to stroke her face, Robert traced the outline of her lips, cheekbones, her eyelids and brows, as if he were trying to record every inch of her face into his memory forever. He cupped her chin in his hand and coaxed her face to meet his. The tenderness of his kiss sent chills down her spine. The gentleness with which he touched her and held her made the tears she'd been able to hold back earlier to finally spill down her cheeks. She felt so good! To her surprise, when she looked at him, he too was filled with emotion, his face somewhat contorted, trying to maintain his masculine control.

"I've finally found home." Robert uttered.

No longer able to maintain control, they both openly cried as they clung to one another, arms and legs firmly wrapped around each other, as they tenderly rocked.

CHAPTER X

In the morning Leslie woke remembering last night's emotional, sensual events. She could still feel his hands on her body, stroking her in secret places, arousing a level of sexual ecstasy she'd never experienced before. While Darryl had always been very tender with his lovemaking, he had kept things on a traditional note. The idea of being sensuously kissed in the manner that Robert had done was something she'd only read about, never thinking she'd ever experience it herself. The scent of his cologne still clung to her body, reminding her that last night was very real.

Inside her steamy hot shower she closed her eyes, relishing in the heady aroma of jasmine and strawberries. The wonderful fragrances softly penetrated her senses as she generously lathered herself. The gentle loofah sponge reminded her of the gentleness—the softness of Robert's kisses. She touched her own face, trying to recapture the feeling of him stroking her cheeks while he examined the contours of her face. These thoughts caused delicious chills of pleasure to ripple swiftly through her loins. She realized that full consummation had not occurred last night, and thoughts of Bryan's failed attempt came to her mind, causing her to suddenly feel bittersweet. Uncertainty and doubt crept along the edges of her mind. Suddenly, she was grateful that the water of her shower had become cool, forcing her to leave her aquatic sanctuary and her doubts behind.

She dressed quickly, wanting to share her morning with Anastasia and get her impression of Robert and Malcolm.

"Hey, Mom, you got back kind of late last night. You have a good time with Robert?" Anastasia was eyeing her mother curiously—did Leslie look different? She certainly felt younger.

"Yes, Robert and I had a wonderful evening together. We usually do. What did you think of him and Malcolm?"

"I liked both of them. Malcolm's kind of smart even though he's just a freshman," she said, laughing; then just as quickly she sobered. "You look like you're serious about his dad. Are you, Mom?" Leslie knew how worried Anastasia was about this relationship but she hoped she was happy for her, too.

"You know I've always tried to discuss everything with you and I want your opinion about this too. Yes. I like him a lot. I don't know exactly where this relationship is going but we are serious about each other. That's one of the reasons why we included you and Malcolm in our plans yesterday, since we're both concerned about what you guys think. Do you have any problems with Robert? You know, if we seriously hooked up, would you be okay with that?" Leslie held her breath. Anastasia's feelings and her answer were important to her.

"Ummm. I'm not sure yet. I haven't been around him enough to say for sure. But he's okay, I guess. Are you thinking about marrying him?" Anastasia's voice rose an octave and her eyebrows lifted in a questioning expression.

"We haven't discussed anything that deep yet, but you never know. We've obviously got a long way to go before we explore that. Besides, you know I also have feelings for Bryan. I'm going to have to talk to him about this too. It's only fair that he know how far this thing with Robert has gone."

"Why? Mom, Bryan's hardly ever around and he doesn't seem all that interested to me. Besides, you see Robert more than him anyway. Oooh, check Moms out. Trying to be a player!" Anastasia teased her.

"I am not trying to be a player. It's just that I've had this thing—whatever it is—with Bryan for a lot of years. I don't know what's going on with him. But I guess I should tell him I'm seeing someone that I'm getting real serious about. See what he says." Leslie paused, "The last thing I want to do is hurt his feelings. He's been my friend for a long time. He deserves to be told."

"Mom, I'm not trying to be mean, but Bryan seems weird to me. Like he doesn't quite connect, like he's never really here—you know, kinda distant, out there." Anastasia made a funny face and was gesturing wildly to demonstrate her point.

"He seems that way to you because you've always pushed him away. But he is our friend and he was there for us when Grandpa and Grandma died. Remember?"

"Yeah, I remember. He helped a lot. But Mom, does that mean you've got to be stuck with him?"

"No, it doesn't. But I feel a certain connection—an obligation to him. I care about him a lot. I just need to talk to him, that's all. It'll be all right, don't worry." Leslie said, more to reassure herself than Anastasia.

"I knew you'd replace Daddy one day," Anastasia mumbled. "I guess I better get ready for that, huh."

Leslie looked at her, startled.

"I can never replace your father. I wouldn't want to."

"Well, what do you call it?"

"It's called moving on with your life, continuing to live. And I know it's hard for you to understand, but your father and I talked about this."

Anastasia gasped and shrieked, "You talked about Bryan!"

"No, silly. We talked about what we would do if either one of us died. We were especially concerned about you . . . and we decided that if anything horrible happened to either one of us, we'd continue to be human—to live and love if and when it presented itself."

"So he gave you permission to replace him, right, Mom? Is that what you want me to believe?" she said on the verge of hysteria and rage.

"Stop saying that! I hate that word. You can never replace one person with another. There are special qualities that only your father had. I shared with him a special first love that I will never, ever forget. I loved your father. I still do."

Tears sprang to Anastasia's eyes and she sniffed, rubbed her eyes exactly as she used to when she was a little girl fighting sleep. Leslie's heart jerked as that clear image came to her. Her little girl was growing up and she was unhappy. Leslie felt tears begin to form hot and intense in her own eyes.

"Yes, I still love him and he gave me the greatest gift of all . . . he gave me you."

She hugged her and Anastasia at first resisted the contact. Leslie refused to let go until she felt some kind of response. Finally, she felt slim arms begin to raise as Anastasia embraced her. She clung to her mother, silently weeping.

"I miss him, Mom," she mumbled into her mother's neck, her breath hot against Leslie's skin.

"I know, baby, I do too. But can you understand I still want to love and be loved?"

"I guess," she responded, peeling away as she searched for

91

tissue.

Leslie wondered what to say next, noting that the moment had passed as a look of rejection came over Anastasia's face.

"What are you planning to do tonight?" Leslie asked, as she began to straighten up the kitchen, no longer able to meet the eyes of the daughter who seemed completely unwilling to understand or compromise, whose moods seemed to swing from one end of the spectrum to the next.

"Probably hang out with Kyndra like always. Maybe go to the mall. With the way you've been gone lately you'd never know if I broke curfew," she said as she actually smiled at her mother, her personality swinging again.

"Don't fool yourself, girlfriend. I'd know," Leslie retorted, shaking her finger at her in a playful manner. "How many times do I have to tell you I have a special kind of mother radar. I know when you come home late even if I'm not here to see you do it. Don't forget that, girl. Mother radar." She laughed then, thankful that her mood had shifted. She hoped Anastasia would never violate curfew, fairly certain that she had enough respect not to do that.

"Yeah, right, Mom, mother radar. That's a good one. Kinda like that other word you use, stupidism. You sure know how to make them up, don't you."

"Okay, girl, don't try me. Trust me, you do not want to have my mother radar bust your behind, now do you?" She tried to look serious, but they both ended up cracking up over her silly words.

The telephone rang, breaking in on their playful banter. Anastasia picked it up, and Leslie felt a little annoyed. She wanted to answer the phone; she hoped it would be Robert.

"It's lover boy, Mom." Anastasia teased, wiggling her hips.

"Give me that phone, girl." Leslie grabbed the phone and

gestured as if she were going to smack her upside the head.

"Hello."

"Good morning, Leslie. Did I catch you at a good time?"

"Good morning. I'm just talking to my daughter, schooling her again about my mother radar. You know about that, don't you?" Leslie asked with humor in her voice. "You've probably got it yourself, but it would be called daddy radar, am I right? You know what I'm talking about?"

"Umm, I think I do. Why? What brought on this conversation?"

"She was just informing me that since I've been out late myself, I wouldn't know if she broke her curfew. I had to remind her about mother radar. She knows what I'm talking about." Leslie looked at Anastasia and scooted her out of the kitchen so she could talk to Robert in private.

"I hope I didn't keep you out too late. I lost track of the time. I called to thank you for the evening."

"You're very welcome. I thoroughly enjoyed myself."

"How are you feeling today?" Robert asked.

With a sultry voice and sexy smile Leslie answered, "Good. No, actually I'm feeling great. I feel like a woman in love. And what about you?"

"Like we've got some unfinished business. So . . . what's on your agenda this evening? Can you get away for a while, come to my place?"

"Maybe. What's up?"

"Malcolm's spending another night with friends. So I thought I'd barbecue a mean steak for you and let you taste the best microwave potatoes in the state of California."

"Umm, microwave potatoes, that sounds so delicious," Leslie mocked him.

"You trying to tell me you don't think I make good 'taters?

Oh, I can throw down on some microwave 'taters," Daffy Duck retorted.

"Gawd, I swear you haven't got any sense."

"And that's what you love about me, right?"

"Hmm . . . perhaps," she coyly replied.

"So, how about it?"

"Steak and 'taters sounds good. I wouldn't miss a meal like that for the world. Actually tonight would be good because Anastasia has plans. Maybe her friend will spend the night. In that case, believe me, I will not be missed. What time?"

"Eight o'clock."

"Okay—"

"And, Leslie," he interrupted, "Don't be late."

"Have I ever let you down before? I'm always on time."

"You have never let me down and I can't wait to see you."

⚜

Robert hung up hoping he wasn't being too pushy. She was on his mind twenty-four, seven. He hadn't felt this way in a long, long time. One of his worst fears was of falling in love again and not having his feelings reciprocated. He did not want to make a fool of himself by going crazy about some woman who wasn't crazy back.

⚜

At 6:30, Leslie was standing butt naked in front of her closet. She didn't know what to wear to Robert's house. Something kinda sexy, she thought, but she didn't want to give him the wrong idea. On the other hand, what wrong idea would that be? Damn, the man had already tasted her in his own delicious way. Umm. She thought about his hands and his mouth. Oh, what a great lover she knew he would be. Perhaps she would find out tonight just what kind of lover he was as his sample intrigued her. Last night, her mind had silently begged him for more, a request that had not passed her lips. She thought about the fact that they had not fully consummated the act, although she wanted to so very badly, and was, in fact, waiting intent and eager, desiring that to happen. Then images of Bryan plagued her as she remembered again how her experiences with him had often led to disappointment and unfulfilled desire. Was Robert just like him? she wondered. A trickling of doubt crossed her mind as her heart went to war against her mind. Her intellectual self fought with her emotions. Her body knew that any man who could stimulate her to orgasm, without intercourse—who cared about her pleasure more than his own, that translated into someone who was good and sensitive, an unselfish lover.

She decided not to allow those negative thoughts to spoil her evening. The task at hand was deciding what to wear. Period! She wanted to pick something comfortable, yet alluring. So she selected a cashmere red sweater which seductively dipped in the front and black slacks. She slipped into a comfortable pair of black mule shoes, then examined her makeup and clothes one last time as she headed for the door. She stopped by Anastasia's room where she and her girlfriend were doing several things at once—listening to music, talking on the telephone (probably to some poor, not-very-mature boy) and to each other, while simultaneously painting one another's toenails. How can they concentrate on all this stuff at one time? Leslie thought.

"I'll see you two later. Stay out of trouble while I'm gone." They barely looked up at her.

"Oh no doubt, Mom. Besides, what kind of trouble can we get into on a Sunday night? We'll be fine, you go have a good time. And, Mom . . . tell Robert and Malcolm I said hi."

"I will. I'll see you two later." Leslie smiled, surprised at how quickly it seemed Anastasia had accepted her relationship with Robert after their brief discussion.

❦

Leslie arrived at Robert's house, excitedly anticipating another beautiful evening with him.

"Hi."

"Hi yourself. Come in. I just pulled the steaks off the grill. We can eat in a few minutes." He stepped aside to allow her entrance.

"It smells wonderful in here," Leslie said as she wandered in. "I didn't think I was very hungry but smelling that food is making my mouth water."

Once she was inside the confines of his home, an immediate feeling of comfort came over her. The high-vaulted ceilings opened up the room, where lots of greenery gave it a look of warmth. The living room was clearly masculine but not without a few feminine touches. The decor he'd chosen was contemporary chic. A cozy leather sofa, the color of maple syrup, was flanked by two oversized cream-colored arm-chairs. A unique glass coffee table sat low to the floor. It was a definite conversation piece. It was glass and wood, having odd angles and shapes; a triangle-shaped piece of wood flanked one corner, while in the center, the glass sat atop a round tubular base that then stretched to meet a rectangular piece of blond wood at the outer edge. Just trying to understand the design alone, she thought, would give one pause to admire it and wonder about who designed it.

She continued to peruse the room. The walls were covered with beautiful artwork. She studied and admired the stoic expressions on the faces of Africans in native garb. The artwork appeared to be original; it was definitely unique and she thought it said a lot about its owner's personality. His sense of style was very distinctive.

The living room displayed a stunning assortment of African memorabilia; an exquisite parade of staffs, canes, statues, and masks also lined the walls. Strategically placed where track lighting hit its angles just right stood a huge bronze statute of an African king and queen adorned in full headdress. It sat atop a tall black lacquer pedestal. It was glorious, a magnificent tribute to the regal elegance of the room. Leslie was overwhelmed by its graceful beauty.

"Oh, Robert, I love your African art. It's beautiful."

"Thank you. I've collected these works from different parts of the world. I try to visit the African-American art galleries in every city I've ever travelled to and, as you can see, I have quite a collection," Robert explained as he gave her a brief tour of the room. "Got this one in Atlanta," he said, pointing to the statue. "This is my way of admiring and worshipping my ancestors. I also never want my son to lose sight of where he came from, what our people look like and what they stood for before they were brought to this country as slaves. Proud kings and queens. Warriors."

"I'm very impressed with your collection."

"Yeah, me too. Can I have a kiss?" he asked while drying his hands on an apron that read *Master Chef - Hard At Work.*

"Yes."

She aggressively threw her arms around his neck and kissed him with telling intensity. As they stood nose to nose, they searched each other's face. Leslie felt as if she were drowning in a sea of desire. She enjoyed the feel of his body so close to hers. She released him as with sudden clarity she remembered what he was supposed to be doing.

He quickly retreated back to the kitchen.

"Would you like a glass of wine?" Robert asked.

"Sure, I'll get it while you're finishing up there." Leslie walked around him to open the refrigerator. A bottle of Chardonnay, her favorite brand, was sitting on the shelf.

"There're some wine glasses in the freezer. Use them, okay?"

"Okay," she said, impressed that he seemed to think of everything.

She poured two glasses and nibbled on some sliced vegetables that were sitting on the butcher block cutting board.

"You look good in the kitchen, Robert, very comfortable."

"Why thank you. You look good in my kitchen too!" He leaned over her intending to snatch a quick kiss. Instead their lips held and lingered, as he felt compelled to stroke her mouth with a slow, easy motion, tasting the wine, inhaling the scent of her sweet breath.

"Ummm, you taste like peppermint-flavored Chardonnay," he said, comically smacking his lips.

A provocative smile crept over her lips as she wished he would kiss her again. Instead, he turned his attention to a rich-looking sauce on the stove. A smile lingered on his lips too.

"What is that? It smells good."

"Oh, this here's my mama's secret recipe for steak sauce." He was doing a very poor imitation of a Southern drawl. She began to laugh again at his silliness. It seemed there was no end to the laughter and sheer joy of simply being with him.

"Secret recipe, huh. Now, how did you get it?"

"Oh, I stole it."

Leslie looked at him and he had such a serious look on his face that she couldn't help laughing. An infectious laugh began deep in her belly; the wine she had been sipping suddenly erupted from her mouth, spewing all over the room. All of a sudden they both were laughing so hard that they couldn't catch their breath. They were gasping and bending over at the waist. They stopped to wipe their eyes, looked at each other, then simply started all over again. This unexpected explosion caused both of them to start laughing even harder until sated and holding their aching sides, they got their laughter under control.

"I'm so sorry for spitting wine at you. I wasn't expecting that response, or that face. You are crazy!"

"Well, next time cover your mouth, woman; you almost added an extra ingredient to my sauce." He playfully shooed her away from him, and she sat on a bar stool, watching him quietly. He was a master in the kitchen, moving with elegant grace, his muscles flexing and retracting as he reached for this or that. He looked so handsome. Leslie sighed.

"What you sighing about, girl? Am I boring you? We'll be ready to eat in a minute, okay?"

"No, I'm definitely not bored watching you. That was a sigh of contentment, of happiness."

"Oh. Well, I'll have to keep that in mind. I just hope I never hear a sigh that sounds like boredom when we're in bed together."

He looked up at her then and their eyes locked. Yes, they were going to finish what they started yesterday. And believe me, I'm not going to sigh from boredom, no, not a chance, Leslie thought, as her entire body seemed to respond with a glow of sweet anticipation.

❧

"Dinner was excellent, Robert, thank you. And the 'taters, now you weren't lying about making some good 'taters. What did you put on them to make them crispy like that?"

"Crispy, they weren't crispy, was yours crispy? Mine wasn't crispy, must have put an extra ingredient on yours." He said all this in one rapid sentence which made Leslie laugh. He leaned toward her and kissed her, slowly, deliciously tasting her. When Robert pulled away, Leslie was slightly winded, her breathing irregular and rapid. A warmth spread to the center of her as she ached for more. Fire and desire, the voices of Rick James and Tina Marie suddenly sprang to her mind. That's how she felt, on fire!

Robert stood then, taking her by the hand as he led her to the rear of the house where the master suite was. When he opened the door she gasped at the size of the room; then she noticed candles that were burning in the corners of the room while from the stereo a medley of music echoed softly. She wondered when he had set this up. Surely this CD and these candles had not been burning the whole time she'd been there. Those questions flew out of her mind as Robert began to kiss the back of her neck, as he stroked her arms. When he started doing that she didn't care when or how he had set up this mood. She closed her eyes and leaned into him. He knew what to do. She responded, trembling at his touch. His hands were putting gentle pressure on her outer thighs, gliding up and down, up and down, in a mesmerizing fashion. She moaned, turned around to lace her arms around his neck, to taste his mouth, to press her breasts against his chest. She knew what to do, too. She lifted her leg and straddled his thigh, gently rocking her hips back and forth in a sensual motion. He lifted her sweater over her head, and through her bra he captured her breasts and teased her until her nipples stood erect. She reached behind her to unhook her bra for him. He gazed at her, looking as if he were in shock from her touch. She raked her fingers through the waves in his hair, gently guiding his head—his lips—back to her now moist, erect nipples. He sucked gently, biting softly, bringing her close to an orgasm simply by stimulating her breasts. She pulled away to step out of her shoes, unfastened and then wiggled and squirmed out of her pants. She bent to take them off. When she bent over his hands began to stroke her bottom. Leslie froze in this position, giving him a chance to explore her if he wanted to. Although she was normally timid and shy about her body, tonight her fear was gone. Her desires were so strong that they had taken over—a possession that was complete and raw.

Robert fell to his knees and with his teeth pulled her panties down. He inhaled her scent. Dizzy with excitement, he resisted the urge to be immediately inside her love.

He stood before her and allowed her to undress him. She looked him in the eyes, unbuttoned his shirt and periodically placed a sensual kiss upon his lips. His eyes began to slip closed as he began to relax, surrendering to her touch.

"Don't close your eyes," Leslie said, shocking him with the huskiness of her voice.

"What—"

"Keep 'em open. Watch me."

"Watch you?"

"It will be even more intense if you do. Trust me," Leslie said, surprised by her own boldness.

He had never experienced this before—a woman asking him to keep his eyes open so she could watch his reaction. She kneeled before him and even as she worked the buckle on his belt and unzipped his pants, she continued to gaze at him. His magnificent manhood sprang out, proud, erect and strong. She continued to look him in his eyes, at his erect member and back to his eyes. All the while she was easing his pants off. God, she was good! Robert thought.

He stepped out of his pants. Leslie kissed his knees and stroked the backs of his hard calves, working her way up the backs of his thighs. She closed her eyes then and flicked her tongue out quickly—snakelike—here and there, tasting him, teasing him. She gathered his member in her hand and softly, with purposeful strokes, caressed it—back and forth, back and forth.

He closed his eyes and moaned, enjoying the feel of her soft hands upon him. Suddenly, she took him in her mouth. She circled his head, then took all of him deep inside her mouth. Her mouth was hot and wet. It felt like heaven. Over and over and over again she continued to tease him until he thought he might explode. He pulled away then, gathered her in his arms and laid her on his bed. Instinctively, she pulled her knees up to allow him entrance.

Instead, he fell to his knees and kissed the inside of her thigh, nudging her mound with his fingers. Softly unfolding her sex, he slid his finger into her and she arched. Carefully, he took the very center of her between his lips and began to blow. He continued a blowing, sucking rhythm, until she was completely swollen, signalling her oncoming orgasm. The intensity of her explosion rocked her whole body. She quivered and moaned his name over and over and over again. He slipped on a condom and entered her. A perfect fit. They rocked together in perfect unison. He was completely lost in ecstasy inside her warm embrace, enjoying the see-saw motion of their hips, thrusting deeper and deeper until finally—together they exploded.

That was what Leslie remembered as she drifted off to sleep, a satisfied smile on her face.

CHAPTER XI

All week long Leslie thought about Robert; remembering details of conversations they had enjoyed, his masculine scent as he moved close to her, the taste of his lips, the softness of his touch. All this was vivid in her memory. The way he held his head to the side when he talked to her, the sly way he worked his face into a smile. She had to admit that she loved everything about him. He had called her several times during the week to say hello and see how her day was going.

As Leslie was intently reading some material, her intercom buzzed, startling her.

"Leslie, there's a package here for you. Want me to bring it in?" Jessica said.

"Yes, please bring it in. Thanks."

The sentencing hearing for Horace Brown was just a few days away and Leslie continued to study the law to find a way to convince the judge to reduce his jail time to time-served.

She continued to read, her excitement building as she thought about the possibilities this new information she'd found could bring to her case.

"Here you go." Jessica said, placing a large heart-shaped box with a huge red ribbon in front of Leslie.

"Oh, my goodness! What is this?" Leslie exclaimed, smiling delightedly.

"Looks like chocolates to me. Somebody loves you, huh?" Jessica teased.

"What a nice surprise! I wasn't expecting anything."

"Well, read the card, see who's thinking about you today. And I'd say they're thinking about you in a big way," Jessica said as she left Leslie alone, closing the door behind her.

Leslie snatched the card from under the ribbon, not recognizing the handwriting, and read its contents aloud, "Thanks for spending a magical evening with me. Robert."

She held the card close to her heart, closing her eyes as a flood of memories leapt to her mind. She carefully pulled the red ribbon off, noting that he even remembered that red was her favorite color. She lifted the lid, laid aside the protective plastic wrap and instantly the scent of milk chocolate, dark chocolate, coconut and raspberry filled her nostrils. She looked at the beautiful assortment of chocolate and couldn't decide which one to sample first. Like a child too excited to choose, she just closed her eyes and pulled one out, placing it in her mouth. She savored the smooth milk chocolate coating her tongue before it slid down her throat. She groaned with pleasure. Jessica tapped at her door, interrupting her dramatic, private performance. Feeling a little embarrassed, Leslie held the box out to her.

"Want some?"

"Sure. Wow, looks like all my favorites are in here."

"Mine too. But Lord knows I do not need an extra ten pounds riding these hips."

She placed the box on the corner of her desk, telling Jessica to let others know they were free to come enjoy a piece or two.

Robert's gesture made her feel so good, as her feminine

senses were awakened by every word he spoke, or deed he performed. The contents of the note again made her smile as she read it again, placing it discretely in her purse. She loved this attention and she hoped he would never stop.

Thinking about Robert was something she had been doing a lot of lately. She knew she had to stop soon or her law practice was going to suffer. She had a full case load, which often included conducting depositions. In addition to working on her pro bono case with Horace Brown, she also had to take care of preparation for deposing the CEO of a company another client of hers was suing. There were times when she'd allow an associate to attend depositions for her but this new case she was working on was only to be handled by her.

She set aside her research for Horace's matter and began to prepare for taking this deposition, wading through mountains of documents and other testimony. She studied documents for so long that she just couldn't concentrate anymore, let alone prepare an accurate, thorough outline for the questions she wanted to ask. Finally she gave up and decided to take a walk to clear her head and help align her thoughts.

Downtown San Diego with its majestic skyline and ocean views was the perfect setting to simply escape. The ocean's calming effect always helped ease her mind, so she headed toward Harbor Drive. Leslie walked with her head up, taking deep cleansing breaths, gazing periodically at the sky, admiring the ocean's expanse and the beautiful dark blue coloring it mirrored from the sapphire sky. She was quickly approaching the building that Bryan worked in. She remembered then that she still needed to talk to him. She made an impetuous decision to drop in on him.

"Leslie Hughes to see Bryan McKay. Is he available?" Leslie asked the receptionist at the front desk.

"Let me check. Is he expecting you? Do you have an appointment?"

"No, I'm sorry, I don't have an appointment, but if he's busy I'll call him later. I just wanted to say hello."

"Okay. I'll let him know you're here."

While the receptionist called Bryan, Leslie looked around the spacious reception area which had recently been redecorated. Now it definitely had a look of class and money—a powerful aura—which was surprising since this was a one-man office. Bryan employed a legal assistant to do legal research, a part-time paralegal, one secretary, and a receptionist. Most of the extensive work he did himself and often hired investigators to help him when he was preparing a case, but otherwise he had a very small staff. Perhaps that was why he obviously had so much money. Leslie also speculated that his offices looked so rich because he didn't have huge overhead and salaries to pay as her firm did, obviously freeing up major finances for him.

"Hey, girl! What are you doing up here? Slummin'?" Bryan approached her smiling, swiftly kissing her cheek.

"Slummin' is not the word I'd use for this office. It's beautiful. I love the way you redecorated the lobby. Very nice!"

"Thank you. Come on in; I'm between appointments so it's perfect timing."

Bryan led the way into his spacious Victorian furnished office. The massive cherry wood desk and credenza screamed "expensive"—not to mention the original prints, beautifully framed, the richly textured rugs, Queen Anne chairs in deep hues of burgundy with dusty rose accent pillows. His office was even more impressive than the lobby.

"Are you going to stand there with your mouth open

catchin' flies, or you plan on sitting down sometime soon?"

"Oh, I'm sorry. I'm gawkin' like I've never seen a nice office before. Looks like you're doing all right for yourself, Bryan." She sat down and crossed her legs. She noticed that he quickly looked away. Her mind immediately made a comparison between Robert and Bryan. Robert's eyes would have lit up at the sight of her legs. Why didn't Bryan's? she wondered.

"I'm doing okay. Don't let this fool you. I'm just frontin', you know, for the White boys, so I can get all their legal troubles dropped in my lap. You know how it is." Bryan relaxed in his chair, unbuttoned his jacket and opened his arms wide in a welcoming gesture.

"I know how it is, but I'd be afraid to retain you as my lawyer; you look very, very expensive. What's your rate anyway?"

"Three-fifty."

"Damn, I'm only two-ten and that's a partner's rate. Okay, what are you up to and can I get in on it?" For a split second, Leslie's thoughts registered warning, but it was gone before she could really capture and explore it.

"I'm not up to anything and even if I was, NO, you cannot get in on it." Bryan immediately got defensive; his tone was harsh, not a hint of playfulness there.

"Okay, damn. Relax, Bryan. I was just playing with you. I know you're legit." Leslie felt as if she'd been slapped. She looked at Bryan then, trying to coax a smile to lighten the moment.

Bryan's inner bells were starting to go off and he realized

he desperately needed to calm down. He did not want to send her vibes that would make her suspicious or afraid. He had to act as if nothing was wrong. His stomach rumbled and he started to sweat. Feebly trying to avert her attention, he lightly chuckled and graced her with one of his award-winning smiles. "So, Leslie, what's been going on in your life since we last talked?"

"Umm—I've just been working a lot. Got a bunch of depos coming up. As a matter of fact, I should be working on one right now, but I just couldn't think anymore. Thought a walk would do me some good—help clear my head. What are you working on?"

"Oh, nothing much, same old, same old."

"Um, hum." Leslie uncrossed her legs and leaned forward. Bryan thought this was one of those feminine ploys, so he decided to act out the scene with her.

"We haven't seen much of each other lately, Leslie," Bryan said, reaching for her hand, "I'm sorry about that. Things have been kinda crazy 'round here. It's hard being a one-man office. As a matter of fact, I've been thinking about taking on a partner."

"A partner! Not you. You said you'd never do that. I thought you wanted to work alone."

"Well, that was before I got so popular," he said smiling.

"Yeah, you know I'm kind of tired of seeing your face on TV all the time. They sing your praises more than Michael Jordan. The media loves you." Leslie smiled, looking at him with genuine admiration. "Be careful though; they'll turn on you quicker than you can blink your eye. Don't do anything wrong."

"Yeah, I know that's right. I know how finicky the media can be—love you today—hate you tomorrow. And, as we both know, they're quick to crucify a confident, influential brotha like myself. Shoot, I'm scared to even burp in public."

They laughed at the picture he had just painted. The sad part was they both knew it was true. Would things ever change in this country? he wondered. They both doubted it. One of the reasons they had chosen this line of work was to help alleviate the inherent injustice and prejudice that affected the African American community—people who far too frequently get mixed up in the complicated legal maze. Bryan and Leslie knew they were small fish in a very large, prejudicial pond, but they continued to fight anyway. Being Black in America, now that was a challenge. Too often the innocent were convicted and the guilty went free, and the color of one's skin was often the major contributing factor to being found "guilty."

"But seriously, my case load is just too heavy now for me to continue to try and do it alone."

"I heard you're defending Lorenzo Ortez in that murder case. How'd you get that one?"

Damn, she's asking too many questions. I've got to get her out of here. He made an elaborate gesture of checking his watch, hoping she'd get the hint and leave soon.

"It's a long story and one I really don't want to talk about. I'd rather talk about you. Girl, you sittin' over there looking so fine. I miss you."

"I miss you, too. When do you think we can get together for drinks or something?"

"Oh, my schedule is crazy right now. I'm going to have to take a rain check until after this trial is over. This case is really complicated. I've got to give it all my attention right now."

"I understand. Okay," Leslie said, standing to leave, "Let me know when you've got some time and we'll get together then. I better get going—I've played hooky long enough. But, actually, I wanted to talk to you about something," Leslie said, hoping she could at least let him know what was on her mind. As she searched his handsome face willing him to understand, a swoosh of air exploded in the room as the door flew open.

A massive Samoan man barreled in. His posture, navy blue double-breasted suit, with buttons that seemed to strain to stay closed, as well as his stern face gave him a menacing look. Leslie cried out in surprise.

Damn, Bryan thought, not now! He tried to calm Leslie. Her eyes were bulging as fear gripped her.

"It's okay. It's okay," he said as he protectively shielded her, stroking her as his own hands trembled. "Don't be alarmed. This is Bruno, my client's bodyguard."

He turned to Bruno, his voice barely controlled anger. A slight tremor in Bryan's voice and the fact that his fists opened and closed rhythmically, while his jaw twitched and his eyes blazed, was a clear indication of his rage. Bryan was unaware of how threatening he looked.

"I'd appreciate it if you'd knock next time, Bruno. You scared my friend and I do not appreciate it."

"Mr. Ortez has a scheduled appointment with you," Bruno angrily retorted, flexing his muscled arm to look at his watch, which he tapped for emphasis. His voice matched Bryan's. He had a no nonsense, stern, unsmiling face. He was puffy and red and sweat had begun to bead up on his forehead. The extra one hundred pounds he carried, although probably all muscle, was undoubtedly taxing his overworked heart.

"No one is taking up his time. You are a little early. Tell Mr. Ortez to come in; I'm ready for our meeting."

He turned his attention back to Leslie who still seemed shocked by everything that was happening. He gave her a hug and whispered, "Leslie, I'll call you later." He patted her arm, grabbed her hand and stepped around Bruno, escorting Leslie to the reception area. His secretary was gone and while that surprised him, his first concern was getting Leslie out of there.

"Are you okay, Leslie?"

"Yes . . . yes. Bryan, what's going on? God, I'm so scared. Look at me. I'm shaking!" she said, holding out her trembling hands.

"Everything is fine. Please just go. I'll explain all this to you later. Okay?"

Leslie stared at him and for reasons she couldn't explain, he no longer even physically resembled the Bryan she knew. Something was changing him. She didn't budge; she continued to study his face, his eyes which continuously darted around the room. Unable to even speak, she just shook her head.

"Leslie, I've got to take care of this. You'll be fine. I'll call you later."

He gently pushed her out the door.

She stood outside the building still trembling; she continued to chant "calm down, calm down." Finally she felt composed again. She speculated about the whole episode and every scenario she could think of worried her. The same question ran over and over in the mind, "What is going on?" It plagued her for the rest of the day, denying her the peace of mind and clear head she needed to finish her project. She kept seeing Bruno barge into the room with his massive body and beady eyes. She shuddered just thinking about him. Worry lines began to wrinkle her brow and again she wondered if Bryan was okay.

CHAPTER XII

Bryan's meeting with his client's brother, Fernando Ortez, was the scheduled meeting he had been dreading. His instincts were right. From the moment of Bruno's rude appearance to Mr. Ortez's grand entrance, he knew this was going to be a stressful meeting.

"I apologize if Bruno offended you."

"Apology accepted. Have a seat," Bryan said, gesturing to the chair directly across from him. Instead of taking this seat, Bryan watched Mr. Ortez turn his back as he crossed the room to take a seat upon the sofa. He stood and with deliberate slowness unbuttoned his jacket, sat down, crossed his legs, fidgeted with the crease of his pants leg. Finally his eyes lighted on Bryan as if signalling him that he called the shots and now Bryan was allowed to speak.

"If you're more comfortable over there, no problem," Bryan stammered.

"Brief me on the status of my brother's case."

"Well, I'm sure as you might imagine, this case is anything but simplistic, thus making it difficult for me to make any explanation of it brief for you."

"Semantics!" he shouted. "Don't toy with me. I want to

know what you're doing to prepare my brother's defense."

Bryan's temper, which he could usually keep in check, flared, making it difficult for him to speak immediately. He still had not had a chance to get over being angry about the way Bruno had barged in. And now this man had the audacity to shout at him. He cleared his throat in an attempt to brace himself for a very unpleasant encounter.

"Mr. Ortez, there is nothing to worry about. I've got things under control. In fact, I have an investigator gathering evidence at this very moment."

"What have you gathered so far?"

"With all due respect, Mr. Ortez, if I spend precious time now explaining all the details to you, well—that's time I'm not spending preparing things for your brother. Now, I thought you had the utmost confidence in me. Did something happen to change that? And if it did, perhaps you'd like to seek other counsel?" Bryan said using his voice that usually threatened most clients into submission.

Conceding to Bryan's comments, Mr. Ortez's jaw flexed as the two men stared each other down. Finally he stood, extending his hand for Bryan to shake.

"There's no need to speak of obtaining other counsel. Just do a good job. Get him off. I want him home. It will be important to you to have that happen."

He continued to hold his hand in a firm grasp as the two men glared at each other. Bryan searched for something to say but his mouth was dry, and he sensed it would be better for him to say nothing at all. As the words Mr. Ortez had just uttered began to sink in, seeping into his consciousness, he became fully aware that he was grasping the hand of a very dangerous man. Nope, he'd say nothing at all for now.

After Mr. Ortez and Bruno left, Bryan shakily sat down,

loosened his tie as sweat began to trickle down his face. He began to reflect on this case, wishing now he had never agreed to take it on.

The charge against the young man he was representing was murder one. Lorenzo Ortez had killed someone, allegedly in self-defense. That was problem enough, but in addition to the murder charge, Lorenzo was reputed to be connected with some very unsavory members of a Hispanic gang that had been terrorizing San Diego for years. Their membership was steadily growing, as was their ruthlessness. They'd just as soon kill you, step over the body, and continue on to the next illegal task at hand. Becoming bolder and more brazen made them the number one priority for both the FBI and DEA agents. Lorenzo and his brother, Fernando, had many ties with Mexico's drug trafficking and they were very much feared. The event that brought Fernando to Bryan's office was the involvement of his brother, Lorenzo, in a drug deal gone sour. It resulted in the demise of a small-time hoodlum and drug dealer, Victor Travis. Lorenzo had become more and more dangerous, having absolutely no fear of the law. That was evident in the fact that he took Victor Travis out in front of a group of witnesses.

Fernando Ortez, also a very dangerous man, was feared, admired and loathed simultaneously. He had handpicked Bryan to be his brother's lawyer. Mr. Ortez explained that he'd heard of Bryan's victories, had carefully watched his career blossom and his reputation soar. He pleaded the case for his brother in a most passionate, articulate, sincere, and persuasive manner. Fernando cleverly stroked Bryan's ego, convincing him to take the case.

Until Bryan met Fernando, he had only looked at his various victories as small, the result of simply doing his job, certainly not worthy of the kind of scrutiny Fernando spoke of. He worked hard and studied the law inside and out, cleverly finding loopholes and ways to suppress evidence, and he had fun doing it. He actually enjoyed destroying so-called respectable witnesses with bits of adverse information about them that his investigators would uncover. Everybody had dirty laundry—skeletons—and Bryan was ruthless in uncovering whatever it took to win a case. He was, he thought, in a relentless pursuit of justice for his clients. Right or wrong, good or bad.

Bryan was smart and clever, and his ability to gain favorable results for his clients over and over again had obviously attracted the attention of Fernando Ortez. Mr. Ortez had taken an interest in him and, much to Bryan's amazement, when he heard that his brother was in police custody, Bryan was the only lawyer he wanted. Mr. Ortez explained that he would stop at nothing to retain Bryan's services. It was unthinkable for his brother to go to prison; in fact, it was inconceivable. Mr. Ortez knew Lorenzo would die there. Together he and his brother, indeed their entire family, had made many enemies along their path to considerable wealth. Ruthlessness and greed hurled them to their heady success, but not without great risk and gaining many enemies along the way. Past clients, and even customers, were now spending time in penitentiaries and prisons all over the country, as a result of their association with the Ortez brothers. Some were six feet under. But neither Lorenzo nor Fernando counted or cared. Until now.

Bryan recalled so clearly the day Fernando Ortez had

walked into his office with his entourage, plastic smile and determination.

"Mr. McKay, I'm here today because I need a damn good lawyer to help my brother get out of this mess he's in. I'm sure you've heard about the recent shooting near the border. Hell, it's all over the news. Damn reporters!" He paused. "Anyway, that's my brother and I need you to get him off. Bring him home."

Bryan listened intently to the heavy Mexican accent, and he watched this gruff, but self-assured man ask him for help. But his tone and his body language suggested it wasn't really a request. He was clearly irritated, but his demeanor hinted that he was a man who didn't sweat over much, nor was he used to being denied anything. He hadn't even allowed Bryan to speak.

"My name's Fernando. Fernando Ortez. My brother's Lorenzo. And although I know it looks like he's guilty, he's not and I need you to prove that."

"And how do you suggest I do that?"

"I've watched you. Hell, I know all about your reputation, and to me you're the best criminal attorney this town has to offer. I know you're ruthless, and that's exactly what we need."

"I've been called a lot of things, but ruthless, well, I don't believe that is one of them."

"Look, I'm not trying to insult you. I'm just saying I admire the kind of man you are. Now, what'll it take to have you do this?"

"I'm not sure I understand your question."

"Let's cut to the chase. How does a two hundred thousand dollar retainer sound to you. That enough to get you started?"

Bryan suppressed the urge to gasp at the amount which was

just offered to him. A huge retainer like this could go a long, long way. But Bryan was not a greedy man. He was, however, a curious man.

"Mr. Ortez, that retainer is a little larger than I normally require of my clients. Is there some reason why you're offering such a substantial amount?"

"Let's just say I'm throwing in a bonus to have you come work with us. Bring my brother home."

"What are they charging Lorenzo with?"

"I believe it's first degree murder, premeditated, special circumstances, or some such. Hell, I don't know." He waved his hand in the air as if this were unimportant and didn't require his full attention.

"Mr. Ortez, those are very serious charges and in this state, a premeditated charge of murder accompanied by special circumstances would mean your brother could be facing a death sentence if convicted. Are you aware of that?" Bryan tried to stress the seriousness to Mr. Ortez. The dismissal-type mannerisms alarmed him more than he cared to admit.

"I'm not worried about it, not as long as we've got you as our lawyer. They can go . . . well, you can imagine what I was just about to say."

"Yes, I can."

His overconfidence made Bryan suspicious, and his subconscious warned him against his man, but was quickly suppressed as Mr. Ortez continued to flatter and convince.

"You're the best. What have we got to worry about. Some two-bit city attorneys who probably don't know squat about squat!"

"Um huh. Well, I appreciate the confidence you have in me, but a case of this nature often can require a team of lawyers to form a strong defense, and as you probably know, I work alone."

"That's fine. Hell, I don't like too many people in my way either," he said and glanced around the room at his bodyguards. They all nodded in agreement and simultaneously took a step back.

"It's just not that simple, Mr. Ortez. Murder cases are tricky. I'm not sure I can handle it alone, and it's very important to me that any client I take on has everything he needs to ensure a good legal defense."

"I'm confident and that's enough, Mr. McKay," he said harshly. This sudden change in attitude startled him.

"Mr. Ortez, I cannot give you a firm answer on whether or not I will represent your brother until I have some more facts. Now," Bryan said, grabbing a legal pad, "tell me everything you know."

Their conversation had lasted into the night. His bodyguards never left their respective positions around their master. Bryan began to wonder if these men even took a piss without permission! The more they talked, the more Bryan could clearly see holes in the story, and his experience told him that any decent attorney for the city could get a conviction on the amount of credible evidence against Lorenzo. For one, a weapon was found with Lorenzo's prints on it, and secondly, the argument between the men was witnessed by many people. These witnesses probably were already being protected by the police. There had even been a previous verbal threat made by Lorenzo Ortez that was overheard by many. Now this man was dead and Lorenzo stood rightly accused. This was not good. Bryan knew upon reflection that Fernando Ortez was trying to fool him, and that alone was not a good way to start off any case—especially when the charge was murder. If nothing else, it was imperative for the accused to tell his attorney the truth.

And the truth was Lorenzo Ortez was a hot head. He lost his cool at the wrong time and place.

As the evening wore on, Bryan had a sinking feeling that this was not a good idea, but the two hundred thousand dollar figure kept running through his head. But he also realized that only a not guilty verdict would make Mr. Ortez happy. As good as Bryan knew he was, this was going to be the kind of challenge he had not yet faced, the least of which were the eyewitnesses. Just how did Fernando think he was going to get rid of them? He wasn't a miracle worker. His mind raced for answers as Mr. Ortez talked, but he could think of nothing.

Bryan had stopped scribbling notes. He put the pen down and was just about to tell Mr. Ortez that he didn't think he could take the case. As if he were able to read Bryan's mind and thoughts, Mr. Ortez reached inside his jacket and took out a black leather checkbook and first signed his name with a flourish. He briefly stopped and stared at Bryan with determination. Bryan watched his every calculated move. He became mesmerized, it seemed, as his name, a two followed by five zeros appeared. Mr. Ortez with grace and style glided the check smoothly across the desk, stopping right at Bryan's fingertips. Bryan remembered how he had licked his suddenly dry lips as greed reared its ugly head and all his good sense fled.

Bryan shook his head as if coming awake from a dream; reminiscing about his own stupidity made him feel very tired. He rose slowly, as if an old man, leaving his thoughts behind. He reminded himself that he needed a good night's rest so he could prepare for tomorrow and the new challenges this case would bring.

When he arrived home exhausted, feeling despair deep in his bones, he heard a distinctive clink. Someone was in his kitchen. Fear gripped him and he felt his bowels loosen, but in a split second fear turned to rage. He barged into the kitchen expecting to find Bruno lurking there.

Walter turned and smiled at him. "Hi. Thought I'd surprise you by making dinner."

"You scared the shit out of me. What are you doing here?" Bryan's heart was pounding and his head began to hurt from the adrenaline rush, but he was glad it was Walter he was seeing and not Bruno.

"I'm making you dinner. Here, have a scotch and soda." Walter handed a glass to him. "Relax, I'm almost finished." Bryan could see that Walter was a little nervous, too, since he probably knew Bryan might not be happy to see him.

Bryan accepted the glass and watched as his lover prepared dinner. This was indeed a surprise. They hadn't spoken since Leslie's Atlantic City Casino Night affair and that exchange was anything but pleasant. Bryan felt a mixture of pleasure at seeing him and anger because he had waited so long to get in touch with him.

"I guess you figured out I got a little jealous about Miz Thang," Walter said.

"Don't refer to her that way, okay? I don't know how many times I've told you that I need a female in my life so no one gets suspicious. Besides, Leslie's my friend."

"Yeah, well, it looked to me like you was getting just a little too chummy with her."

"There's no need for you to feel jealous. Why can't you understand that?" Bryan was clearly exasperated with having to explain this over and over again to Walter.

"Even though it may sound simple to you, it isn't for me," Walter said, his voice shaky with emotion as he turned from the stove to look at Bryan. "You're supposed to be my man," he said pouting. "I need your reassurance that our relationship is solid. I realize coming out of the closet might hurt your career; that's why I've kept my distance and stayed quiet. But you know what time it is? It's time for you to shit or get off the pot! This drama we're always going through is really getting tired."

"This drama, as you refer to it, is my life and without it we don't have much. So save me your theatrics, okay? I've already had the worst day of my life. I don't need to get into this with you. Not again."

"Okay, okay. I didn't want to fight with you anyway," Walter acquiesced, throwing his hands up as if warding off invisible blows. "But you and I do need to talk about this situation," he said, his voice growing softer. "I just don't know how much longer I can take this—this secrecy and all the lies. You need to know that I'm tired, real tired, Bryan."

"Just be patient with me a little longer." Bryan approached Walter and put his hand on his shoulder. "I've got a client with some serious bank," he said as he reached into the pocket inside his jacket and pulled out the check. "See."

Walter's eyes were wide with surprise. "What'd you do to get that kind of money?"

"Nothing yet. But don't you see that if I pull this one off we'll be set for a while, and maybe a victory with this client will be the ticket I need to come out and not worry about whether I can attract any other business. I'm almost positive that Mr. Ortez will throw lots of business my way and I can be independent after this. Then I'll be free to be who I really am. Just give it some more time, okay?"

"I'll try."

Walter had just finished whipping up his favorite and best dish—basil and garlic mashed potatoes.

"Here, taste them for me." He dipped a spoon into the potatoes and offered it to Bryan. "Do they need anything?"

Bryan closed his eyes and rolled the rich, flavorful, buttery potatoes in his mouth, savoring and identifying the hint of garlic and basil. This gesture of feeding one another, along with a hug, was their silent pact to let things go for now.

Walter was certain that it was time for them to get on with their life together. He wanted to do something to speed up the process, though right now he was at a loss as to what that might be. His patience was rapidly running out and he knew he just had to do something. To hell with Bryan's legal career; they would be able to deal with whatever came along. They'd struggled many times over their relationship and people's reaction to it. These kinds of obstacles had been overcome and they were still together. All Walter really wanted was to be with his man and try to live a happy life. And he was ready to get on with it, no matter what the cost.

CHAPTER XIII

The sentencing hearing for Horace Brown was scheduled for later that afternoon. Leslie prepared her arguments in an anxious manner, hoping the judge would not be too harsh on her client. The burden she felt was great, heavily weighing her down; she hoped her lack of objectivity wouldn't adversely affect her judgment. Even though she knew her client was not guilty of the crime for which he was convicted, she knew she had to be cautious about what she said so as not to reveal the truth.

Gripping her pen tightly she furiously wrote her arguments for a minimum sentence. She thought about the last time she wrote a similar letter full of passion and pleas and, she thought, convincing arguments. She shook her head, knowing that that letter had not worked. God, I hope this one does. No matter what, she would continue to fight to keep her client from spending any more time in jail. That much she knew for sure because as far as she was concerned, two days—no even one more hour—was far too long for an innocent man to be caged like an animal. She glanced at the clock and noticed that it was almost time to go. It was important to her that she spend some time with her client before the sentencing hearing, prepare him for what might happen and attempt to alleviate any overly emotional scenes by either one of them. She picked up her briefcase, her notes and headed for court.

Judge Sherman was known for running a strictly punctual courtroom. When a ripple of whispers began among the observers that he was late, Leslie's heart sank. What could this possibly mean? she wondered. Mr. Brown, eyes downcast, slumped in his seat, his breathing shallow. Leslie lightly touched his sleeve and asked, "Are you okay, Horace?"

Raising his head ever so slightly he said, "Is my boy here?"

Leslie scanned the room, her eyes lighting upon every face, but no Jeffrey.

"I'm sorry, Horace. I don't see him."

His reaction startled her; he seemed to shrink inside himself and one lone tear slid down his rough cheek. Leslie again tenderly patted his arm, whispered, "It's okay. Hang on, Horace. It'll be okay." Doubting her own words, she thought, what in God's name is taking so long? Let's get this over with! She tried to reassure Horace with soft strokes of her hand against the rough textured sleeve of the prison-issued shirt he wore.

Leslie scanned her notes again, trying to distract herself from Horace's misery. The bailiff approached both Leslie and the D.A., handing them notes which summoned them to the judge's chambers. She grabbed Horace's hand, "Listen, I've got to go talk to the judge. I don't know what's going on, but I'll be right back. Okay?" She searched his face for some kind of response. He sat slumped, his only response a slight shrug of his shoulders. Defeated and alone, he seemed not to care.

The bailiff, a tall, muscular man with a stern face, briskly walked down the hallway, ushered them into the chambers of Judge Sherman and quickly vanished. Leslie smoothed her dress nervously and steeled herself for what the judge might say.

Judge Sherman's booming, authoritative voice said, "Ms. Hughes, Mr. Laughlin. Please sit down."

Leslie gingerly approached the nearest chair and sat perched on its edge. The district attorney hurried to a chair and glared with annoyance at Judge Sherman.

"Your Honor, what is this about?" Leslie inquired.

"Contrary to how things are supposed to be done, I was accosted by a persistent young man who insisted that he needed to speak with me. Not knowing what it was about, I had my clerk allow him into my chambers just before we convened. Before me stood a frightened, very remorseful young man, and it turns out he had information about this case."

Leslie still uncertain, hoped the young man would be Jeffrey. She said, "Please explain, Your Honor."

"I'm sure you're aware that your client, Mr. Brown, has a son, are you not?"

Beginning to understand what was happening, Leslie quietly said, "Yes, I am, Your Honor."

"He has explained to me that he was the one driving the car the night of the accident—the accident that Mr. Brown is to be sentenced for today—and with explicit detail, outlined the events of that tragic evening. Obviously, we face a problem with this new confession and information which needs to be explored, Mr. Laughlin."

"Yes, we do, Your Honor," replied Mr. Laughlin.

"Patsy, show the young man in, please," Judge Sherman told his clerk.

A side door opened and Jeff Brown entered the room, tear tracks drying on his mahogany cheeks. He sorrowfully looked at Leslie and then bent his head in shame. His attempt to look grown-up by dressing in one of his father's suits, which was entirely too large, with his tie off-center and knotted in a peculiar way, made him look the picture of youthful innocence and naivety. His dark brown eyes were wide with fear.

Leslie didn't know if she should rejoice or cry. What did this mean?

"After extensive discussions with Master Brown here, it is my opinion that this young man is telling the truth and that the information he provides is very, very credible. It needs exploring, of course, but it is my judgment that the sentencing of Mr. Brown cannot go forward today."

"I agree, Your Honor," Mr. Laughlin interjected.

"Do you wish to move for a new trial, Ms. Hughes?" Judge Sherman inquired.

"Yes, Your Honor. As quickly as possible."

"Mr. Laughlin, is it your opinion that the State is willing to prosecute this case again?"

"I'm not sure, Your Honor. I'll have to check with my superiors."

"You do that. In the meantime, let's send Mr. Brown and his son home."

"Thank you, Your Honor." Leslie beamed.

"Ms. Hughes," Jeff said with a voice that trembled, "I'm sorry for putting you and my dad through all this trouble. He must hate me now."

The anger that Leslie had felt for this young man quickly disappeared as she stood to embrace him. His shoulders trembled as he stiffly endured her hug. She whispered in his ear, "Thank you, Jeff. Your father will be very proud of you for being so brave."

She held him at arm's length, lifted his chin so their eyes

could meet. She knew he was surprised to see tears clinging to her lashes too. Then he awkwardly hugged her—a genuine hug full of sadness, appreciation, and pain.

"Young man," Justice Sherman interrupted.

"Yes . . . yes, sir," Jeff responded, standing at attention.

"You need to understand that your story will be checked out and then the District Attorney here will decide how to proceed. Now, you might get lucky this time, but the older you get the more liable you become for all your actions. Remember that, son."

"I will. Thank you, sir." Jeff extended his hand to Judge Sherman, who firmly shook it. Leslie noticed the glint of understanding in his eyes.

Together, Mr. Laughlin, Jeff and Leslie re-entered the courtroom. Horace Brown cautiously looked up. The smile on his face literally lit up the room. He shakily stood, and Leslie motioned him to sit, which he did, but his eyes never left the face of his son. Once Leslie was seated, the bailiff cried, "All rise! The Honorable Bertram Sherman, presiding. Please be seated."

"Good afternoon, ladies and gentlemen. I apologize for the delay, but we've had some interesting events occur that needed my immediate attention, in the matter of State of California versus Horace Brown."

The courtroom was hushed and Leslie noticed that for the first time, Horace Brown sat up straight in his chair. She sensed he was determined to face his sentencing like a man. She had no doubt that he wanted to appear brave for his son. Her eyes lighted from Horace Brown to his son, noticing for the first time how much alike they looked. She thought about Robert and Malcolm then. Although they did not resemble each other, the love they shared was as strong and binding as the one she'd witnessed between Horace and Jeffrey. Her instincts told her that Robert would react this very same way if their roles had been switched. She felt an enormous sense of pride for both men who totally loved and showed their heartfelt affection for their children.

"Ms. Hughes, do you have a motion?"

Leslie stood. "Yes, Your Honor. Defendant moves for a new trial based on new evidence that has recently come to our attention."

"Mr. Laughlin?"

"The State will file its response once it completes its investigation, Your Honor."

"All right then, I expect your motion for a new trial, Ms. Hughes, within twenty days."

"Yes, Your Honor."

"Mr. Brown, you're free to go."

Horace still remained seated, poised in readiness until Leslie tapped his arm.

"Horace, did you hear that? You can go home!"

"How'd this happen?" he shouted. He turned to look at his son. A rush of fear came over him as rapid images of his son in custody overwhelmed him. His mouth went dry and his eyes bulged, as if straining for understanding. "What did you do, boy? What did you do?"

Alarmed, Leslie grabbed him, quickly saying, "It's all right, Horace. I'll explain everything to you outside. Sit down!" she hissed at him in an attempt to make him understand that he needed to be quiet.

"Ms. Hughes, control your client," Judge Sherman barked. "I can't allow such a disruption in this courtroom." He paused, then continued in a softer voice, "This concludes this matter. I'll expect your brief, counselor."

"Yes, Your Honor. Thank you," Leslie quickly said.

"All rise!" shouted the bailiff.

Everyone in the courtroom stood, some with obvious expressions of surprise on their faces as Judge Sherman left the room. Leslie could see that Horace was still unsure of what had happened. He sat again, a look of shock upon his face.

Leslie gently touched his arm, beckoning him to stand. She ushered her client and his son outside to a secluded corner. Leslie tried to explain.

"Horace, please don't be upset with me for what I've done. Trust me when I say that everything I did was for you and your son."

"Miss Leslie," Jeff interrupted, "can I tell him?"

"Yes, Son, you tell me," Mr. Brown interrupted before Leslie could answer. He was so angry with her he could not even look at her.

"Dad, Miss Leslie wrote me a letter tellin' me all about how horrible jail would be for you. She said it would be good for you to see me as a man who would stand up and face my mistakes. But I was afraid to do that. I was so scared I couldn't even sleep! Then, I realized I had to tell the truth—just like you always taught me to do. She said that if I could live with this lie, then I'd probably go through the rest of my life running and hiding, never being able to tell the truth from a lie. And, Dad, she was right. Besides, I couldn't let you go out like that."

Horace still did not fully understand what had happened, but a smile appeared on his face anyway. Just listening to his son talk, he began to realize what a fine man he would someday be.

"Is this true, Ms. Hughes?" Horace asked. Now able to face her, he continued to smile.

"Well, in a simplified way, yes, it's true. As your attorney I was under a strict obligation to keep the attorney-client relationship confidential. I couldn't tell anyone what Jeff had done. And even though I repeatedly told you that Jeff, because he was a minor at the time of the accident, would not suffer severe repercussions because of his actions, you refused to believe in me or the judicial system. Although I agree that often it does not work in our favor, I urged you to trust the system and specifically, me."

"I know you did, but I know better. I've seen things go wrong too many times when it comes to court stuff. I couldn't trust anybody—not even you—with my son's life."

"We took a gamble when we elected to have a jury trial and we lost. After you were convicted, that made everything much tougher for me because my battle for your freedom was far from over. I had to urge Jeff to come forward. Which," she paused to place her arm around his narrow, young shoulders, "thankfully, he did."

Horace seemed to be completely awestruck at his unexpected freedom. He looked at his remorseful but now brave son, then at Leslie and shook his head, amazed at the picture the two of them made. She fighting for his freedom, and his son struggling to become a man. Tears slowly ran down the rugged lines in his brown cheeks. He gathered his son in his arms, where muffled sobs began.

"I'm sorry. I'm so sorry. I'll never do anything like this again. I promise, Dad. Never again!" Jeff vowed.

"I know, Son. I know. We both learned a valuable lesson in all this didn't we?"

Leslie watched the two as they walked away hugging each other, talking excitedly about what Horace was going to do first. She heard an exuberant plea for McDonald's, then

Vicki Andrews

Burger King and she chuckled, happy that the two of them were able to patch things up so quickly. She was grateful that her plan to overturn Horace's sentence had worked. She knew no matter what, she'd never stop trying to free Horace. It would be like leaving Robert in jail for something Malcolm had done. That was, in her mind, out of the question! She knew that Robert's love for Malcolm was as strong, if not stronger, than Horace's love for Jeffrey. She knew they were both ready to meet the challenges of single parenthood and she vowed that from now on she would be too. Nothing Anastasia could do or say would break her!

CHAPTER XIV

An exquisite bouquet of bright yellow roses arrived for Leslie on a Monday morning. She immediately thought of Robert when she saw them. When she reached for the card, familiar handwriting caught her attention, but for a moment she was confused. The card and flowers were not from Robert; they were from Bryan. She had been so preoccupied with Robert that she had forgotten all about Bryan and for a very brief moment she felt guilty. The card simply said, "The first in a series. Enjoy! Bryan." She picked up the telephone and immediately dialed his number.

"Hi, Bryan. Thank you. I just received this beautiful bouquet. What's the occasion?"

"You must be getting old. You don't remember the gift I purchased for you at the silent auction during the Atlantic City Casino Night? You should be receiving flowers once a month for the rest of the year. Are they beautiful or some tired, dried-up looking cheapies?"

"They're wonderful. As a matter of fact, I had forgotten all about the flowers. It took a while for them to start coming. But they're worth the wait. They are the most beautiful, delicate, vivid yellow roses I've ever seen. And they aren't just buds;

these are open. They're huge."

"I'm glad you like them. It was a gift worth giving. But I sincerely doubt that they are more beautiful than you."

"Okay, Mr. Smooth Talker. I guess beauty is genuinely in the eye of the beholder, huh?"

"Girl, why don't you quit with the forced modesty act, okay? I know you remember." They were off to their usual friendly banter. Leslie realized it felt good to hear his voice.

"And just what is that supposed to mean?" Leslie said with mock indignation. "Are you trying to say I'm not modest?"

Laughing, Bryan responded, "You know I'm just kidding with you. You're one of the finest and, might I add, modest women I know. It's really good to hear your voice. When am I going to get to see you?"

Leslie smiled and with a sultry voice—she couldn't resist teasing him, it seemed—she said, "When do you want to see me?"

"Now!"

"Aren't you working?" she said, alarmed that her comment had boomeranged.

"You know I am, but I can make time for you."

"Is that right?"

"Yeah, that's right."

"Well, unfortunately I don't have the same luxury you do. I can't get away right now but perhaps later. I need to talk to you anyway. How's your evening look?"

"I'm free tonight. Let's meet for dinner and drinks after work."

"Okay, but I'm definitely not coming to your office. The last time I was there I got scared half to death. By the way, how's that situation going?"

"Everything is fine. I straightened him out. You can believe that shit won't be happening again. I promise you that."

"Well, I certainly hope so."

"I'm more worried about you standing me up again than I am about Bruno."

"I did not deliberately stand you up. My daughter's science project knocked me out. I told you that, or didn't you get my message."

"Yeah, I know. But just as added insurance that nothing interferes, can we meet right after work, around six o'clock? Meet me here . . . in the lobby. Is that okay?"

"Sure, I think I can work that out. I have just one stipulation, though."

"What?"

"I need to be home by nine. I promised Anastasia we'd watch a movie tonight. We need to spend some time together. Okay?"

"No problem. I can come back here and finish up some paperwork. Nine works for me. I'll see you here at six."

Hanging up, Leslie pondered her relationship with Bryan. She couldn't really define it. Sometimes it seemed as though he was really interested in her and he would like to be a couple, and other times he was distant and unreachable. She didn't know what to make of him. On the other hand, she had no problem identifying her relationship with Robert. He was crystal clear about his intentions, and Leslie felt a stab of guilt again. Should she be going out with two guys at the same time? Not to mention that Black men definitely do not play that game! And besides, isn't it immoral or something? No, she decided, it was definitely not immoral. After all, she was only intimate with Robert, not with both men, so there really wasn't any risk of being labeled "loose," even by her usually conservative self. But she knew she owed it to Bryan to tell him about Robert and how serious they were getting. Even though having the attention of two men was fun, it was not worth a risk to her reputation or her friendship with Bryan. Tonight she would tell him what was going on.

After work, Leslie decided to leave her car parked in her office building so she could walk to Bryan's office. It was a beautiful, mild San Diego evening and the walk felt good. She was so absorbed in her own thoughts that it took awhile before she noticed the stares she got as she walked down the street, her hips gently swaying in a provocative manner that came naturally to her. She was dressed in a Donna Karan suit of royal blue, accented with a silk scarf tied around her slender neck. It was a lighter shade of the blue in her suit. She felt that she looked good and though she felt confident, she was happily surprised to realize her effect on the people around her.

⚜

Bryan had been watching her approach. He could see she was obviously lost in thought, not paying attention to anyone, barely noticing where she was going. She almost ran right into him. Startled, she said, "Where did you come from? I didn't even see you standing there."

"I know you didn't, pretty lady." He reached for her hand and kissed her cheek. "I've been standing here watching you. Where were your thoughts just now?"

"Oh, I was just sorting out some things in my head."

"Well, I hope it's not anything too deep."

"It's deep all right. Isn't this your car?"

"Yep. I pulled it around so we could get out of here before anything could stop us."

136

"At an expired meter, too!" she teased.

"Let's go before I get a ticket."

"You're brave; you know the San Diego Police Department has a unique kind of radar; they can spot an expired meter from miles away. They're probably on their way to get you as we speak!"

"That ain't no lie. Let's get out of here." He grabbed her hand and swiftly secured her inside his car.

They drove to Seaport Village and settled at the Harbor House for dinner. Bryan noticed that Leslie seemed a bit preoccupied. She had a faraway look in her eyes which troubled Bryan. Something was missing in her smile. Even her usual friendly chatter was strained. Her eyes looked worried, as they often did when something was bothering her— obviously her mind was someplace else and he began to wonder what was bothering her. He didn't think it could be that unfortunate incident that happened in his office with Bruno. He was fairly certain he'd alleviated her fears about that. Then he thought about her health, knowing all about her constant headaches. Or perhaps her problems with Anastasia were breaking her down. He wanted to ask her but he realized at that moment that he was afraid that these might not be the things worrying her, and he might not like what she would tell him.

He wondered if she was seeing somebody and felt guilty about it. He wished he could tell her not to worry. He wanted so badly to share the real him with her. After all, she was his friend and, frankly, he was getting tired of hiding and pretending, especially with her.

"How's life been treating you?" Bryan asked, breaking into her thoughts. "What have you been up to besides work?"

Leslie didn't immediately answer; instead she sighed. Then

her eyes—which had a distant, dreamy air—cleared as she began to focus on him.

"Life's been good. I'm working on another matter that's taking up a lot of my time. It would get easier for me if I could just let my guard down and let someone else do some of the research. But after all I went through in law school, I can't completely let go. I still don't trust people and it's starting to take a toll on me. Even now, although I'm a partner and could fire anyone who performed their job poorly, I'm still not willing to risk my reputation or my clients' to sloppy work and chance. I've got to do it myself." Bryan noticed there were worry lines etched on her face and he felt bad for her.

"You have a legitimate concern, Leslie; you know I know that, but you've got to let go of the trivial stuff. Let somebody else do it. And can their ass if they mess up. You're so strong in some areas, it surprises me when you appear so uncertain, like in this situation. You know you've got power, girlfriend, use it!" Bryan's voice was powerful yet soothing and she knew he was right.

"Yeah, well, even though I've got power, I still feel uncomfortable letting somebody go if they do a sloppy job. It just isn't me. So I'd rather just do the work myself." Leslie shook her head and looked away, and Bryan could see that she felt a deep-rooted kind of sadness. He wondered if this was really all about work.

"I know some people get a kind of perverse pleasure in firing people, but I know that's not you, Leslie. You would never fire someone if it weren't warranted. What I'm saying to you is, cut yourself a break. You've worked long and hard and now you can and should relax a bit and enjoy the fruits of your labor. How many female African-American partners do you know in this town?"

"Not many."

"Exactly. That's my point. You've got good judgment and you're honest, caring and discreet. Count on those qualities to get you through, if and when you have to do the unpleasant stuff, like firing someone if they don't meet your expectations."

"It's just easier for me to let the office manager do that kind of stuff. I'm such a chicken, I don't want to make the decision to drastically alter someone's life by taking their job away. I couldn't deal with the guilt."

"Leslie, have you ever been fired?"

"Yes. A long time ago and I still feel the sting of the rejection."

"Do you think the person who let you go felt guilty, or cared about how their decision affected you?"

"I sincerely doubt it."

"Well then, adopt the same attitude, girl, and hire some help. I'm not used to seeing you looking this tired and preoccupied. You can't do all the research alone."

Leslie smiled at him and Bryan was happy to see her face finally light up.

"I'm okay, really, just needed a few minutes to unwind. The Chardonnay is doing the trick." Gazing out the window, Leslie sighed and said, "No matter how many times I see it, I never get tired of the ocean, this view, or the spectacular sunsets we San Diegans experience."

He followed her gaze, catching the tail end of the sun majestically disappearing, seeming to slip right into the ocean. The sunset was painted with fiery colors of orange and yellow. Shortly, the sky changed to deep purples and royal blues. It reminded him of Leslie's suit. He faced her then. They both had been observing the sunset in silence.

"The colors in the sky almost match your suit."

She glanced at her suit, then up at the beautiful sunset. He was right; it did look almost identical.

"It's truly breathtaking, a great display of color and light. It's calming, you know," Leslie said, turning to look at Bryan, and he noticed the worry lines appear again.

"Leslie, I've got to talk to you about something but I'm not sure how to say it—what the right words should be."

"Were you just reading my mind? I was thinking the same thing, too."

"You know you mean the world to me, don't you, Leslie? I mean I would never do anything to intentionally hurt you. You know that."

"Yes. And I would never intentionally hurt you either. You are first and foremost one of my best friends."

"That's what makes this so hard."

"Yeah, I know what you mean."

They stared at each other, nervous and unsure about how to proceed. Leslie, he could tell, was waiting patiently for him to tell her what was on his mind. Just then a distinctive, small shrill of a telephone began ringing, the sounds coming from inside his jacket.

"You've got a cell phone?" Leslie asked, surprised.

"Yeah, one of my clients insisted I get one. Excuse me."

He angrily jerked the small phone from his pocket and snapped it open. Turning his head he began to speak in low tones. He tried not to arouse suspicion on Leslie's part but he knew he probably was.

". . . I'll be back in my office in a little bit. I'll call you from there. Okay? Right, right. Goodbye."

The waiter appeared, cheerily wrapping up the final details of their dinner, asking if they'd like dessert or coffee. They both declined. Bryan shakily asked for the check, muttering to himself that he had to get back.

"You know what, since my client interrupted our dinner I'm charging this to him!"

His tone was unusually harsh, he knew, but in his aggravated state he could not seem to help it.

"It's no problem, Bryan. Is everything okay?"

He did not answer her. Instead he snatched the check from the table and abruptly stood. He held out his hand to help Leslie stand. He was not going to lie to her.

Sadly, he realized their moment for sharing secrets was lost and they would have to talk later. Bryan drove Leslie back to her office, giving her a fierce hug, making excuses for his hasty departure, all of which he noticed she graciously did not seem to mind.

"Say hello to Anastasia for me."

"I sure will. Don't work too late, Bryan."

Bryan felt somewhat melancholy, especially since it seemed Leslie understood his tortured feelings. Again, the thought struck him that maybe she was seeing someone. Fear of losing her cherished friendship stopped him from asking, and he chided himself for being such a coward. Next time, he told himself, next time he would tell her about Walter, no matter what, and he'd release her from feeling any obligation to him. He realized he couldn't betray Leslie any longer.

CHAPTER XV

The air seemed thick and oppressive to Bryan when he returned to his office suite. He thought it felt that way because the case he was working on was getting on his nerves and, more to the point, making him nervous. The full-scale investigation he had launched into the backgrounds and stories of the people who were eyewitnesses to the hot-headed, stupid, and reckless murder by Lorenzo Ortez were all solid. Not one witness seemed to have a shaky background he could use to throw the jury off the real issues by attacking that witness' credibility. Bryan switched on the light and was startled that his investigator, Marcus, was sitting at his desk, in the dark.

Marcus was a small man who wore thick glasses, so thick that Bryan was certain his driver's license must declare that he was to be considered legally blind. He stood about five feet two, had an unnaturally large head, hands and feet. His eyes always seemed to dart around a room. Bryan both admired and hated this man. He admired his keen ability to trace people, to sniff things out. But Marcus was also known for pulling pranks and being theatrical. Bryan only tolerated him because he was very good at what he did.

"What are you doing here, sitting in the dark, scaring the shit out of me, man?" Bryan said angrily.

"Don't wet your shorts. I ain't been here long and besides, you needed someone to look out for your, shall we say, best interest, by babysitting your little office here."

"What are you talking about? Why does my office need babysitting?" Bryan asked, exasperated by the man's nasal tone.

Marcus held up a small, button-size gadget in his hand. Bryan had no idea what it was. "Somebody left you a little present. Something to remember all your conversations by. I found this, shall we say, little bug, in your telephone."

Bryan stared at it wide-eyed, astonished that his office had been bugged. Before he could ask the question of who put it there, Marcus said, "I came to tell you that there are some rumors floating around that the Ortez people are not too happy with our, shall we say, investigation," Marcus slurred.

Bryan, although frightened, was also totally annoyed, as he always was with Marcus. He had this unnerving, constant use of the phrase "shall we say," and it irritated the hell out of Bryan. "I don't have time to try and pull information out of you, Marcus, so spit it out. What rumors are you talking about?"

"You hear 'bout that case where they found that doctor stuffed in a barrel of cement off I-5?"

"Yes. I heard about it."

"Well, the details which the police are keepin' to themselves are, shall we say, morbid."

"Morbid—"

"This guy was one of Fernando's doctors, who supposedly diagnosed an ugly mole on his back as cancer. So, get this, they gave him a Columbian necktie."

143

"What the hell is a Columbian necktie?"

"It's where they slit the throat from ear-to-ear, then pull the tongue out through the slash."

"Damn!"

"Anyway, the guy's mouth is sewn shut. Guess what's inside?"

"God, I don't think I want to know."

"His eyes! Man, he stuffed the guy's eyes inside his mouth. Not a pretty sight, no pun intended."

"Unbelievable. I didn't read that in the paper."

"And you probably won't. San Diego P.D. ain't stupid. They keep details like that to themselves. Anyway, that's the kind of crazy shit Fernando does. It shows everybody what he'll do if he don't like something ya say or do."

"What's all that got to do with me?"

"Look, I been helping you out for a long, long time and I wouldn't want to see anything happen to you. So, I been hearing that Mr. Ortez will not be very happy if we are unable to—shall we say—release his dear, sweet brother from his stupid crime. And from the looks of things, it's not gonna happen. We are in deep shit. And as I just told ya, it's not a good thing to piss this guy off," Marcus concluded, eyebrows raised, a lit cigarette extending from his lips. It bobbed up and down with each word he spoke and put Bryan in a semi-hypnotic trance, watching the smoke rise and swirl. Shaking his head to ward off the spell, Bryan said, "We are in deep shit! What's that supposed to mean?"

"It means I ain't been able to come up with nothing that helps this case. It means I think your boy is going down. It means your ass, shall we say, is grass," he said, raising his voice as well as the color in his face. "Look, I don't mean to scare ya, but word on the street is, if Mr. Ortez doesn't have his brother back in the fold again, somebody's going to pay for being inadequate in their quote—legal representation—unquote."

His words slammed into Bryan with a force that actually took his breath away as the reality of the magnitude of this man's power and fury fully and finally registered. All the rumors he'd ever heard about Fernando Ortez and his brother were nothing compared to the gruesome picture Marcus had just painted.

His client with deep pockets was more than a dangerous man: He was a man without a conscience. It obviously didn't matter if his brother was guilty; what mattered was his freedom and if it didn't happen, Mr. Ortez would take it out on Bryan. Bryan contemplated Marcus' words. His legs turned to rubber. He was scared out of his mind, but he was not about to go out like that. Bryan mentally tried to devise a plan to get out of this mess. He sat at his desk, his hands visibly shaking, while his stomach rocked and heaved.

"Well, I'll just withdraw from the case. I'll say I've had a serious family matter come up that will take me away for several months."

"Not gonna work."

"Why not?"

"You can bet your last dollar he knows all about your family. And if he don't, he'll find out."

"Well, what about an illness that makes me bedridden?" Bryan threw this thought on the table, hoping against hope that Marcus would agree this was a great plan.

"What are ya gonna have, AIDS or something? Whatever it is, it better be life threatening. Nothing short of that will save your ass from these guys, especially if they realize you're faking. This family has connections everywhere. Now unless you're able to get a doctor to—shall we say—fake some medical records for you, that won't work either."

Bryan's temporary euphoria flew away like a startled bird; his heart sank; every possible thought to get out of this mess was futile. He simply did not have the resources to ward off an attack if Mr. Ortez decided to launch one against him.

"Well, I've got to get him off my back. There's no question about it. We've got to find something to make that happen," Bryan said, running his hands through his hair, fear gripping him. "Something's got to happen in our favor in this case. Why'd that stupid ass Lorenzo have to beat the hell out of the guy, then shoot him in front of a bunch of people? Damn, what an idiot!"

Bryan continued to pace the room, his strides harder and wider.

"I can't make witnesses disappear; they're already in police protective custody. Shit!" Bryan slammed his hand on the desk. He loosened his tie. The heat of fear rose like a volcano, leaving him feeling as if he were strangling.

It was not beyond Bryan's ethics to do whatever it took to win, but in this particular case, it was crucial that he find something to gain a not guilty verdict for Lorenzo Ortez.

Long into the night Bryan and Marcus talked. Each avenue they took and decided to walk down—to explore—would abruptly stop, leaving them facing yet another dead end.

Bryan's trial, the trial written about in all the San Diego newspapers, reputed to be the "trial of the decade," began on a rainy day. The weather seemed to punctuate the dreariness, the hopelessness Bryan was feeling.

Bryan dressed in what he called his "lucky suit," a navy blue Will Smith double-breasted silk suit. He had made it a tradition to wear it on the first and last day of every trial. He considered it lucky because up until now he had never lost a case when he wore this suit. Now, he wondered if he'd be buried in it.

He arrived at the courthouse early, sat at the defendant's table and began pulling legal briefs and documents from his suitcase, meticulously lining them up for use as each witness came up. The jury selection had been long and tedious; he tried mightily to dismiss many jurors whom he did not feel would favor his client, but early on he ran out of peremptory challenges, not to mention every other challenge he was allowed by law. But now, thankfully, that part of the process was over. It was not his ideal jury. The only acceptable jurors, in his mind, would have to consist of elderly people who were illiterate and prone to falling to sleep frequently. He nervously chuckled as his mind's eye imagined such a thing. He had failed miserably in getting a jury that would be pro-defendant. He glanced out the courthouse window at the steady downpour of rain as gigantic waves of despair made his heart flutter unnaturally and beat precariously. He had not picked a winner this time. And he feared the loser would be an innocent man—himself.

From the beginning, everything that could go wrong, did. The judge, Judge Grady, seemed to hate Bryan, and he didn't hide his loathing for Lorenzo either. This became painfully obvious to Bryan as the judge overruled each and every possible objection he raised. He sank in his chair for the tenth time that morning, risking a glance at Fernando Ortez who just glared through him, as if he wasn't even there. Not a good sign, no, not a good sign at all.

ക്ഷാള

Leslie, while certainly busy with her own practice, continued to follow Bryan's trial, a trial consistently referred to as one of the most intriguing in San Diego's history. Everyday she'd watch the news—with an uneasiness, which surprised her—clips of highlights of the trial on late-night newscasts or she eagerly scanned the San Diego Union-Tribune for details of the previous day's events. Some days the articles she read were very worrisome, and she wondered how Bryan was holding up. The reporters seemed to be relentless in judging Bryan's and his client's credibility in the media. It seemed to her Bryan was definitely not getting a fair shake. He was, after all, simply doing his job. A job she knew not many people would have undertaken.

There were comments about the solemnness of the jury, who occasionally threw periodic glares of disapproval Lorenzo Ortez's way, and he, in return, glared and stared at them, a move that was rightfully perceived as his attempts to intimidate the jury. Judge Grady, who was known for running a no-nonsense courtroom, had to admonish Bryan that his client would be taken from the courtroom if he continued this unacceptable behavior. There would be none of that in his courtroom, he advised, further admonishing the jurors to keep eye contact with the defendant to a minimum.

Leslie knew Bryan had a tough battle to wage if he also had to struggle with an unruly or uncooperative client. She'd set the paper down or turn away from the television set with worry lines across her forehead, while an unnatural state of disquieted alarm came over her as she worried incessantly about Bryan, and what this trial could do to his impeccable reputation.

❧❧❧

Little did she know how justified her fear for Bryan was. At the end of each day, Bryan would rush back to his office to meet in closed-door sessions with Marcus, who was still working hard to uncover something that would pull Lorenzo Ortez from certain execution. And each day nothing worth pursuing happened.

The final day of trial came, and Bryan breathed a heavy sigh as he stumbled from his bed, feeling grouchy and mean from too little sleep and too much work, to his shower. He closed his eyes, and for the first time in years, prayed that the solemn jury would find his client not guilty. He sank to his knees, water streaming down his face as he begged God to allow him to be successful today in raising reasonable doubt . . . and save his own life.

The day crawled by in a torturous anti-climax of closing arguments. Bryan appeared, as always, a confident and compelling speaker. He only hoped beyond belief that he'd left a seed of doubt in the minds of the non-responsive jurors. And now the moment of reckoning had come. Even though he'd prayed desperately to God that morning, nothing—not even the Almighty above—could strengthen Bryan's weak knees or still his hammering heart as he stood waiting for the fateful jury's decision.

"Have you reached a verdict?" Judge Grady inquired.

The foreperson rose and said, "Yes, we have, Your Honor."

"What say you?"

"We the jury, in People versus Lorenzo Ortez, find the defendant Lorenzo Ortez, not guilty of the charge of first degree murder."

That's the last thing Bryan remembered before he fainted.

CHAPTER XVI

Bryan stood on the courthouse steps with his now-free client smiling broadly but a bit nervously into the cameras of the fascinated media. He loved victory. He had worked harder and fought dirtier than anyone would ever know to get this client off. Having his life depending upon the successful outcome for this case tended to make one work harder than you could ever imagine you ever could or would, he mused.

The man standing beside him was guilty of the crime he was charged with, but Bryan didn't care. His job was to defend. Guilt or innocence was not his concern; it was the jury's job to decide that. But his mind nudged him that that wasn't exactly true, at least not in this case. His client's not guilty verdict might have been finagled, fabricated. As much as he didn't want to think about it now, his mind kept returning to the night not too long ago that he was forced to meet with Fernando Ortez.

He remembered how he almost had a heart attack the night he and Marcus were in his office discussing strategies when the door burst open and in came Bruno, followed by Fernando. While Bryan blinked and gaped at him in complete surprise, with the flick of his wrist Marcus was dismissed. He scurried out, not even risking a backward glance at Bryan.

Fernando had cleared his throat in an exaggerated manner, then informed Bryan, matter-of-factly, that he could not win this case, that all his confidence in him was well . . . it was gone. He would take matters into his own hands.

"Don't worry," he'd said, "I've taken care of things." He refused to disclose how he had taken care of it, and frankly Bryan was too afraid to ask. He didn't want to know. Knowledge of any sort of jury tampering or bribes could cost him his license to practice law and forever tarnish his reputation. That's where Bryan drew the line. He would not allow this gangster to take his life's work away from him by doing something as stupid as bribe a juror and then tell him about it! Although Bryan tried, rather weakly, to steer Mr. Ortez away from doing anything that could jeopardize the case, Fernando Ortez, in his customary fashion, didn't care what Bryan thought. All he demanded was that Bryan continue to work long and hard. Everything would be fine, just fine. His words continued to echo inside Bryan's head.

Bryan remembered how Fernando had smirked at him then. At that moment he had wanted to shove his fist down his throat. But he didn't do anything. He just sat there as meek as a lamb and prayed for this ordeal to end soon. Although he knew he was afraid of this man and his power, he had not realized the extent of his fear until he passed out cold on the floor after the jury's verdict. He already knew this case was not a winner, and once he heard the not guilty verdict, it caught him by surprise. At that moment, he surmised exactly what Fernando had meant by he'd "taken care of it." It was highly probable that he'd used devious methods to free his brother.

CHAPTER XVII

The legal community in San Diego was a tight little circle of lawyers who knew who was doing what, who represented whom, and even who was being sanctioned or disciplined for small to large infractions. It was no surprise how quickly news of Bryan's latest victory hit the streets and became the latest thing to gossip and speculate about. Leslie had heard people theorize about his possible association with the Mexican mob, even murmurs that he was dishonest. She heard questions about his morals and his professional ethics. From the beginning, this case was a no-win situation and everybody knew it. Now, even people who once admired Bryan wondered about him. His reputation was rapidly being soiled, tarnished.

Leslie listened and endured the laughter and jokes surrounding the fainting episode after the verdict was read. She tried many times to even defend his position, but to no avail. Actually, little did anyone know, including Bryan, that she was in the courtroom that day, attempting to show support for Bryan, and she was extremely alarmed when he passed out. Something about it felt so wrong. She tried to get to him, but the crowd pressed in around him and a bailiff stopped anyone from trying to approach the area where he had fallen. The courtroom temporarily erupted in madness and Leslie stood by feeling helpless. She, along with all the other attendees, was escorted from the room. She took a backward glance, and was happy to see that he was sitting up, taking sips of water from a paper cup someone had handed him. His client, she noticed, just sat there and watched him with a look of disdain upon his face.

Since that day, even though it had only been three days ago, he was on her mind. She needed to see him; she had to talk to him. It was very important to her to be able to look in his eyes. There, she believed, she would be able to read the truth. What was this fainting all about? Was he sick, scared or worse? she wondered. Something was terribly wrong; she knew that much.

They had been in contact with each other minimally since the beginning of this trial. Leslie knew he was too busy to see her but she had tried to reach him anyway, several times. His secretary always politely informed Leslie that his calendar was full and that he would not be able to see her for several weeks. Finally, today, Leslie decided to take another chance and call him. This time she'd try him at home.

The telephone rang and Bryan jumped again. He'd just placed it gingerly in its cradle after speaking in hushed tones with his investigator, Marcus. The word on the street was "not good" as Marcus had suspected. He urged Bryan to leave town. Never once during the conversation did he say "shall we say," and although that euphemism normally irritated Bryan, the absence of it unnerved him even more. He had listened intently to Marcus. It was incredibly hard to believe what he was hearing.

"It's not good, my friend."

"What do you mean?"

"Let's just say that I'm willing to kick in a few thousand dollars to get you away from here—far, far away, as quickly as you can pack underwear and a t-shirt or two."

"I can't just leave. I've got to fight this—whatever it is— I'm fighting. Tell me the details, please Marcus, what you know."

"Details aren't necessary at this point, my friend. It would be a waste of precious time."

The remorseful tone he used was enough to strike a blow of huge proportions into Bryan's groin.

"What do you mean?"

"I'll help you anyway I can. Just leave, Bryan. Leave now!"

He heard a soft click as the line was disconnected. He knew Marcus had simply hung up. There was nothing more he could say.

Still reeling from his conversation with Marcus, Bryan was stunned when the phone rang again. Part of him for a split second hoped it was Marcus calling again to say "sike" or "gottcha"—telling him that it was all a joke. But he seriously doubted that Marcus would do that to him. Even though he was a jokester, he knew the stakes were too high to joke about anything now.

Bryan couldn't suppress the sinking feeling of pure, stark fear that was working its way up his spine, leaving a tart, metallic taste in his mouth as the shrill ringing of the telephone began again. He had to answer it, he knew that. Fernando or Lorenzo could be calling him, and he wondered if they he might even know that he was there. He feared antagonizing them any further, so with trepidation Bryan picked up the phone. His legs seemed to be filled with lead, his hands were limp and moist from perspiration. He felt incredibly weak when he placed the phone against his ear.

⚜

"Hello . . . hello!" Leslie said. "Bryan, are you there?" Leslie knew that someone had picked up the phone but they hadn't said a word. She could hear heavy breathing, then—

"Leslie," he muttered. "I . . . I . . . was expecting another, uh, call. Uh, uh, how are you?" Bryan sounded strange to Leslie. His voice was strained and his tone had a lifeless quality that frightened Leslie. She was suddenly very terrified for him.

"Bryan, what's wrong? You've been on my mind all day. I've been so worried about you. Is everything okay?"

The compassion and concern in Leslie's voice sent a wave of unexpected emotion surging through him. Bryan began to whimper and mumble, his sentences disjointed, muddled and incoherent. Leslie tried hard to concentrate and not panic, but she understood only portions of his words.

"I'm . . . sc . . . sc . . . scared, Leslie. I've—"

"You've what, Bryan?"

"People, hurt—"

"What people, who's hurt?"

"Going to—Leslie . . . oh God, I think I'm going to—"

"What Bryan, what—you're going to what?"

A loud blast rocked the phone right out of Leslie's hand. The deafening sound startled and unnerved Leslie. In that split second she instinctively knew it was a shot, and it sounded as if someone had shot directly into the telephone. Leslie screamed and dropped the phone. Grasping for control, Leslie snatched the phone from the floor. Wide-eyed and terrified, she continued to listen. The gurgling sound she heard caused bile to creep up the back of her throat. She stifled the urge to vomit and willed herself to calm down. She could hear Bryan struggling to breathe.

"Bryan! Bryan! Bry—an!" She screamed his name over and over and over again, completely losing the battle to remain calm. Her screams sent Anastasia running into the room.

"Mom! Mom, what happened? Why are you screaming?"

"Anastasia, quick–go upstairs and call 9-1-1. Bring me your phone—I need to get help for Bryan, he's hurt. Hurry, get the phone. Now!"

Anastasia ran from the room, rounding the corner on a dime. She grabbed her phone and raced back to her mother, dialing 9-1-1 while she ran. When she reached her mother, an operator was on the line.

"Someone has just been shot, I think, at my friend's house. I'm on the other line with him now and . . . and, he's making strange sounds. He can't talk."

Leslie rapidly told the operator where Bryan lived. The operator instructed her to stay on the line with her friend until help arrived. Leslie began to speak softly into the phone, trying to reassure Bryan. She didn't know if he could hear her, but she could hear him. The noises she heard caused her hands to go numb. She was cold with fear. Bryan sounded somehow slimy. He kept making a gurgling, hissing, wet smacking sound. It was awful. She knew he had to be hurt very badly. What had happened? Had someone shot him while he talked to her? What was he trying to tell her? Had he shot himself? She was crooning words of reassurance into the telephone, hoping they would reach Bryan's ear. Finally, she heard the distant cry of an ambulance and then a thump and bump before the door was smashed. Help had arrived.

"Ma'am. We've got it now."

"Is he okay? What happened?"

"Ma'am, he's in serious need of attention. We're working on him now. Looks like a gunshot. I've got to hang up. If you can meet us at the hospital, we'll need someone to help us with identification, et cetera. What's his name, ma'am?"

"Bryan—Bryan McKay."

"Okay. Ma'am, you may have helped save his life. I've got to go."

A finality of deaf silence replaced the sounds she had been hearing. Leslie continued to hold both telephones, one in each hand, as a glazed expression covered her face. Then she began to shake uncontrollably as the effects of shock took over. Anastasia began to cry. Leslie heard her daughter's sobs. They seemed to come from a tunnel far, far away. At last she held her arms out to her.

"Mom, what happened to Bryan?"

"Baby, I don't know. We were talking and I heard a loud bang. Dear God, it sounded like a cannon. I've got to go, baby. They need me to give them information about him."

Leslie realized then she was still holding the phones, and she could hear someone saying, "Ma'am, ma'am. Please pick the phone up, ma'am." It was the 9-1-1 operator.

"I . . . I forgot I was still holding the phone in my hand."

"Ma'am, I'm sure you're pretty shook up right now, but you need to pull yourself together. Your friend needs you. The paramedics have just informed me that they are taking the victim to St. Luke's Hospital. Can you meet them there?"

"Yes, yes I can. I just need to get my keys. Where are my keys, Anastasia?" Leslie asked in a timid, confused voice. She couldn't think clearly and she was thankful Anastasia was there to help. Anastasia gently took the phones from her mother's hands, helped her stand up and quickly went to find her keys. Leslie began to wring her hands, trying to generate some warmth, but she was very, very cold.

"Here, Mom. I found your keys and your purse. I'll drive you, though, okay, Mom? You look like you should rest before we get there," Anastasia said taking control, something Leslie badly needed, and led her out the door.

&

St. Luke's emergency room was nothing like the one depicted on TV shows. No one was running around; there were no people bleeding in the hallways. It seemed calm. Leslie walked in with purposeful strides, feeling in charge again. She inquired at the admissions desk about Bryan's whereabouts. Her peripheral vision caught movement, and then, as if in a dream, she slowly turned and saw Bryan frantically being worked on in a small room. A nurse had just rushed out and Leslie caught a glimpse of Bryan's bloody face.

"Oh, my God! There he is. Oh God, oh God!" Leslie's calm exterior dissolved; she grabbed the counter and began to cry all over again. Anastasia was quickly at her side and led her to the seating area.

"Mom, please Mom, don't cry. They're working on him, Mom. He'll be okay. He's got to be. Come on, Mom, think good thoughts. Please, Mom, don't cry," Anastasia said, urgently speaking to Leslie.

Leslie knew she had to get herself together. She couldn't fall apart like this. Not now. She forced herself to breathe deeply in an attempt to calm herself. What in God's name happened? Who could have done this to Bryan? Those questions were all Leslie could think about. She prayed for Bryan, fervently asking God to save his life.

Leslie and Anastasia spent hours in the waiting room of the hospital. They had received very little information about Bryan's condition. Was he dead or alive? Leslie didn't know and she was afraid to ask. She had no idea how to contact Bryan's family about this horrible tragedy; oddly it was then Leslie remembered that Bryan rarely spoke of his family anymore. She decided to wait until morning to notify his secretary and perhaps she would know who to call. She hated to be the one to tell her this awful news, but who else was going to do it? She hoped the police didn't ransack his office looking for reasons why this thing happened; it would terrify his secretary. She was a quiet, older lady, and Leslie thought a commotion like this might not be good for her health.

The hours slipped by and Anastasia fell asleep. She was stretched out on a very uncomfortable-looking couch. Leslie had created a makeshift pillow for her out of her sweater. She was holding Anastasia's hand as she slept. The constant contact was reassuring, especially since she kept getting the shakes; great tremors would whip through her and she simply needed the comfort of a human touch. She thought about calling Robert but she wasn't sure what to say to him. "Hi, I'm at the hospital where a guy I'm also dating is lying with his head half blown off. Can you come comfort me?" What in the world would she say? Although she knew Robert to be very sensitive and kind, she was afraid to push him into another realm, one where visions of mistrust might shatter their relationship. If she were in his place, how would she feel? Probably the exact same way she imagined Robert would act, suspicious. How could she tell him that Bryan was really only her friend? She knew a part of her loved him too, and she feared Robert might pick up on that and misinterpret it. She talked to herself, reasoning that the love she felt for each man wasn't the same. How could she get Robert to see that?

She recalled that although at the beginning of their relationship she'd told Robert all about Bryan, since they had gotten more serious, she hadn't spoken about him anymore. Robert probably thought Bryan was out of her life.

She stood and began to pace the room. She watched Anastasia sleep; her body rhythmically rose and fell, and she heard a barely audible snore. She wanted to wake her, just so they could go to the cafeteria to get some coffee or go outside for some air, but as she watched her, she looked so peaceful she didn't have the heart to wake her. It was three o'clock in the morning, and Leslie was surprised that the long day and the shock of everything hadn't lulled her to sleep too. She was far too wound-up to sleep. Instead, she just continued to pace back and forth waiting for word about Bryan.

The following morning, Leslie and Anastasia were returning from the hospital cafeteria where they had eaten a fairly decent, inexpensive breakfast. The coffee was strong, exactly what Leslie needed. She'd only catnapped since she had gotten there, and lack of sleep was starting to make her cranky and weary. As they approached the lobby, she noticed an extremely agitated man speaking wildly to the information clerk, who seemed unable to understand who he was asking about because he was talking so fast. Leslie thought she heard him say McKay, and she turned to look closely at him. It was

Walter, one of Bryan's friends; she recognized him from the party.

"Walter? Mr. Brody, is that you?" Leslie approached him and noticed the wild look in his eyes. When he focused on her face and voice, he managed a bleak smile of recognition.

"Leslie. Thank God, somebody I know. What happened? Is he all right? Is he dead? Oh God—is he dead?" Walter was so distressed that he appeared completely out of control and Leslie felt sorry for him. Taking his hand, she led him to a nearby chair. Glancing back, Leslie noticed that the clerk actually looked relieved.

"Walter, Bryan is not dead. At least I don't think so. We've been here all night and we haven't heard much." Leslie tried to sound calm even though she didn't feel that way. She explained all that she knew to Walter. She tried very hard to be professional, speaking to him factually, her tone businesslike. Walter looked at her as if she were crazy.

"Leslie, this is just too much to take. How can you be so calm? I'm a wreck and I haven't been to sleep since yesterday."

"Why were you up all night?" Leslie asked.

"I work nights and I stopped by Bryan's this morning and some macho man cop detained me for hours. I thought I was going to have to kick his ass! I was so pissed they wouldn't let me go. Excuse me, baby, I don't mean to use bad language in front of you," he said, acknowledging Anastasia's presence.
"Oh, Walter, this is my daughter, Anastasia."

"Hi."

"Hi, baby. She's pretty."

Anastasia and Leslie exchanged a look as Walter continued to tell them his experience this morning. A cop had stopped him, asked him numerous questions about who he was and why he was there. They had actually put him in a patrol car!

"Oh, I almost went to jail this morning. Like'd to have me some Kentucky Fried cop ass, you hear me! If I'm lying, I'm dying! Trying to detain me. Accusing me!"

"Do you know who did this or why this happened?" Leslie asked. Her tone was slightly accusatory and she could tell Walter noticed it. That's when he completely lost it. Leslie didn't know what to do. He waved and flailed his arms. Anastasia gave her mother a "What did you do?" look and Leslie shrugged.

"I'm sorry—I'm making a spectacle of myself, aren't I?" Walter said, peering at Leslie through bloodshot eyes brimming with tears. "I just can't take it anymore! Everybody keeps thinking I could have had something to do with this. I didn't! I would never hurt him. He means too much to me. I . . . I love him." Walter wailed.

Leslie's mouth dropped. Anastasia was blinking fast as if she'd been slapped. Leslie asked her to excuse them for a minute. Her daughter walked away shaking her head.

"You what? What do you mean, you love him? Love him like what?" Leslie whispered.

"Oh man, I didn't mean to say anything. This is all too much. If he lives he's going to kill me for this. Please, Leslie, don't say anything to anybody," Walter pleaded.

"So you do mean what I think you mean?" Leslie could hardly believe what he was saying. The reality of the situation slammed into her head and she felt the beginnings of yet another headache. "Walter, are you and Bryan lovers? Is that what you're telling me?" Her voice rose to near hysteric pitch.

"Yes. And calm down, Leslie. He wanted to tell you but he didn't know how. I told him, hell, I'll tell her, but he always refused. You know how you lawyers are. Y'all wouldn't take kindly to him if you knew." Then he went from being accusatory to questioning. "Do you think someone found out? Do you think that's why this happened to him?"

"I don't know but I doubt it. Why would anybody try to kill him for being involved with you? That's ridiculous—" But her thoughts trailed off to explore that very possibility. As insane as it was, maybe somebody did know and didn't like it. There were so many people who hated gays and lesbians.

"Look," she said, "I seriously doubt that that's what happened, but if that was it, do you know who knew about the two of you? I certainly didn't," Leslie added with sarcasm.

"Nobody knew. Bryan and I were very discreet. It was important to him that we stay undercover. I never completely agreed with him, but I tried to respect his wishes. The only time I bucked him on it was when I showed up at your fund raiser, that Atlantic City Casino Night thing—the night I met you. I had to see what you looked like. I knew he had been spending a lot of time with you, and I was worried that he might be swinging."

"Swinging? What does that mean?"

"It means going both ways, girl. You never heard of it?"

"Yes, I've heard of it, but never quite like that, not that terminology."

"Well, call it what you want, girlfriend, I was worried. So I decided to check you out, but when I saw how angry Bryan was that I came, I knew he wasn't compromising us for you." He looked at her rather sheepishly. She could tell he was sorry he had to be so blunt.

"I knew he was angry with you and up until now I couldn't figure out why." Leslie folded her arms and added, "I'll be damn—he's gay."

"Does that matter? I mean, damn, he's fighting for his life

right now and his being gay has nothing to do with that. Don't be so insensitive, Leslie." It was Walter's turn to act indignant at Leslie's responses and actions.

"I'm sorry." Leslie caught herself, "You have to know that I am shocked, though a few things are making perfect sense now."

"Things like what?"

"Like he never did more than kiss my cheek, except one time. He was rarely overtly sexual, not in all the years I've known him. No wonder he seemed more like my girlfriend than a boyfriend. Damn." Leslie's voice trailed off again.

"He liked you a lot, Leslie. I also happen to know that he had a great deal of respect for you too." Walter's voice was solemn, laced with sadness.

"Do you realize you're talking in the past tense?" Leslie inquired, with her eyebrows raised.

"Oh God, I didn't mean to do that." He jumped up then and started to pace. Leslie just watched him. It's going to be a very long day, she thought.

CHAPTER XVIII

While Leslie contemplated her long day with Walter, Robert and Malcolm were enjoying a game of basketball. Malcolm had thought he could beat his father, but Robert fooled him. He took him to the hoop, showed him what time it was, and then said, "Don't ever think you can beat your daddy!" That was the first game.

Malcolm surprised him and took the second game by two points. A beautiful three-pointer cinched it for him. He looked at his dad and was smiling as if he'd really done something. They enjoyed being together, playing their favorite sport. If they weren't watching basketball on T.V., they were playing it. Robert had even had a court built on his property so they didn't have to leave home. He watched his son shoot the ball; he had good form, strong legs and a good eye. He squared off and shot the ball from various points on the court, missing only a few. Robert advised him to go to the hole, shoot some free throws. But there, his form was a little off. Robert walked over to his son, smiling, and showed him how to bend his knees just a little bit while bouncing the ball. He then showed him how to concentrate on the exact point of entry for the ball, flex his wrist, and then swish, it would go smoothly in; didn't

165

even touch the backboard, all net.

"Son, that's the way you do it!" Robert bragged.

"Dad, I keep trying to do it like that but I always need the board to sink it. What's up with that? What am I doing wrong?"

"Here," Robert said, motioning for Malcolm to throw him the ball. "Stand here. Watch me again. Concentrate on the point just above the center of the rim. See it?"

"Yeah, I see it."

"Okay, now concentrate on that point of entry but don't hit the board." He threw the ball. "Swish, each and every time it goes right in. Like magic. Now you try it. Remember what I said." Robert stepped aside and watched his son's form, balance and his concentration on the hoop. Bounce, bounce, bounce, then swish; it smoothly landed right in the net, no backboard help that time.

"All right!" Malcolm shouted, running over to give his father an excited high five.

"See, I knew you could. It just takes practice. Here." He threw the ball to him, "Do it again, Son." Robert was enjoying his time with his son. He was proud that he took instruction well.

The day was hot and slightly humid. Beautiful San Diego weather. He decided to take his son out for a quick driving lesson, then go for some ice cream. Baskin-Robbins sounded really good to both of them right about now.

"Come on, Son, let's shower real quick and go for a drive. You hungry?"

"No doubt, Dad, no doubt. You know I'm always hungry. Especially after beating my dad. That makes me ravenous!" Malcolm teased. Robert smiled at his son. He knew that Malcolm thought he was a good player—even for an "old man." Malcolm genuinely loved listening to his father tell him about his college days on the basketball court. Their family room was full of trophies he had won, and every time Malcolm looked at them, he yearned for some of his own. Robert had assured him that one day the walls would be lined with his trophies too. Malcolm already played for an independent team. It wasn't connected with his school, but Robert supported him and made sure he got to each and every game and practice. Even when he was tired, Robert still took his son and attended all the games.

Every now and then he'd say, "I can't wait till you start driving, Son; all these games are wearing me out!" But Robert knew he wouldn't miss a game for the world. Sometimes Malcolm didn't feel like going, but Robert encouraged him, built up his excitement for the oncoming game, and then he was ready to play. It never failed. Even though Robert often said the same old thing, it seemed to inspire Malcolm to want to play hard and particularly play hard when his Dad was watching.

They finished dressing about the same time. Father and son were surprised when they met up in the kitchen and had both decided to wear almost exactly the same thing. They pointed at each other and started laughing. Robert loved the way they had the same mind set sometimes. Robert felt young and healthy—they could almost pass for brothers. Well, in Robert's eyes anyway.

Malcolm noticed that his father looked happier lately. Especially since he'd met Leslie. Malcolm thought about his own mother then. He knew he was adopted and he knew his mother was just a teenager when she had him. Robert had explained to him that she'd later been killed in an automobile accident. His grandmother had tried to take care of him, but her advancing age and limited income had prevented her from doing so. They never knew who his father was; his mother would never tell. Robert told Malcolm what little he'd known about the beginning of his life, but Malcolm sometimes secretly wished and then he'd wonder about his grandmother, whether or not she was still alive and why she hadn't kept him. But most of all, he thought about his mother. He struggled sometimes with the pain of losing her. He said a little prayer every night asking God not to take his dad. But now that his dad had Leslie, for some reason Malcolm was less afraid. His dad was happy and that made him happy, too. She was kinda fine, so Malcolm didn't mind her being in his Dad's life. He could share—in fact he wanted to share. Since Robert met Leslie he'd been even more animated in his discussions with Malcolm about girls. They could be so weird sometimes. But lately he'd started noticing how good they looked. They usually smelled great, especially Laurie who was teaching him how to kiss. Oh, yeah, she could kiss really good. He had told his dad about her. His dad listened intently and gave him some advice on how to treat her. His dad was cool. Yeah, his dad was real cool.

"Son, what are you daydreaming about? Don't you want to drive?" Robert was standing there dangling the keys; Malcolm, lost in thought, hadn't even noticed that his Dad was going to let him drive.

"Oh, you know I do. Thanks, Dad." He grabbed the keys and slid into the driver's seat, suddenly feeling mature and serious. His dad always told him, "Son, driving is serious business. You must always keep your mind on the road. You are now responsible for a lot of people's lives. Okay?" Malcolm took his dad's speech seriously. The thought of having a car accident made him serious and somber whenever he took the wheel. He never wanted to hurt anyone like his mother had been hurt. Never, ever.

He adjusted his mirrors and the seat—his dad had slightly longer legs than his—then put the car in gear. He backed slowly and cautiously out of the driveway. Concentrating hard, both hands on the wheel, exactly as he'd been taught, he held the steering wheel with a death grip until his father said, "Now, Son, lighten up. You are in control of this machine. It is not in control of you. Don't hold the wheel so tight. Relax a little. Take your time. We'll be fine. Okay?"

"Yeah, Dad. Okay. I'm kinda nervous. It's been a while since I drove. Man, I'm tripping!" Malcolm said with a light laugh, chuckling at himself and his sudden case of nerves. His stomach was churning. He had to get over this fear. Every time he got in the car to drive, a vision of the mother whom he didn't remember appeared.

"Dad?"

"Yes."

"Can I tell you something?"

"You know you can. What is it now? Is that girlfriend of yours teaching you something else?" Robert said, teasing.

"No, Dad! It's not even about her. It's about—" he hesitated.

"Go on, Son, you know you can talk to me about anything. So, what's up?" Robert turned to face his son, his hand draped casually around the seat.

"Well, it's just that . . . man, um, well, I don't want to sound like no sissy or anything, or like I'm crazy."

"Son, just say it. You know I'm not judgmental. Speak your

mind. Go on." He sensed his dad's encouragement.

"Okay." He cleared his throat. "Every time I start to drive I see a woman's face. Always the same woman. I think it's my mother. And I get scared. It's like I think she's warning me or something. It's a trip, Dad. I don't know what's going on." His voice had a noticeable tremor now and his dad was concerned.

"I'm not sure what that means. Let me think about it for a minute—"

"Am I crazy, Dad?"

"No, no, Son, you are not crazy. I think what happens is your subconscious, always mindful of the accident that took your mother away, floods you with memories of her. I'm not sure, but maybe she comes to your mind like a guardian angel, letting you know she's with you and with that knowledge you are extra careful. She helps you to do that."

"You think my mother's helping me?" Malcolm questioned.

"Sure. I think she probably helps you all the time but you are particularly aware and sensitive to it when you're driving. Let her guide you, Son; don't be afraid."

"My mother's guiding me. Ain't that a trip!" Malcolm said. "Well, Mom, thank you. I won't let you down."

Robert patted him on the back and winked. "That's it, son. Talk to her."

In only a few minutes, they arrived at Baskin-Robbins and Malcolm carefully parked.

"Dad?" Malcolm looked at him, eyebrows arched.

"Hmm?"

"How serious are you about Leslie?"

"Very serious. I'm glad we're talking about this now. I wanted to talk to you about this anyway. Let's get some ice cream and talk about it."

They both ordered double scoops of chocolate, chocolate

chip ice cream. Malcolm had his on a cone, but Robert got a cup. Malcolm knew the girl serving them, so while Malcolm was busy talking to her, Robert went discreetly outside to sit and enjoy the day. His mind was rapidly clicking, deciding how to say what he needed to say to his son. Leslie was his woman, an important part of his life. There wasn't a day that went by that he didn't think about her or want to be with her. His son needed to know that.

"Dad, why'd you leave me?" Malcolm asked when he found his father outside.

"Because you were talking. I let you talk. And by the way–"

"What?"

"Your rap is weak!" he said laughing, slapping him on the back.

"Dad, nobody says 'rap' anymore."

"No? What do you young folks say?"

"It's called spittin'."

"Spitting, ugh, that sounds nasty."

"Spittin' game, Dad, we "spit at girls." You know 'get at 'em,' not rap. Now, that's weak," Malcolm said, laughing. "Besides, I've got a girlfriend, remember?"

"Yeah, I remember. Spittin'! Man, I must be getting old 'cause I don't get it."

"That's all right, just don't use words like 'rap' around my friends. They think you're cool, and that would blow your image. Anyway, how serious are you about Leslie, Dad?"

"I've been sitting out here thinking 'bout how to tell you this. So rather than make myself crazy thinking up the right words, I'll just say it—I love her. I can't imagine the rest of my life without her in it. I'd like to one day soon ask her to be my wife. How do you feel about that?" Robert failed miserably at trying to sound calm. He spoke rapidly, and then he noticed his palms were sweaty. He was nervous. This was the first revelation he had made to his son voicing how serious he was about her.

"Man, I don't know what I think. I guess I'm surprised a little. You haven't known her that long, Dad."

"That doesn't matter. My instincts tell me she'll be a very good wife. Our conversations, life experiences and stuff like that tell me she'd be perfect for me—and you."

Malcolm jumped in. "Me? I'm too big to need a mother. I'm fine. We're fine all by ourselves, Dad."

"I agree. But what you don't realize yet, because you're so young, is that a man sometimes needs more. Son, I'm extremely proud of who you are but soon you'll be gone. A grown man, going to college, making your own decisions. And I'll be alone. I'd like a chance to have both you and the woman I love under the same roof. And that includes her daughter, of course."

"Dad, she's going to graduate soon. She told me she's going to college somewhere on the East Coast," Malcolm said matter-of-factly.

"I know that. Leslie and I have talked about Anastasia's plans, and she's told me her fears about her going so far away to college. It worries her. And I've told her about your dream of attending Howard. She's excited for you."

"She is?"

"Yes. Son, like I just told you, we talk about everything. She's important to me. But how you feel is important, too. I'm not saying I'm going to do this tomorrow but I want you to think about it. And it would make me happy if you accepted her and Anastasia into our lives." Robert looked intently at his son. Malcolm's eyes were troubled. He kept turning away from direct eye contact.

"Well, you think about it, Son. There's no rush. Okay?" Robert was disappointed that things hadn't turned out the way he would have liked.

The drive home wasn't quite as animated as before. They were both solemn, lost in their own thoughts. Every attempt Robert made to lighten the mood hadn't worked. He knew Malcolm was struggling with the information he now had to process. Robert understood that it would be difficult for his son to give up having him all to himself, but life had a way of always changing. Malcolm had to be prepared and ready to meet the challenges and changes as they confronted him. This would be a start.

Once they entered the house, Malcolm immediately excused himself and went to his room. Feeling somewhat distraught, Robert felt an urgent need to speak with Leslie. All of a sudden he needed to hear her voice. She would utter words of reassurance—tell him that everything would be okay. While he doubted he'd tell her the exact content of his conversation with Malcolm, he still wanted to talk to her. He picked up the telephone and called her at the office.

"Leslie Hughes, please."

"I'm sorry, sir. Ms. Hughes is not in today. Can someone else help you?"

"No. Will she be in later today?"

"Not to my knowledge. I understand there has been an emergency and she's not expected."

"An emergency . . . not her daughter I hope."

"No, sir. All I was told was that she's at St. Luke's Hospital with a friend. Is there a message you'd like to leave?"

"No, no message."

Robert stared into space trying to identify who could possibly be in the hospital. What "friend" could it be—her best friend, Michelle? Rather than continue to sit there and speculate, he made a hasty decision to try and find her at the hospital. Maybe she needed him. He first checked his answering machine to see if she'd left a message. The message light was not blinking. Robert went into his son's room to tell him he was going out for a while, but when he knocked on the door, he didn't answer. Listening intently at the door, Robert heard no movement inside. Maybe he's asleep, he thought. Carefully, so as not to wake him, Robert opened the door. His son was lying across the bed, staring at the ceiling, his earphones turned up full blast; Robert could hear it from across the room. In a sullen gesture he removed the earphones.

"Huh, Dad?"

"I'm going out for a while. I'll be back. You okay?"

"Yeah, Dad. I'm okay."

Robert nodded and started to close the door.

"—Hey, Dad."

"Yes, Son."

"It's okay with me. She's cool. Go for it." Even as he said the words, Robert noticed Malcolm's eyes mist over.

Crossing the room in quick strides, Robert sat on the bed. He reached to hug him and in return his son embraced him, too.

"I'm glad to hear you say that." They quickly hugged again and Robert left the room with a lighter step as joy seemed to propel him.

The drive to the hospital was emotional and a much needed release for Robert. He had gotten his son's approval of the woman he loved. There were no words to adequately describe how he felt right now. He couldn't wait to see Leslie to tell her what had happened. Lost in his thoughts of joy, he almost forgot where he was headed and why. His sixth sense nudged him. Something told him that maybe he shouldn't show up here. It might be an intrusion. How would Leslie feel? What was she going through? And would his arrival be welcomed? Too late, he was here. This hospital was usually so crowded there never seemed to be enough parking spaces, but he lucked out and found one right away.

Walking the corridor, searching for the E.R.—he figured that must be where they were—he immediately saw Anastasia. She looked tired and worried. He headed over to her.

"Anastasia—"

"Oh hi, Robert. How'd you know we were here?"

"Your mom's secretary told me. I hope I'm not intruding."

"I'm sure you'll just add to the drama that's already going on around here. Mom's over there." Anastasia pointed to Leslie who was talking to an extremely handsome man who seemed very distraught. Robert wasn't sure he should approach them, but Anastasia's use of the term "drama" drew him to them anyway.

"Leslie—"

"Robert, what are you doing here?" She wrapped her arms around him.

Robert noticed a puzzled look on the stranger's face and freed himself from Leslie's embrace to face him.

"Hi, I'm Robert, a friend of Leslie's. And you are—"

"I'm Walter. Walter Brody." The two shook hands and Robert could tell he sized him up.

"Robert," Leslie interjected, "this is Walter, a good friend of Bryan. Bryan was shot last night while I was speaking to him on the telephone." It took Robert a moment for her words to sink in, for he was too busy glaring at Walter, trying to gauge how much he cared for Leslie.

"Who's Bryan?" he finally questioned once he again focused on Leslie.

"A business associate and a friend," she said. "He's in critical, but stable condition right now. He's still not out of the woods though."

"Leslie, may I speak to you alone for a minute?" Robert asked, but continued to dart glances Walter's way.

"Sure. Excuse us, Walter." Leslie walked away with Robert and he kept wondering how to ask if she was involved with Bryan—or Walter.

Before they had a chance to talk, a mob of reporters pushed and shoved their way into the hospital corridor. Someone shouted, "There she is!" All at once a sea of reporters surrounded them, thrusting microphones in her face. Lightbulbs flashed, and everyone seemed to talk at once.

"Ms. Hughes, is it true that Bryan McKay was shot last evening in his home?"

Leslie, obviously unaccustomed to such assaults, was taken aback. She quickly recovered.

"There has been an incident, yes."

"Were you with him at the time of the attack?"

"Not physically, no." Leslie answered vaguely.

Robert was elbowed out of the way. However, he could hear perfectly well as Leslie answered questions that were being shouted at her from all angles.

"Is he alive?"

"What motivated the attack?"

"We understand he was in his home; were you there too?"

Leslie put up her hand to stop the questions and try to gain some control over the situation.

"I can only answer one question at a time. Please allow me that." The crowd settled down a little.

"Mr. McKay was involved in an incident last night. He was in his home and I do not know why this happened. No details are known at this time. The last update I was given was simply that he is in surgery."

"Is he expected to survive?"

"I haven't been told that yet."

"What's your relationship to the victim? You've been linked romantically to him in the past. Aren't you his girlfriend?"

At that question, Robert's heart sank. He now knew the answer to what he suspected. Without a look back at Leslie, Robert turned and slowly walked away.

❧

Leslie watched as Robert left the corridor. She couldn't even stop him. The reporters were surrounding her, shouting numerous questions at once. Finally, security escorted them out for disrupting the hospital. Leslie sighed as she sat and pondered the implications of this situation with Robert. Her brow wrinkled and her mood darkened. She paced the now quiet room. Her ears buzzed and she still could see little dots of light that continued to dance long after the flash of the cameras had stopped. She went through everything in her mind. Robert hadn't even given her a chance to explain, nor did he hear her answer to the question regarding her relationship with Bryan. Somehow this whole situation had to be explained. She could have strangled that reporter who asked her such a personal question: Was she romantically linked with Bryan? She never had a chance to tell Robert, to explain to him the true nature of their relationship. Now she feared he'd gotten the wrong idea. There were several times during their courtship that she had wanted to tell Robert, to break off this triad she had going, but the right words never came to her. And, admittedly, she was enjoying the attention of both men too much to cause any alteration of it. Now that she knew about Bryan's sexual orientation, she knew he wasn't a threat to her relationship with Robert, but Robert didn't know that. And now she worried if she'd get a chance to tell him. He looked both angry and disgusted when he stormed away.

The dilemma that faced her now was how to tell him that yes, she had been dating Bryan at the same time she dated him, but he needn't worry about it, because he's gay. Would he believe that scenario? And even if he did, would he forgive her for not being exclusively his? The last thing she wanted right now was to lose both men. Bryan's condition was precarious; in fact, he might not make it. If he died, his death would haunt her for a very long time. How could she be involved with someone who, now that she really thought about it, she hadn't really known? I mean, he's gay! How come I didn't pick up on that? I must be slipping. Or was she too busy getting her ego stroked that she hadn't paid attention? Her mind swirled and dipped and dived from one question to another. She was so deep in thought that she hadn't noticed that a doctor was talking to Walter about Bryan's condition. Anastasia grabbed her arm and pointed in their direction.

"Leslie, I'm glad you came over. The doctor was just telling me a little bit about Bryan's condition."

She listened as the doctor included her in the conversation.

"I was just telling Mr. Brody that Mr. McKay has suffered severe trauma to the head, which may result in brain damage.

We won't know the true extent of the damage for perhaps a couple of days. There's a great deal of swelling that needs to be monitored. His condition is critical. Rest assured he will be closely monitored for the next several days in ICU. So far, he is still in a coma. And right now, that's a good thing. His body needs time to heal, and it heals best when a person is unconscious. His reflexes are minimal and a CAT scan shows little brain activity. I have to be honest, it's not looking good, but he is still alive. He appears to be in excellent health and if he's a fighter, that should help him a great deal. I understand you helped direct the paramedics to him." He turned to Leslie.

"Yes. Yes, I did."

"Well, the help he received so quickly probably saved his life. Their quick response and immediate attention were essential to him being in the state he is in now—alive."

"Well, Doctor, that's good to know."

"We'll try to keep you posted. Now if you'll excuse me, I've got rounds to make."

They thanked the doctor and watched as he walked away. He had left them with more questions about Bryan and his chances for survival than answers. He hadn't allowed them an opportunity to ask many questions. But Leslie was so stunned by everything that had happened, she couldn't formulate a decent question if her life depended on it. Right now her mind and heart were in turmoil.

CHAPTER XIX

Robert left the hospital in an angry huff. As he made his way through the throng of people thrusting microphones with cords snaking their way around his ankles, he became even more irritated. Damn, he thought, I had a feeling I shouldn't have come here. I should have kept my first thought and stayed the hell away from this hospital. An unreasonable feeling of betrayal enveloped him. He didn't know the facts and at this point that didn't even matter. His pride was wounded. How could people think Leslie was that man's woman if she wasn't? Something was obviously going on. With a quickness that startled him, it seemed as if all his hopes for a lasting relationship with Leslie were shattered. He felt as though a big piece of his life had just broken into fragments, a million tiny pieces.

He loved her. Now he was unsure of her love for him. There was something going on with this man—this Bryan—more than she ever let on before. He began to reflect on the fact that she hadn't called him when this whole thing happened. Earlier he had wondered why, now he knew. She didn't call you, dummy, because that's her other man, his irrational thoughts told him. He thought about all the things he'd just heard, and he wondered if she had just been playing games with him—deadly games that aimed for and shattered his heart. He couldn't believe what was happening. It was all too much to even absorb. How could such a great day turn so ugly? He wondered if it were possible that he was being unfair. He knew Leslie and she wasn't the kind of woman who would betray him like this. Her interest in him and the way she made love to him was far too intense for somebody playing games. When they made love he knew she was not only giving him a chance to taste and explore her body, she was also giving him a little part of her soul. He tried to convince himself that her feelings were genuine because to think otherwise, he knew, would destroy him.

Once he finally reached the parking lot, a news van was haphazardly parked, partially blocking in his car just enough to make getting out a nightmare. As he angrily rocked the car back and forth, slamming the car into first gear, then reverse, turning the wheel right then left, he finally was able to leave. His tires screeched as he sped away from this nightmare. He approached a red light, tapped his foot, drummed his fingers across the steering wheel, then fidgeted with his sleeve. He did not want to think about his behavior, but his thoughts kept drifting back to the look of shock on Leslie's face as he backed away. Now that he had a chance to breath and assess the situation, he started to feel ashamed for abandoning her when she probably needed him by her side to help her through this ordeal, especially since those reporters had practically assaulted her. But again those words—"You've been linked romantically to him in the past. Aren't you his girlfriend?"–rang in his ears. A profound feeling of loneliness wrapped itself around him. In his mind, he had planned a future with Leslie and her daughter in it. He had even made room for them in every aspect of his and Malcolm's life. Now this! He was dazed, disoriented and confused. He drove around for a time, not really knowing where he was going; his thoughts swung like a pendulum. One minute he'd be firmly convinced of her love and commitment to him, then the next, he would be skeptical. Fear of rejection was not letting loose of the death grip it had on his heart. He was not going to deny that he was hurt; he couldn't because the second he glanced in the rearview mirror, he saw the painful expression on his face. Did she betray me? he asked himself aloud.

From the airwaves, he heard the distant lyrics of a song he once loved to sing. ". . . Love don't love nobody. It takes a fool to learn that love don't love no one."

"Ain't that the truth," he said aloud as he snapped the radio off. Damn!

⚜

Leslie, Walter and Anastasia were allowed to each spend a little time with Bryan. He looked horrible. His head was swaddled in bandages. His eye was puffy, bruised and swollen, and a purplish color. His appearance reminded Leslie of Cyclops, a monster who was depicted in an old scary movie she remembered from her childhood. She glanced at Anastasia who uttered a soft whimper. Leslie, overwhelmed by the sights and sounds, again began to cry. The once handsome face that the media loved so much was probably permanently disfigured. She prayed to God to please let him live; she didn't give a damn about how he would look, she just wanted him to pull through this.

As soon as they left the confines of the ICU, Leslie noticed how tired and drained Anastasia looked. She pulled her into her arms and whispered it was time to go home. They had spent two days at the hospital. Anastasia had never left her side. Emotionally they were exhausted. They drove home in silence, each one lost in her own thoughts and worries about what all this meant. Finally, Leslie reached for Anastasia's hand, seeking its soft warmth.

"Baby, thanks for sticking with me. I know I must have scared you when this whole thing happened. I don't know what I would have done if it hadn't been for you."

"I just did what you've always taught me to do. I kept a level head and helped you when you needed me. I knew how to do it because you've always done it for me. I'm a good imitator, Mom."

"Yes, you are. But some of what you did was your own very good instincts. So give yourself some credit."

"Mom, what do you think is going to happen to Bryan?" Anastasia voiced Leslie's fear.

"I'm not sure, honey. The doctors didn't tell us much. But that really doesn't matter because we are going to be praying for him. They probably don't know the power of prayer like we do," Leslie said, continuing to lovingly stroke Anastasia's hand.

"I've been praying real hard for him, Mom, so hard I feel like I could sleep for days."

"Me too."

"I feel bad 'cause I wasn't always nice to him," Anastasia said, her voice dropping to a near whisper. "I hope he doesn't die. He wasn't that bad; he was okay."

"Neither one of us can regret anything we've done in the past. Let's just go forward from here. Bryan understood how much you missed your father. He was just trying to help both of us through that.

"Did I hear that guy Walter right? Is he gay?"

Leslie searched for the right response. Finally she said, "Apparently he is."

"You didn't know?"

"No, I didn't, but I guess that doesn't matter. Right now, I'd like to focus on something else. We are not going to think about anything other than prayer. We're going to keep on praying for Bryan's recovery, and we're going to pray for ourselves too." Leslie said.

"Why for ourselves—asking for forgiveness?" Anastasia replied, remembering with regret how ugly she'd always been to him.

"Forgiveness, yes. But also because we'll need God's strength to help us through this no matter how it turns out. If he lives, he'll need lots of love and support, and if he dies we'll need strength to agree with God's decision to let him go."

"I never thought about it that way, but I guess you're right, Mom." Anastasia's voice trailed off as she stared out the window.

Leslie continued to hold her hand, hoping that another tragedy was not going to touch her daughter again. She was learning life's hard lessons too early. Loss was never easy to take.

When they got home, Anastasia retreated to her bedroom and Leslie checked the answering machine. It was full of messages—messages she didn't want to hear; she simply did not have the strength to listen to them. She erased them all after listening to the first three which were all ambitious reporters trying desperately to get a more in-depth scoop on Bryan's condition, on Bryan's connection to the mob—connection to the mob, what's that all about? Leslie wondered.

Then another message asked her what were the chances of Bryan making a full recovery. What am I now, a doctor? How am I supposed to know that! She shook her head in disgust. Then a smile crossed her face as she made the foolhardy decision to delete all the rest of her messages without listening to another one! She'd never done that before. It felt great to ignore responsibility for a change.

Little did she know she erased several messages from Robert.

When she finally eased herself into bed—grateful to be home—Leslie's slept fitfully. She kept hearing the blast of a gunshot ringing crystal clear in her ear. She dreamt she was running after someone who had no face, but whoever it was carried a huge gun, and as irrational as dreams go, it resembled a cannon. Suddenly, the faceless person turned and pointed the gun at her head. She opened her mouth and uttered a silent scream. She woke then, covered in sweat that cooled her skin, her bedding in complete disarray. Her blankets were actually wrapped tightly around her, hugging her waist, a result of the thrashing she'd been doing. Her breathing was rapid and her pulse somewhat irregular, making it more difficult for her to untangle herself while she gasped for breath. She feared she was having a heart attack until finally she calmed down. She paced the room, threw some cold water on her face. She looked at her reflection in the mirror almost not recognizing herself. She felt very old then.

There were so many things happening that she did not understand. She wished she could talk to Bryan, find out what was really going on, and have him explain why he thought this tragedy happened. But sadly, she knew she could not. There was a strong possibility that she might never know the truth because Bryan might die.

She knew she would not go back to sleep tonight, so she sat quietly by her window gazing into the night, thinking about her life and wishing Robert were here to comfort her. She glanced at the clock. The thought of calling him crossed her mind. She actually ran her hand gently over the telephone that sat on her nightstand, yearning to hear his voice, but she didn't want to wake him. She was unsure of exactly what it was she wanted to say to him anyway.

Memories of his startled face came back to her now—stark and clear, and the fear of losing him came over her. Actually she was afraid that she might lose both Robert and Bryan. Bryan, her dear sweet friend, had come to mean so much to her over the years, but their bond was certainly never as deep—as stirring and reaching to her soul, as the one she had developed with Robert. She loved both men. She knew that and she felt a measure of deep sorrow for Bryan. Not only because of his current plight but because he was unaware that he had also lost her.

Something about the Ortez matter kept haunting her. The very real fear she'd felt that time in Bryan's office came over her again. She should have stayed that day; she should have voiced all her concerns at that moment. But she didn't. She had been suspicious of Bryan's activities the minute she set foot in his luxurious office, but she hadn't asked the right questions. She thought that she might have somehow been able to prevent this from happening, especially if she were clearer on who Bryan's clients were, and knew what his new extravagant lifestyle meant. Instead, she had only wanted to talk to him that day about her relationship with Robert. She

186

remembered that as stunned as she was about the explosive entrance of Mr. Ortez's bodyguard, she recalled now how she had missed another opportunity to expose her feelings for Robert. It all seemed so trivial now.

She slipped on her bathrobe and crept silently down to the kitchen, deciding that something hot might induce more pleasant dreams; she was tired of the terrifying perils that happen at midnight. She put hot water in the tea kettle and waited for it to sing.

Sometimes everything was crystal clear in the middle of the night, she thought. I love Robert as much as I loved my husband. She smiled then, thinking about how fortunate she was to be in love, not once but twice in her life. She thought it could never happen again. Robert had made her believe in love again. He was so open with her about his feelings, so much so that now she was ashamed of herself for holding some things about herself back. What was she thinking? Even though she knew she had mentioned Bryan to Robert before, she had never really told him the depth of their relationship or that she was dating him. Even though the flirtation had been going on between them for years, the fact was, they were never really serious. Bryan was never a threat. But she knew Robert did not know that. She hadn't told him and she didn't understand why she hadn't shared this information with him.

A low, slow whistling startled her from her thoughts. She grudgingly lifted her weary body from the chair and grabbed the tea kettle before it had a chance to screech and wake Anastasia up.

She poured the steamy hot liquid into her favorite mug. As she sat down, another fact hit her, the very real realization that Bryan was gay. She couldn't believe it, but it was true. She was surprised about it and deeply hurt by the fact that he had obviously been deceiving her for many, many years. And she in turn had deceived him by developing an intimate relationship with someone else behind his back. And for that she knew she had to face the music, but it wouldn't be melodious like the beautiful, soft stirring of a harp. In her mind's eye what she heard was the crashing sound of a cymbal. Holding her head in her hands, feeling the beginnings of yet another headache, she regretted so many things. Another headache, another sleepless night and she didn't see an end in sight for the peace of mind she once owned and treasured. She remembered her girlfriend Michelle's familiar words, words she'd always uttered when she was in a jam. "Now what you goin' to do, girlfriend?"

CHAPTER XX

The following morning Leslie was in considerable pain. A sleepless night, coupled with tumultuous thoughts and the traumatic events she'd experienced, left her feeling out of sorts. Now she wished the million—yeah, had to be at least a million—tiny, marching men would get out of her head. She felt as if grains of sand were imbedded in her eyeballs. She rose slowly and with considerable effort made it to her bathroom. She peered at her reflection and saw eyes that were bloodshot and puffy. She knew no amount of makeup would make her look any better. To top things off, she was also out of Visine. She moaned. This whole thing was taking a serious toll on her body, her mind, her soul. The painful headaches always began behind her eyes, pressure building until she felt sure something was expanding inside her head, causing incredible pain. She had gotten to the point that she was swallowing aspirin or any other pain reliever by the handful, and after awhile, all that did was reduce the thunder inside her head to a dull ache. The persistent throbbing seemed to be forever present. She promised herself to get it checked as soon as this mess was over with.

Anastasia poked her head in.

"Hey, Mom. I'm leaving for school," she shouted, then slammed the door. Leslie heard her footsteps retreat before she could even respond.

She was disappointed that Anastasia hadn't even waited for an answer; she hadn't even looked for Leslie. If she had, she might have been surprised at how awful Leslie looked. She sat on the edge of her bed feeling defeated and extremely sad. She picked up the telephone and dialed Robert's number. Malcolm answered before the first ring was completed.

"Hi, Malcolm. This is Leslie."

"Hi, Leslie."

"How are you doing, sweetie?"

"I'm fine. Uh, Leslie, my dad's already gone if you wanted to speak to him."

"Oh, okay. I did want to talk to him. Would you please tell him that I called? It's important."

"Sure. Gotta go, or I'll be late for school. Bye."

"Goodbye." After making this call she had thought she'd feel better; instead she felt worse. She grabbed the bottle of Motrin sitting on her nightstand and headed to the kitchen for coffee. Should I be mixing the two? she wondered.

After spending a quiet few minutes alone, she dressed slowly, methodically, in an effort to go to the office to see what was going on there. She knew she needed to at least check in. After missing several days of work, things were probably backing up. When she arrived, everyone who approached her was sympathetic and sent well wishes, their prayers and good thoughts to Bryan. Some were walking around looking shell-shocked, probably wondering about their own mortality and vulnerability. Some questioned whether this was a random act of violence or someone sending a message to lawyers. Considering the amount of hate mail they received periodically, she couldn't blame them for their fears. She just chose not to entertain those thoughts.

Finally allowing herself to take the advice Bryan had given her long ago, Leslie delegated as much of her workload as she could to people she trusted, and she relied heavily upon her secretary to handle everything else for her. As was so rudely but poignantly pointed out to her, life was too short to sweat about this kind of stuff. So she passed it on and didn't give it a second thought. Her staff was competent and things would get taken care of properly and timely. She left after about three hours and headed back to Bryan at the hospital.

Walter was dozing in a chair next to Bryan's bed when Leslie walked in. She was told by the nurses that Bryan had still not come out of the coma and that he had experienced a rough night. Leslie wasn't sure what that meant and she was afraid to ask. She entered the room and was again overwhelmed by the sight of all the machines bleeping, hissing, dripping, and all attached, in some form, to almost every area of Bryan's body. Tears welled in her eyes again. His head was still wrapped in bandages, only one eye visible, and it was also a mess. The tubes and wires scared her although she knew each one of them served a purpose in helping to sustain Bryan's life and nourish him. When she peered at them, giving them a closer inspection, they seemed to run in and out of every possible orifice on Bryan's body, and that frightened her. What if suddenly one or all of them stopped? The bleeping monitors and swishing respirator made her involuntarily shudder. She stood by the bed and held Bryan's left hand, the only part of his body that was free of a contraption. She began to speak to him, using a gentle tone of voice, attempting to coax him into opening his eyes. Walter heard her voice then and awakened. He looked bad, too; he obviously had never left, was wearing the same clothes she'd seen him in days ago.

"Hi, Walter."

"Hey, Leslie. How long you been here! Oh, I was out, wasn't I?" he crooned in his sing-song, slightly feminine voice.

"Not very long and yes, you were out." Leslie said, smiling. "Walter, why don't you go home for a little while, freshen up, get some sleep. I'll stay here with Bryan until you return." Before he could protest, she added, "Walter, you can't get sick, too, and, believe me, you will if you keep up this pace," Leslie said with concern.

"Oooh, girl, no, I can't leave. What if he wakes up when I'm gone, then what? He'll just end up getting upset and I don't want that to happen. He's got to know I'm here."

"Walter, even if he does wake up while you're gone, I'll call you immediately and I'll tell him you were here and that you'll be right back. I'll tell him, Walter, trust me. Go home, get some food, rest up and change your clothes." Attempting to sound humorous, Leslie added, "You'll scare him back into a coma if he sees you looking like this."

"Oh, no you don't, Miz Thang. I know I've been here for several days, but do I really look that bad?" Walter's righteous tone turned to genuine concern for his appearance.

"Walter, you don't look bad, you just look, well, tired and frumpy. Your clothes are a wrinkled mess. Just shower and change, eat something and then come back if you have to. But it really would be better if you also got some sleep. Trust me. I won't let you down; I know how much you care about him.

I'll call you the second he opens his eyes. Okay?"

"You promise?"

"I promise. Go on now. The sooner you leave the sooner you can be back. I won't leave his side until you return."

"All right then, I'll go, but I'll be back." He paused, then glanced at his watch. "I'll be back this evening, but sooner if he wakes up. Now, call me." He hurriedly wrote his number down and Leslie noticed his hands were shaking. He either had consumed too many cups of coffee or he was still very shaken by everything that had happened. She felt shaky herself.

Leslie lowered herself into the seat Walter vacated. She began again to gently cradle Bryan's hand in hers, and she watched him in his deep, deep sleep, willing him to wake up with each stroke of her hand against his.

She imagined that Walter had been doing this very same thing, talking to him, uttering words of encouragement and love to help bring him back. It surprised her how deep his commitment to Bryan was, and she wondered how in the world the two of them had been successful in hiding this kind of passion and commitment. It had to be more difficult than anything she could ever imagine. When she just looked at Robert, she knew her eyes lit up and her body language told more than any words she could say. It was a pity they had to suppress their feelings simply because society wouldn't accept the nature of their relationship.

When she thought about love, any kind of love, mother for child, man for woman, brother for brother, or even the love one could have for dogs and cats, what stood out most was the unconditional love, the devotion and dedication they expressed to that love. That's what made it special and everyone could see it.

She thought about commitment, something most men and women seek to find and sincerely want in life. Because of that, she questioned what difference it really made if they were of the same sex. Love sees no color; it hopes all things, believes all things, endures all things. At least that's what the Bible said. If this were really true, then why was their love wrong? Love is love. Plain and simple. But nothing was ever simple, she knew that. It was difficult to love anyone, sometimes even your child, but that didn't stop people from doing it or from continuously searching for it, sometimes all their lives, trying time and time again, seeking to find a love like the one she was seeing displayed between these two men. Even she wanted it, craved it and now feared she'd lost it.

She thought about Robert then and her heart began to ache. She exhaled a heavy sigh, admitting to herself that she wanted what Walter and Bryan had. She wanted someone who would again care deeply for her, as Darryl had.

She gently squeezed Bryan's hand then and softly began to speak to him.

"Bryan. Bryan. Wake up. I'm here. . .You've been asleep long enough. I need to talk to you. Wake up, Bryan. I miss you. I'm waiting for you." She sighed, "What am I going to do without you? Huh? Who's going to keep me in line, make me laugh? Huh? Who?" She spoke earnestly to him as tears formed in her eyes and began to fall. The idea that she might lose him, never talk to him again, was very painful. Her chest ached as she tried to suppress the sobs of anguish that rocked her body. She sniffed. "Wake up, Bryan. Pleeezzzze," she whispered to him, distressed. "Open your eyes, Bryan. Please, Bryan, come back."

As Leslie cried at Bryan's bedside, Robert was going through his own hell and personal torment. Even though he had called Leslie and left a message asking for her forgiveness for his actions at the hospital, she hadn't responded. Not a phone call saying kiss my ass, see you later alligator, nothing! This silence was interpreted by him as rejection. He could not bring himself to contact her again. It was hard enough for him to try and comprehend the recent events, which had literally turned his life upside down, much less begin to entertain the idea of groveling at her feet.

Robert hated that he was so moody and grouchy, but nothing he did could make the ache in his heart go away. He couldn't explain, much less face, the reason for the apparent break up between himself and Leslie to his son. What could he say? He had to be strong. No woman had ever brought him to his knees before, and he wasn't going to let that happen now either. He kept telling himself, I am a strong Black man; I can handle this. But if he was so strong, why then did he feel so weak? He clung to his manly pride with every inch of his being and he felt it was the one thing that would keep him from doing something stupid, like call her or go see her, or even inquire as to how her friend (or was he her lover) was doing. Had he died? he wondered. And God forgive him, he didn't really give a damn about him.

This feeling of abandonment and betrayal was so intense that he felt that if he had to live another day experiencing this loneliness, going through it without Leslie, he would lose his mind! Damn, I never should have gotten involved with that woman, he thought, but he remembered all too vividly that day he'd first seen her at the school. The feelings he had then were so strong, and that compulsion to meet her and get to know her was still there. That he could not deny. Was she his destiny? He wanted to give up on love, summing it up as fruitless and unnecessary, but he knew he could not do that. Leslie was now as much a part of him as Malcolm was. He wanted answers but, admittedly, he was scared what the answers he got might be.

⚜

Leslie fell into an exhausted sleep, still cradling Bryan's hand in hers. She had said everything imaginable to him. When her appeals and supplication were complete, she rested her head beside him as fatigue overcame her. She didn't notice or feel it when Bryan's hand twitched. She was dreaming about making love to Robert on the beach. A warm, tingling sensation began to build between her legs, sexual readiness— a dampness—awakened within her. She throbbed with longing for Robert. She woke then, feeling embarrassed at the vividness of her dream, hoping she hadn't moaned out loud. Slowly, she opened her eyes. Her head was pounding, and she felt a now familiar ache deep behind her eyes. Gently she rubbed her eyes which were sore and sensitive. She stretched and glanced at her watch. She looked at Bryan. He was staring at her and he was smiling. It startled her so that she lost her balance in mid-stretch and fell to the floor.

"Bryan, you're awake!" she screamed. She couldn't believe she had slept through his awakening. Tears of joy sprang to her eyes. Bryan weakly gestured for her to hug him, unable to fully raise his arms to encircle her. Crying uncontrollably, Leslie sobbed in his arms, mumbling incoherently. Finally, after several minutes, she regained control of herself.

"Welcome back," Leslie sniffed.

"Where am I?" Bryan's voice was very thick, like a wad of

196

cotton had been placed there. He recognized her; that was a good sign.

"You're at St. Luke's Hospital," Leslie responded in a whisper. She was so startled she had difficulty finding her voice. "Bryan, I need to get the doctor, tell them you're awake." She started to leave.

"No, don't go. Tell me what happened. How'd I get here?" Leslie wasn't sure if she should tell him what had happened since he didn't remember. Would it hurt him to know so soon? she wondered.

"Bryan, I'll answer all your questions but I've got to get a doctor in here. We've been waiting a long time for you to wake up." Standing to leave, Leslie tried to remain calm but felt panicked because she wasn't sure if he was going to push her to tell him everything. "I'll just be a second." She patted his hand and hurried from the room.

"My, my! Well, you've finally decided to rejoin us," Dr. Richman exclaimed when he followed Leslie into the room. He was clearly pleased that his patient was at last awake. He proceeded to examine him, checking his eyes, his pulse and listening to his heart. He asked Leslie to leave the room for a few moments, then gently turned Bryan over, exposing his bare bottom. Leslie heard him ask Bryan to cough before the door softly swished closed. She hurried to the bank of telephones and dialed Walter's number. He answered on the first ring, as if he had been standing on top of it. Leslie wondered if he was anticipating her call.

"Walter, I've got great news!" Leslie shouted.

"What? Is he awake? Did he come out of it? Can he talk?" Walter fired his questions in rapid succession.

"Yes. He just woke up. The doctor's with him now. Get down here as fast as you can!"

197

"Don't you even worry about that, girlfriend, I'm on my way!" The phone went dead in her hand; he hadn't even bothered to say goodbye. Any other time she would have been angry that he'd hung up on her like that, but today she was too overjoyed to let that upset her.

She picked up the phone again, intending to share the news with Robert. She rapidly dialed six digits, then stopped. Robert's not talking to me. He probably could care less that Bryan's conscious, she thought. She put the phone down and walked away, not even bothering to retrieve the quarter that returned after she aborted the call. She hung her head, disappointed and embarrassed. She returned to her post outside Bryan's room, noticing that the doctor was still with him. Her euphoria was gone. It was funny how quickly it had faded away. The joy she felt at seeing Bryan staring at her was fabulous, but when she measured her inability to share her happiness with Robert, it hurt so bad. All the emotions that ran through her now were so unsettling she felt as if she were on a roller coaster ride. She didn't know if she should scream and shout, throw up her hands with euphoric delight or cry and tremble with fear, wishing the ride would soon be over.

CHAPTER XXI

Leslie arrived home eager to tell Anastasia that Bryan was awake. After that, all she wanted to do was go to bed and bid farewell to this emotionally taxing day. She hoped Anastasia had already eaten dinner, leftovers from yesterday's dinner, so she could creep to her room. She entered the house through the kitchen, which she noticed was still a mess from this morning's breakfast preparations. Where is she? Leslie thought, wondering why she hadn't done her chores. Before she could entertain the idea of climbing into her bed for a quick nap, she shrugged out of her shoes, rubbed her aching feet and quickly flipped through the mail. She noticed the light flashing on her answering machine. She pushed play, absently listening while reading the latest Publisher's Clearinghouse boast of making her the next Ten Million Dollar Winner! Don't I wish, she muttered, as she threw it away.

"Ms. Hughes. This is Mr. Berkley at JC Penney in Serena Mall. Could you please call me immediately? I have an urgent matter to discuss with you. Please call 555-1234, ext. 154. Thank you."

Leslie stopped. Mr. who? She pushed the button again to replay the message, jotting down the number. Leslie's heart sank as the realization that this probably had something to do with Anastasia flashed in her mind. After scribbling the number, she turned abruptly and ran up the stairs two at a time. No Anastasia. She hurried to the garage to find what she already knew to be true; Anastasia's car was gone. Gathering herself, Leslie returned to the telephone and punched in the numbers. She sighed in frustration. What now! she thought.

"JC Penney security, Officer Berkley speaking."

That's when Leslie gave herself permission to be upset. She actually felt heavy and clutched her chest as she sat down.

"Officer Berkley, this is Leslie Hughes. You left an urgent message for me to call you."

"Yes, ma'am. How are you this evening?"

"I'm not sure. How should I be, Officer?" Cut the niceties, let's get to the purpose of your call, Leslie thought.

He lightly chuckled, "Well, ma'am we have your daughter here, Anastasia. She was stopped for shoplifting and we need you to come pick her up. Although we're not planning to charge her at this time, since she is a minor, we must release her to a parent or guardian or, in the alternative, she'll be taken to juvenile hall."

Releasing a sigh, Leslie managed to speak.

"What did she take?"

"Well, she was with a friend, who, by the way, did not help her or even know what she was doing. Anyway, she took two pairs of shorts into the dressing room, placing one inside of the other. She exited the room with only one pair of pants. When she left the store we stopped her and recovered the merchandise which," he paused, "she was wearing under her skirt."

"I don't believe it," Leslie whispered.

"Excuse me, ma'am. I didn't hear you."

"I'll be right there. Is Anastasia nearby, can I speak to her?"

"Yes, ma'am, she's right here."

"Hello." Leslie heard a trace of belligerence in Anastasia's tone.

"What is wrong with you? Is this true? Did you try to steal something, for God's sake, Anastasia?" she impatiently demanded, wanting answers to all her questions at once. She knew the truth but was unable to accept it.

"Mom, could you just come and get me? I want to get out of this place."

"Come and get you!" Leslie shouted. "I've got a good mind to let you stay there. I can't believe you did this!" Losing all her control, Leslie slammed the receiver into its cradle, picked up her purse and headed out the door.

By the time Leslie arrived at the store, she was completely drained. Her face showed signs of rage and pity, worry and sorrow. She felt as though she'd aged a lot in the half hour it took to get there. She felt defeated, that she was a bad parent, that she was doing something terribly wrong when it came to her daughter. Shoplifting! I can't believe it!

After going through a maze of a store under construction, Leslie finally found the door marked "Security" and attempted to enter. The door was locked. She shook her head and knocked hard enough to hurt her knuckles. Tears sprang to her eyes as she gently sucked on her sore, reddened knuckles.

A young man answered the door. He was smiling. That pissed her off. Here she was in tears, feeling like the world's worst parent and he was smiling!

"Ms. Hughes."

"Yes, were you expecting someone else?" she said, using a sarcastic tone. It was out of character for her to be so unprofessional; she was definitely tired.

"No, ma'am." He extended his hand for her to shake. "I'm Officer Berkley."

She gripped his hand and shook it more firmly than she'd meant to. "Hello."

Leslie spotted movement out of the corner of her eye. Anastasia sat sulking on a wooden bench. Leslie was enraged by her slouch.

"Ma'am, I've got some paperwork I need you to sign before we can release her. But before we do that, would you like me to tell you again what happened?"

"No, I would not." Turning to Anastasia, Leslie continued, "But, you can, Anastasia. Tell me what happened."

Still slouching, Anastasia began to mumble her story, still acting a bit defensive. Leslie snapped.

"How dare you sit there slumped over, talking to me like you've lost your mind! Sit up. Or better yet, stand up and talk to me!" she shouted impatiently.

"I can't," Anastasia said, using her soft little-girl voice. She lifted her arm to show her mother that her delicate brown wrist was securely encased in steel. She had been handcuffed to the bench.

The sight of her daughter in handcuffs like the numerous criminals she'd had represented over the years was too much for her to take. She moaned, "Oh, God."

She was so ashamed and embarrassed, and suddenly so very, very tired that she felt on the brink of an emotional collapse. She wasn't ashamed of the emotion she was showing in front of her daughter or this stranger—this officer—who had deemed it necessary to handcuff her child like a common thief (even though at this moment she was a thief). She was more ashamed of the level to which Anastasia had chosen to stoop. Was she trying to prove something to herself—to

Leslie—her friends, what? Leslie didn't know. She covered her face with both hands in an attempt to hide the humiliation she felt for both of them.

"Ma'am, I'm sorry. We do that to everybody we bring in. It's just a formality. Sometimes the kids try to run. I'll take them off now. I'm sorry, ma'am," He apologized, not knowing that Leslie was upset about many, many things.

"I'm okay, just please take them off her," Leslie requested. Officer Berkley handed her a clean tissue and the papers she needed to sign, then walked away. Leslie could hear the metal chains clink and rattle as the cuffs were opened and released. She knew the sound too well and never in her lifetime did she ever think she'd hear that distinctive tinkling sound and it have something to do with her child. She couldn't bear to watch him take the cuffs off. She tried to concentrate on the words floating in front of her as she scribbled her signature for Anastasia's release.

They left the office in silence. Leslie didn't know what to do. She thought about grabbing Anastasia and shaking her as she'd done once when she was a little girl after she'd run into the street, barely avoiding an oncoming car. That probably wouldn't work, she thought, as she continued to hurriedly leave the store, her thoughts running in many different directions at once. She had so many questions, but this was not the time or the place to pose any of them. Anastasia abruptly stopped and said, "Mom, my car's this way. I'm going this way," she said, pointing toward an exit that wasn't the way Leslie was going.

"You'll do no such thing. You are coming with me out of this store and away from temptation. Now come on and don't say another word to me, Anastasia."

Leslie continued her angry, quick strides through the store.

Once they were safely inside the confines of Leslie's car, she turned to face her daughter.

"I don't know what in the world made you do what you just did. With everything the two of us have, there is absolutely no way you can justify your actions to me. Do you have any money in your purse right now, Anastasia?"

"Yes."

"Let me see how much money you have."

Anastasia retrieved her wallet and tried to covertly count its contents. Leslie snatched the wallet from her and grabbed all the money out of it.

"Hey!" Anastasia said, surprised by how quickly her mother had snatched it.

"Don't you 'hey' me, young lady." Leslie retrieved a twenty, two tens and two one dollar bills. Forty-two dollars. The item she had tried to steal was thirty-five dollars. She had more than enough money in her wallet.

"Since you're acting like you have no money, I think I'll keep this," Leslie said, tucking the money in her shirt. She threw the wallet at Anastasia. It struck her lightly in the chest.

"Ow!"

"Shut up!" she screamed. "Do you hear me, just shut up. I've got a good mind to slap you. Do you hear me? I . . . want . . . to . . . slap . . . you!" she said, dragging out each word. "I haven't hit you since you were a little girl and even then I only tapped you on your behind through your diaper. Now I seriously want to knock you down. I have taken just about all the mess from you I intend to take. You thought we were at war before, well, let me tell you something, you ain't seen nothing yet!"

Suddenly Leslie grabbed her head, as wave after wave of pain assaulted her. Her head was hurting so badly, she could hardly see. She sat for a long time just holding her head and rocking herself gently to calm down; gingerly she massaged her temples through closed lids, her heart full of sorrow.

"Are you okay, Mom?" Anastasia timidly asked. Leslie put her hand up, directly in Anastasia's face as if to silence her. Slowly and with deliberateness she said, "Like you care how I feel. I asked you to be quiet."

"Dag, all right. I just thought you looked bad, like you needed some help or something," Anastasia said in a sassy tone of voice. Before she knew it, the same hand Leslie had held up to silence her now slapped her, hard against her cheek, leaving a slight red welt. Anastasia's face began to burn. Her eyes smarted and began to tear in response to the pain.

Leslie stared at her daughter, surprised by her own actions. She stared at her hand—the one that had just struck her child—the one person she loved most in the world, and suddenly she wished all of this were a dream, a very bad dream. None of this could be real, she thought. I've never hit her. Never. She wanted to apologize but instead young eyes that were tearing and staring at her probed older, tired ones— eyes that were haunted, drawn, weary. Anastasia realized the depth of her actions and with that realization a remorseful look clouded her face.

They continued to stare at one another, neither speaking, hardly breathing. Then suddenly, they both began to cry.

"Anastasia, please just go to your room. I don't want to hear any music, your TV, or anything else for that matter. When I feel better, we'll talk. Right now, please just get out of my sight!"

Anastasia left the room without uttering another word. Leslie could not believe what had happened. The good news she'd received about Bryan was now being overshadowed by the thoughtless, stupid actions of Anastasia. Everything seemed to be spinning out of control. First, this terrible accident of Bryan's, then being estranged from Robert, now this. She couldn't take much more. As strong as women were expected to be—especially Black women—this series of events was getting to be far too much. Was there going to be any relief in sight? she wondered.

Her head throbbed and then she had to add to the list of her problems, her health. She knew her eating habits were not the best. Though she was slightly over her recommended weight, she didn't think that could be the problem. Maybe my blood pressure is up; it runs in the family. I'd better have it checked before I have a stroke or something. Now that would top off things nicely, wouldn't it? Have a little stroke, she thought, chuckling to herself at how stupid having a "little stroke" sounded. Yet somehow the irony of such a thing happening would not surprise her at all. Life was playing games with her now and she was losing!

She decided a cup of tea might help soothe her nerves and her head. She filled her tea kettle with water, gazing out the window, listening to the night sounds, daydreaming about simply running away. She turned off the tap, lit the stove and sat at her favorite place near the window. Gingerly she laid her head down, fighting the urge to cry again. She felt all dried up. Not another tear would be shed by her today. Besides being too exhausted to cry, crying only caused her head to pound harder. Instead, she closed her eyes and wished someone would come take her away, like a dreamy Calgon commercial. Take her away from all this drama and into a life much more settled and happy.

The tea kettle began a slow rumble; then the loud scream of the boiling water whistled through the spout. Slowly Leslie rose to retrieve a chamomile tea bag from the sleek black canister set. Since she was attempting to make herself feel better, she searched through the cupboard to find her favorite mug, a mug Anastasia had made for her years ago. Looking at its immature design made with a slightly crooked mold caused Leslie to think about the time when Anastasia was smaller and easier to control. A time when she loved her mother and would give her sloppy wet kisses while her tiny arms encircled her neck. That seemed so very far away now. Instead of looking forward to special surprises like this one that Anastasia had shyly placed in her hand after returning from summer camp, she only looked forward to more teenage craziness. Her daughter just didn't seem to be her daughter any more. All that sweet innocence was lost somewhere in the folds of her teenage confusion and rebellion.

Still lost in thought, she poured the hot, steaming water into the ceramic mug with the tea bag already inside. Absentmindedly, Leslie set the kettle back on the stove, then inhaled the rich, strong-scented herbal fragrance. She felt instantly calmer. Instead of sugar she searched for the cute little bear-shaped honey jar. As soon as she'd placed her hand on it the doorbell rang. Now what? she thought. Ignoring her tea, she hurried to the door. She was so distracted that she hadn't bothered to peep at her caller and threw open the door with a frustrated growl.

"Hello."

She couldn't believe that he had come to see her. She stood transfixed. And with a suddenness that surprised her, she threw herself into his arms, and although she'd just promised herself there would be no more tears today, she began to cry.

"Robert! I can't believe you're here."

"I'm sorry, baby. I'm so sorry for letting so much time pass with this misunderstanding between us," he murmured, planting sweet kisses along her hairline and cheek. Finally their lips met and everything was all right with Leslie's world again.

"Do you think we should go inside? Your neighbors might begin to talk if we don't." Robert chuckled as he gently pried Leslie's body off his.

"Yes, yes, come in. I'm so glad to see you."

"I've missed you."

"Things have been terrible lately, just awful, and I wanted to call you, to tell you everything, to apologize, but I was afraid."

"Why were you afraid? I told you before I would never hurt you."

"I was afraid you'd push me away. I know it looked like I betrayed you with Bryan, but it really wasn't even like that. I . . . I . . ."

"You don't need to explain that to me right now. What I'd rather know is, how are you doing? How's Anastasia?"

"Today I'm not doing so well and neither is Anastasia. She got into some serious trouble today. I'm so embarrassed I don't even want to talk about it."

"What happened?"

"I haven't even had a chance to absorb all of it myself. When I got home this evening, I had an urgent message from a security officer at Serena Mall. Anastasia was caught stealing. I had to go down and get her."

"What?"

"My exact words. I don't know what she was thinking, or

why she'd do such a thing. She had money, Robert; she always has money."

"Then I guess it wasn't about money."

"No—"

"It was about trying to get your attention. For some reason she felt the need to resort to something stupid like this to get it."

"I give her my attention," Leslie replied, somewhat offended. "As much as I'm able anyway."

"Oh, I know you do. This is not a criticism of you or your parenting. I just happen to know that kids do stuff like this to get attention, especially kids like ours who are well off—who have everything they need."

"I'm losing my baby to an unseen force—a problem I don't understand."

"She'll come around. In the meantime you need to set down some rules for her to follow."

"I've got plenty of rules for her. She just isn't cooperating with me, and I can't be with her twenty-four hours a day; Robert, I've got to work. My practice is suffering as it is because of the amount of time I've been spending with Bryan at the hospital."

"Sounds like you're spreading yourself too thin. Take some time off, spend it with Anastasia and get some rest. You've got dark circles under your eyes." Robert swept his finger under her puffy eye very gently; then he pulled her into his embrace. "It was my goal to take that sad look out of your eyes. Now I'm afraid I've helped put it back."

"I'm not going to lie; it's been rough. I missed you so much, so very, very much."

They clung to each other, gathering strength and warmth from each other, each inhaling the scent of the other and enjoying its distant familiarity. As he held her, they began to sway back and forth, just as they'd done at the beach, each remembering that they had declared finding home in each other's arms.

Robert kissed the top of her head, laced his fingers between hers and led her back to the kitchen. The tea kettle still hissed a muted whistle. He led her to the table.

"Looks like you were making tea."

"Um-hmm. I was. It's probably cold now."

He poured out what she'd started and began to make another cup for her, adding just the right amount of honey.

"Got any beer?" he asked as he opened the refrigerator door.

"Nope, but I've got wine. Help yourself," Leslie said, while admiring the broadness of his shoulders as he stooped to retrieve the bottle. An uncontrollable feeling of tranquility fell over her and she knew she was hopelessly hooked on him. She vowed never to allow a day to go by that she didn't at least talk to him.

"Malcolm sends his love," Robert said once he was seated opposite her.

"Tell him hello for me. Did he tell you I called?"

"No," he said surprised. "When did you call?"

"Several days ago."

"I didn't get the message. I thought you weren't returning calls."

"What in the world made you think that?"

"I left—oh, about five messages on your machine. You never responded to any of them."

Leslie frowned, trying to find a reason why she'd hadn't gotten them. Then she remembered. "Did you call me the day you saw me at the hospital?"

"Yes, I called to apologize. Why, is there some significance to that day?"

"When I got home I was inundated with messages from reporters. After I listened to some of them, I simply deleted the rest. I did that impulsively. There were messages from you!" she said softly smiling.

"Yes. But that's okay. I'm here now and that's all that matters. By the way, how is your friend doing?"

"He's better, much better in fact."

"Do they know who did it, or did he do it to himself?"

"No, we still don't know who shot him or why. He definitely didn't shoot himself."

"I didn't realize lawyers could have those types of enemies, enemies that attempt to take you out. I hope you're safe."

"Don't worry about me. I don't think this had anything to do with Bryan being a lawyer, although I do think it had to with one of his clients."

"Maybe. Leslie . . . what exactly does he mean to you?"

Sighing heavily, Leslie searched for the right words. "Where do I begin?"

"At the beginning," Robert coaxed.

"Okay. When I first met you I told you about Bryan. We've been friends for years—we dated—he was what I considered to be my boyfriend—my man—but once I met you all that changed. Especially once I realized that the relationship I had with him was not complete. It lacked intimacy and love and . . . and"

"Passion?"

"Yes, passion. And now I know why."

"Why?"

She took a deep breath and plunged ahead. "Bryan's gay. I just found out," she said, noticing Robert's grave facial expression. "Once I did, everything fell into place. It all makes sense now."

"Gay! God, please tell me you never slept with him!"

"No. We never consummated our relationship. And believe it or not, I was content with things the way they were."

"This is a little difficult to understand," he said, his face a mask of confusion. "How could you be involved with someone and not make love to them? I mean, that's a natural progression of things in a relationship."

"I know it seems crazy, but that's the way it was. And I liked it. I didn't want to be sexually intimate. I wanted a friend, a companion, and I had that with Bryan. We tried to make love once and it was a disaster. I thought it was because he wasn't really attracted to me, you know, in that way, and I wasn't attracted to him either. He is a goodlooking man, but something about him sometimes made me cringe when he got too close. And we never even spoke about our failed attempt at lovemaking. We just continued our relationship the way it was. We were companions, someone you could rely on to be your date whenever a bar association dinner or something like it came up. It—we—were comfortable."

"You are the sexiest woman I know. If you had told me about this before I would have told you he had to be gay. There is no way a heterosexual male could be with you and not want to enjoy every inch of you." A spark of desire twinkled in his eyes. They stared at each other, unable to speak, until Leslie looked away.

"Thank you for saying that. I have to tell you that you—you brought out a depth of need in me I thought I'd squelched, especially after Darryl died. In your arms—in your life—I discovered a whole new me. I found out I could love again. I know so much more about myself since I've been involved with you. I am a sexual person. Believe me, I didn't realize that before."

"Come here." Robert said scooting back his chair to allow her to sit upon his lap. "Let's seal our making up with a kiss and a promise."

"What kind of promise?" Leslie asked as she straddled his lap, smiling.

"A promise to always talk to each other about what's going on in our lives. Always. Okay?"

She didn't answer him with words. Instead she looked intently into his eyes until she could clearly see the depth of his feelings for her. She kissed him with an intensity of emotion that made her feel weak. She embraced him with all the passion she felt for him, vowing to forever be true to him, to allow him into the private corners of her world and through words only spoken in her head, she promised to also always be true to herself.

CHAPTER XXII

Leslie returned to her normal work load at the office after it was clear that Bryan would be okay. She made an emotional decision to attempt to also handle Bryan's case. She began by harassing the police for answers, demanding a more exhaustive investigation into the shooting. The extra hours she was putting in at the office began to put lines of worry on Leslie's face.

Robert met her for a quick lunch and as soon as he saw the strain upon her face, he again had an overwhelming desire to make it go away, if he could. He decided that more than anything he wanted to take her away from everything for a while. He could think of no reason for her to object, especially since she was still experiencing a somewhat strained relationship with Anastasia. He thought they definitely needed a break from one another. Bryan was doing well and no longer needed her constant attention. So, in his funniest voice, he'd ask her.

"Mi cherie—let me take you away from all of this."

"What?—"

"Me—I am better than Calgon. You see, with Calgon you close your eyes to soak and tell it to 'take you away.' And then once you open your eyes, you are still there. I, on the other hand, will take you away and when you open your eyes you will be relaxing in a suite in La Jolla or Del Mar or Dana Point. Madam, what say you?"

"I say, yes, yes, yes and when, when, when!" Leslie exclaimed, bouncing up and down excited as a genuine smile finally lit up her face.

"Soon, baby, real soon. I promise."

He immediately set all the plans in motion to take her to one of the most elegant hotels in San Diego, located just off the Pacific Coast Highway. Leslie had rejected the idea of being very far away from either Bryan or Anastasia. Robert was just grateful that she had agreed to go at all. He was going to spoil her. He made reservations for them to stay in the penthouse.

They arrived early afternoon, excited and happy to be alone together even if it was only for a few days. Robert handled checking the two of them in, registering them as if they were husband and wife.

From the moment of their arrival Leslie was struck by the beauty of the hotel. The lobby was elegantly decorated in a contemporary manner. Shiny black marble floors gleamed, while in the center a large round table displayed an enormous floral arrangement filled with exotic flowers giving off a potpourri of heady fragrances. Just to the right of the arrangement was a simulated cascading waterfall. In the pool that formed below were very large, bright goldfish, the biggest ones Leslie had ever seen. She watched them swim back and forth, seeming to be completely content with their aquatic lives. Water splashed her, sprinkling droplets of cold water on her face. She closed her eyes, enjoying the sporadic touch of coolness on different parts of her body, shoulders, arms and face.

෭෯෨

Robert watched her transform before his eyes. Her anxious demeanor was now replaced with a look of quiet peace. She was the most beautiful woman he'd ever known, especially when that beauty radiated from her face and her body was relaxed, and the smile that could put any commercial model to shame was present. This was going to be a special weekend for them. He had every intention of making it so.

He crept up beside her, slipped his hand into hers and led the way to their suite.

෭෯෨

The inner lobby displayed a spectacular glass elevator trimmed in brassy gold, surrounded by plants and flowers encased in black lacquer plant stands. They stepped inside and were both surprised at how quiet it suddenly became once the doors were closed, silencing the sounds of the waterfall below. With a briskness of wonderful weightlessness, it lifted them up thirty stories to the penthouse suite. Robert pulled her into his arms and kissed her with a soft tenderness that brought feelings of serene happiness to both of them. They continued to embrace as the elevator smoothly lifted them to the top, while in full view below, curious patrons watched them.

From the penthouse Leslie and Robert admired the grand view of the Pacific and the surrounding beauty of baby blue skies with scattered, billowy white clouds. Sailboats here and there, racing jet skis and every now and then a surfer would appear. Leslie stood on the balcony and gazed at the waves that seemed to beckon her to come take a swim. The sun, bright and distant, warmed her face. She felt very calm as her mind and body began to relax. Knowing Bryan would be okay in particular made her feel so much better. Her relationship with Anastasia had gotten slightly better after the shoplifting incident, coupled with Leslie's attempts to pay more attention to her. The two of them had talked about Anastasia's fears and the loss of her father and how to deal with it. Leslie explained that doing shocking things was not the best way to handle her feelings. Leslie realized how much Anastasia needed help to be more confident about her appearance. She encouraged her to take off the heavy makeup and let her natural beauty shine. All these things Leslie thought would eventually lead to her enjoying once again a daughter who was loving and respectful.

"What are you thinking about?" he asked as he wrapped his arms around her.

"Oh, just about how beautiful San Diego is . . . And," she said as she turned around, lacing her arms around the broadness of his shoulders, "how great it is to be here with you."

"I'm glad you agreed to come."

"I'm sometimes so amazed at how insightful you are. You knew I needed this time alone, away from everything."

"Of course I did, I'm not blind!" he said as he touched the tip of her nose, then kissed it.

"No, what I mean is, not only did you notice but you did something about it. Sometimes that doesn't happen. Some men wait for the woman to tell them what they need. You didn't."

"Did I earn some brownie points?"

"Definitely."

They sat together on a rattan swing. He held her hands inside of his.

217

"Tell me about your dreams."

"My dreams! What are you talking about?"

"What do you dream about, what are your fantasies?"

"Freaky fantasies?" she asked, smiling, one lone eyebrow raised in mock sleaziness.

"Hmm, now that you mention it, freaky fantasies sounds nice." He laughed and kissed her mouth. "No, baby, I'm talking about fantasies about your future, or a wild idea you have that you'd never think would come to fruition. A fantasy that would change your life."

"Oh, that kind of fantasy. Okay. But don't laugh."

"I won't laugh. Tell me."

"Lately, I've been thinking that I'd love to write about my life, my career, my marriage, his death, my daughter, having a companion who turns out to be gay," she said as she laughed, "and now I'd love to write about finding love, finding you."

"Sounds more like a movie to me. *Leslie's Adventures!*" he said while holding his hands up as if he were displaying a marquee. "But seriously, I think that's a good idea. You have had a fascinating life. But you might want to keep me out of it."

"Why?"

"Oh, there's nothing really interesting about me, certainly not enough to write about."

"Ahh, but there is. If you could read my mind, decipher my thoughts, you'd see there is so much about you I want to say. Maybe I'll get a ghost writer to say it for me. That way I'll know she'd get the essence of my feelings expressed just right!"

"I have no doubt in my mind that you're perfectly capable of uttering just the right words to say how you feel. You don't need a professional. All you need is yourself and the guts to do it."

"You think so?"

"Yes. I have the utmost confidence in you and everything you do."

"You're a sweet talker, Robert."

"I'm your man."

"You know I love you. So much so that at times I feel my heart's going to burst from experiencing so many, many things, emotions, pride . . . passion."

"Ahhh, passion. I remember when you ran from that word."

"Me too. That was a long time ago. Now I run to it. I run to you, for you are my passion."

"See right there," he exclaimed, pointing at her. "That phrase should be in a book."

"Well, who knows, maybe one day it will."

As the afternoon slipped into the evening and they had tired of talking, Robert suggested they get dressed and have a four-course dinner prepared by the hotel's award-winning chef.

The realization that soon she and Robert would be dressing and undressing together caused a fine line of sweat to appear across her upper lip, while moonshaped lines of wetness formed under her arm pits. Her stomach heaved and tumbled as if she'd just plunged off a high diving board. She crossed her legs and began kicking her foot rapidly back and forth. This would be the first time she'd ever dressed in front of any man since the death of her husband. It would also be the first time she would wake up and not be alone. She was fully aware of how flawed she was upon waking. He'd be able to see her in her imperfect nakedness in full daylight, not shadowed by

219

Vicki Andrews

dark lights or candlelight, and this made her suddenly aware that he might find her somehow to be too defective.

She excused herself and hurried to the bathroom. She closed the door behind her, her chest rising and falling in rapid succession as she willed herself to calm down. This was a first for her. She couldn't remember ever experiencing a panic attack before now. She should have mentally prepared herself better for this moment. Although she knew this would happen—sleeping with and then waking up with Robert by her side—she hadn't allowed herself to feel the full impact of her decision to come here. She undressed quickly and stepped into the shower, hoping she could be done before he realized what she was doing.

The shower was enormous. She was surprised to see that it had two shower heads, one in front and one behind. It was large enough to accommodate two people, and while for a second that idea sounded intriguing, then just as quickly it became scary. I'm acting like an adolescent, she scolded herself as she stepped inside. She breathed a sigh of relief, then closed her eyes to enjoy the hot water that cascaded over her face, while behind her the sharp needles of pleasurable warmth rushed down her back. The double-headed shower's waterfall was loud and muffled any other sounds. She did not hear Robert when he joined her. He reached out to touch her, startling her. The soap slipped from her hand and crashed to the floor, while at the same time she uttered an involuntary yelp which surprised both of them.

"I'm sorry, Leslie. I didn't mean to scare you."

"I . . . I wasn't expecting you to join me," she stammered. Robert bent to retrieve the soap and gently began to rotate it through his large palms, gathering a nice lather. He had a seductive smile on his face that didn't escape Leslie's notice.

220

"Here, let me wash your back. Turn around," he gently encouraged.

As she did so, her mind and body molded to his touch. She exhaled slowly and reached to rest her palms against the cool tile while the water soothed her from side-to-side. Her head hung loosely between her shoulders as he continued to massage the soap into her back, kneading and stroking rhythmically her wet skin. She was no longer self-conscious about her body as she allowed the warmth of his hands to calm her spirit. As his hands began to wander down her spine to settle upon her buttocks, he began to alternate between kneading her bottom and her upper thigh. Eventually, his hands guided her to open her legs so he could wash and stroke the inside of her thighs, his thumb slightly grazing the center of her. Each rhythmic motion brought her closer and closer to ecstasy.

"Rinse," he said in a throaty voice that brought her back to reality.

She became spellbound by the sights, sounds and smells of their shower together, forgetting about her inhibitions. She began to lightly trail his back with her fingertips. She was considerably shorter than he, her face reaching the middle of his chest. She began to suckle his nipples, aware of the sensitivity of this spot. He groaned as his manhood responded to the delicate licks she placed there. She massaged soap into his chest where light wisps of dark hair became curly. She played with it, running her finger through the hair with one hand while the other applied firm, even strokes to the swell of his round behind. He picked her up, and she wrapped her legs around his waist, deeply kissing him, clinging to him, seeming to be drowning in the sensuous essence of him.

The water began to run cold as the quick shower Leslie had

intended to take turned into a very long, sensuous affair. Robert released her but continued to kiss her mouth and throat, uttering guttural sounds in her ear.

"Let's get out of here."

He exited first and passed a thick terry cloth towel to her. They dried in silence. Their steamy shower had fogged the mirrors, distorting and blurring their image. Leslie was glad she couldn't see her own face. She knew it would be tinged with lust and desire.

She was unsure if she should drop her towel and prance around naked or leave it on. Thankfully, the hotel provided monogrammed bathrobes which she spotted hanging on the back of the door, so she slipped one on. Robert simply wrapped his towel around his waist. He took long, purposeful strides to the wet bar.

"Want a drink?"

"Sure. I'll have whatever you're having."

Leslie stood near him, quietly watching him stoop and bend, retrieving and filling glasses. She crossed her arms and rested her back against the counter. He handed her a drink and she sipped it. She softly purred her approval. It obviously was a minor gesture that caused him to fill with desire all over again. He kissed her, enjoying the cool contours of her mouth. He captured her body—actually pinning her—leaving her nowhere to go as he gently pressed her against the counter. She wrapped her arms around his neck and felt him begin to rise again. She moved her hips then and lifted her leg with an urgency for him to be inside. Their kisses became more intense as his hands trailed her thighs and she stroked his back, still moist from their shower. He loosened her robe and the two of them watched it slip provocatively from her shoulders to the floor. She yanked and pulled at the tight knot he'd put in his towel, laughed because she couldn't get it off easily. Meanwhile, he continued to place kisses all over her face.

"Robert, we're never going to make it to dinner if we start fooling around again."

"Oh, don't worry, we'll make it. We'll make it a night to remember . . . come here."

He led her to the king size bed where their kisses became more urgent, longer, and deeper as their breathing became labored and they began to sweat. She lay atop him, gyrating her hips suggestively and he groaned. His hands gripped her buttocks, then trailed up her back, then around to fondle her breasts. She lifted herself up so he could capture one in his mouth. The hot wetness of his mouth was so soft and sensual, she felt close to losing all control. She threw back her head and rocked on top of him, moaning with sheer pleasure, marveling at his touch. He stroked her everywhere, the heat from his fingertips leaving a trail of desire blazing through her. They made love that was so very intense that when her orgasm gripped her, it actually brought tears to her eyes. The feeling was inexplicable. It was simply magic!

Much later, when they were completely satisfied, they agreed to shower again but this time they decided to do so separately, laughing and teasing each other, knowing that they would not finish the task if they tried to do it together.

Leslie put on a yellow satin bra, then began to search for the pair of panties that matched. She could have sworn she had packed them but they weren't there. She sensed that Robert watched her, and she knew he noticed the frustrated scowl that had crossed her face as she gave her full attention to the search. A loving smile appeared on his face and, suddenly, he laughed out loud.

"What's so funny?"

"You. What are you looking so intently for?"

"Ummm, a pair of panties I have that matches this bra perfectly. I know I packed it. Oh, forget it. They're not here," she said, dropping the suitcase lid after she retrieved an alternate pair.

Robert again softly chuckled, shaking his head. Finally he said, "I've always wondered about that."

"What?"

"Why women put so much effort into their underclothes, although it looks real nice, matching and everything. But the bottom line is, when the lights go off we're trying our best to get you out of that stuff as quickly as possible, without tearin' 'em. We really don't care whether they match or not."

"That's because you guys are animals!" Leslie teased him as she stepped into them. "I mean, why can't men appreciate the woman's desire to make sure she's perfect from top to bottom, inside and out?"

"Because," he paused to kiss her lightly, "my darling, we only care about gettin' to the goods and quick! Besides, most women don't realize their beauty, or that the attraction we have for them is not in how they've coordinated an outfit. It's their unspoken inner beauty that counts."

"Oh, so you're attracted initially to someone's mind?"

"Now, I didn't say that. In your case I was attracted to your calves flexing in your high heel pumps, your hourglass figure in that purple dress and most of all, I was stopped dead in my tracks by your eyes. No, I take that back. It was your smile and that cute little dimple that plays peek-a-boo when you talk. Yeah, that was it."

"Get outta here. Flattery will get you everywhere."

"And you know this!" he said while wrapping her tenderly in his embrace. "Now, let me see that dimple."

Leslie crossed her eyes and stuck out her tongue. Teasingly she said, "Make me!"

And before she knew it they were making love all over again. As the sun slipped away, disappearing in a glorious display of color, and the moon appeared to light a star-studded night, they watched. Leslie peered at the moon and then said, "Nothing could be better than this. Nothing." Robert nodded his head in agreement.

Finally they ordered room service and fed each other in bed. A sumptuous feast of succulent prime rib topped with a generous portion of sauteed mushrooms and onions, asparagus tips and a baked potato stuffed with butter, sour cream and chives was eloquently presented to her in silver domed dishes, removed with grand relish by Robert. A basket of hot bread glazed with honey butter was also part of their feast. They ate with enthusiastic enjoyment while Robert made sure Leslie's glass of chilled champagne remained full.

Later, for dessert, strawberries were slipped into their final glasses of champagne. Content, satisfied, and slightly inebriated, Leslie slept while he watched her. As her breathing changed and she flinched a couple of times, she fell into a deep sleep wearing a smile of contentment on her face.

CHAPTER XXIII

Several months later, Leslie was visiting Bryan again. They had a rare evening alone. Walter had returned to his deejay gig, giving them time to have a long overdue heart-to-heart talk.

"Leslie, I'm glad we're finally getting a chance to be alone. I need to talk to you about Walter and me." Bryan said.

"Okay. But you know we really don't have to talk about it. I know all I need to know." Leslie reached for Bryan's hand. "I completely understand everything now."

"I'm sorry, Leslie. You don't know how many times I wanted to tell you about my life. I could never get up the nerve. I was afraid you'd hate me and I'd lose your friendship. I couldn't stand for that to happen."

"Bryan, no matter what, we will always, always be friends. After all the things we've been through—all we've helped each other with—you didn't know that nothing could separate me from you as a friend?"

"You never know with stuff like this. People can turn on you with a quickness when they're faced with sensitive issues like a person's sexuality, especially since society views the love between homosexuals as unnatural. You wouldn't be the first, nor probably the last, friend I've lost once it's revealed that I'm gay," Bryan said sadly. "With you, Leslie, I just couldn't bring myself to risk it. Please forgive me for not trusting you enough to let you know who I really was."

"Don't even sweat it. I forgive you even though you know you were tripping. Right? You know that," Leslie teased.

"Yeah, Leslie, I guess I was just tripping."

"Are you happy to be getting out of here tomorrow?" Leslie asked, changing the subject.

"You know that's right. I can't wait to get home to my own bed where I can get some peace and quiet. These damn people wake you up all hours of the night. How do they expect people to heal?" Bryan's voice rose. "I mean, damn, can a brotha get some rest in here!"

Leslie laughed at him. Yep, the old Bryan was back as headstrong and sassy as ever.

"You know, I overheard that there are going to be reporters here when you leave. "Are you prepared to face them?" Leslie inquired.

"I guess I'm as ready as I'm ever going to be. I know they're going to crucify me. I'm gay; therefore, I doubt I'm adored anymore."

"Well to hell with 'em!" Leslie exclaimed. "You are still the same wonderful, brilliant attorney you always were, and your sexual orientation does not change that. So if they turn on you for that reason, well, they can just go—" Leslie was heated up and started to screech a long line of expletives.

"You know what, Leslie?" Bryan interrupted.

"What?"

"You are sexy as hell when you're mad. If I was straight, I'd be real turned on right now," Bryan said mischievously, rapidly raising his eyebrows up and down in a continuous lascivious leer.

"Oh, I bet you say that to all the girls. I ain't studin' you, Bryan!"

Leslie pretended anger as she lightly shoved Bryan's arm. She truly did love this man. He was her friend. Even his comment made her happy because it meant he hadn't begun to take everything seriously, and he still held on to his dignity and pride. He knew who he was and now he was prepared to show the world that he accepted it.

"Bryan, I'm in love."

"I know."

"How do you know?"

"It's written all over your face, and that little swishy walk you've got, well, it's got a lot more swish now. I knew a man put that extra twist in your hips, girl. I'm gay, not stupid."

Laughing, Leslie simply gave him a hug.

"I never could hide much from you."

"Can you hide me from tomorrow's circus? I hope it's not going to be crazy. What am I going to say if someone throws a 'faggot' remark at me?"

"You don't have to say anything but 'no comment.' I'll talk to the press while you and Walter keep right on steppin'. Since I'm representing you in this matter they can direct their questions to me, and they better not ask me anything stupid!" Leslie's eyes flashed with anger.

"Ooooh, girl, I'm scared of you," Bryan said.

With that, the discussion ended and Leslie went home. She promised to return early the following day to be by his side when he was discharged.

One of Robert's daily rituals was to watch the evening news, always amazed at the things people could do to one another. Sometimes it was downright sickening what he saw and heard, but nevertheless every day he had to know what was happening in the world around him.

Robert had turned away from the television to continue to wash a head of lettuce when he heard an announcer mention, "Prominent San Diego attorney, Bryan McKay, was released today from St. Luke's Hospital." He turned his attention back to the television to see Leslie strutting down the hallway, cameras flashing, answering questions that were rapidly being thrown at her. His mind briefly flashed on the last time that had happened and he released a slight shudder. He stopped what he was doing. Revulsion and regret were immediately replaced with pride to see his woman, a vision of professionalism and beauty, answer their questions with grace. Beside her was Bryan in a wheelchair, and holding his hand was the handsome man he'd seen Leslie talking to the day he went to the hospital. He now knew him to be Bryan's lover, Walter.

"Dad, there's Leslie," Malcolm said, interrupting Robert's thoughts.

"Yeah, I see her. Turn it up, I can't hear what she's saying." Malcolm did.

"Mr. McKay's condition was extremely critical after the April 30th shooting," the announcer was saying. "He is currently doing much better, having undergone extensive physical therapy to learn to walk, talk and use his limbs again. Our sources tell us that he'll continue with daily rehabilitation."

"Are you representing Mr. McKay?" a reporter shouted.

"Yes. We intend to pursue with relentlessness the person or

persons who made this attempt on Mr. McKay's life. We are working in conjunction with the San Diego Police Department to find a suspect. Once that information is ascertained, we will vigorously prosecute, seeking the most severe punishment under the law," Leslie said, looking straight into the camera as if she were vowing personal revenge.

"Are there any leads?" another reporter questioned.

"Due to the nature of this matter, I cannot disclose that information at this time."

"Is it true that Mr. McKay is a homosexual and this attack may have been motivated by that fact?"

"The motive for the attack is unknown, so I cannot comment on that. We are hopeful that Mr. McKay's sexual orientation is not the issue here. What we're concerned with, as should be all the citizens of San Diego, is that someone maliciously attacked, shot and could have killed Mr. McKay, and that, in and of itself, is unacceptable. A person's sexual orientation should not provoke an attempt on his or her life. This type of homophobic paranoia must cease. And if that was the motivation for this attack, we will make an example of this person. Our country and this city will not tolerate violence of this nature." Gay and lesbian activists who had gathered shouted their approval.

"It's alleged that you and Mr. McKay were lovers, too. Did this revelation come as a shock to you?" a female reporter shouted.

Leslie turned, scanning the crowd to find the person who had the nerve to say such a thing. When their eyes met, Leslie chose to speak to her with deliberate emphasis on each and every word. "Mr. McKay and I were never lovers." Leslie stopped, looked directly from the reporter into the lens of the camera and added, "We have been friends, colleagues and

230

confidantes for many, many years. I admire Mr. McKay for his brilliance and for his thorough representation that he's always given to his clients and to this city. And I would hope that the city of San Diego recognizes the jewel they have in him." She paused and took Bryan's hand in hers. They shared a look of quiet kinship.

"Again, let me reiterate that Mr. McKay's sexual orientation is irrelevant. Now, if you'll excuse us." With that Leslie sashayed away. Reporters still tried to get comments from her but she, Bryan and Walter moved quickly through the crowd.

"You tell 'em, baby!" Robert said.

"She looked good, Dad, didn't she?" Malcolm said.

"She always looks good to me."

"Did you ask her yet, Dad?"

Robert stared at his son and shook his head. "Not yet. Soon though, soon. Hey, come help me finish dinner."

"I wonder how Anastasia will feel if we become a family," Malcolm asked as he retrieved a knife and began to slice a tomato.

"Well, from the way she's been acting, she probably will be none too happy. Leslie tells me they have had difficulty even speaking to each other since the incident at the mall."

"What happened at the mall?"

"Anastasia stole something and got caught. Now she's angry because Leslie grounded her for a month. She also took away her driving privileges."

"Ooh, I bet that hurt. But what she did was real stupid, Dad."

"I agree. But Anastasia's going through something right now and the two of them have got to work it out. Until they do, I don't think I should ask Leslie to marry me . . . Let's eat."

"Yeah, I'm ready to get my grub on!" Malcolm shouted as the two of them prepared heaping plates of spaghetti, salad and hot, buttery garlic bread.

CHAPTER XXIV

Anastasia sighed in her sleep. She tossed and turned as a clear vision of her mother floated before her. She dreamt that her mother was at work. She had just taken a handful of aspirin, her neck snapping back as she swallowed all of them; then she gulped water. It seeped from the corners of her mouth. Then she carefully lowered her head to her desk and mumbled, "I can't take much more of this. Why is my head killing me?"

When Leslie finally lifted her head, she faltered. Anastasia, even in her unconscious state, wrinkled her brow. She knew that something was terribly, terribly wrong. In slow motion, Leslie's hand floated until it reached for the phone. The vision of her hand was very clear. Anastasia could see its pretty brown coloring and the prominent, protruding veins. Then suddenly she jumped as a spasm of excruciating pain obviously gripped her. Without warning she collapsed in a heap, crashing to the floor, bringing the phone with her. Anastasia jerked and began to mumble, "Mommy, mommy."

Then she saw Jessica, her mother's secretary, come rushing in. She screamed her name and ran to her side. Leslie did not move. A small dribble of blood began to seep from her nose.

All at once a bunch of people appeared. They were yelling and screaming for someone to call 9-1-1. Did anyone know CPR? Was she breathing? Panic began in waves, temporarily reducing the calm, cool attorneys Anastasia knew her mother's co-workers to be into screeching, scared-to-death fools.

A man wearing a uniform rushed in and took control. He put his face very close to hers and then he held her limp wrist. He said her breathing was shallow and that she was unconscious. "An ambulance has been dispatched and is on its way," he shouted. People stood around watching her lying there very still, not moving. She heard voices chanting "Leslie, Leslie!" But there was no response. Even Anastasia mumbled her name. Her eyes were squeezed shut and she made a violent turn in her sleep.

When she shifted, the scene of her dream changed. She saw anger on the faces of the people who watched her mother. They were furious about the delay and actually raised their fists as if about to start a riot when the fire department arrived. They pushed and shoved people aside in an effort to get to her. She still had not stirred. The paramedics began to strike her chest, then blow air into her mouth. Anastasia recognized that they were administering CPR. They took her pulse, lifted her eyelids, and listened to her heart. They asked what her name was and again a chant of "Leslie! Leslie! Leslie!" began, as if a host of cheerleaders had joined them. The comedy didn't mix well with the enormity of the situation, but it was consistent with the irrational nature of dreams. Anastasia watched but her mother still did not respond. A stretcher appeared and she was lifted onto it.

Anastasia still did not wake as the continuing drama unfolded behind her closed eyelids. She felt helpless. A grim-faced doctor appeared. With a shake of his head and eyes downcast, he simply said, "I'm sorry."

Anastasia did not understand his words.

"Leslie never regained consciousness," he continued. "She died of a massive cerebral hemorrhage, an aneurysm. The continuous headaches were a warning sign that she was too busy to heed. Her daughter, who had been causing her so many problems, is also the reason for her untimely death."

"Me! Me?" Anastasia said in a trembling voice. Then abruptly both Bryan and Walter's faces floated above Anastasia's. They were openly crying, trying to hug each other and her at the same time. Anastasia shoved them, screaming, "Get away from me!" As soon as her palms met Bryan's chest, it suddenly became very hot and the scene abruptly changed.

Anastasia was walking around a graveyard. She headed to a patch of earth that would receive her mother. The weather's too nice, Anastasia thought, as she gazed at the dazzling yellow rays of the sun. Her mother's best friend Michelle appeared and held her hand; then she lifted her chin.

"Anastasia," she said in a dreamy voice, "I know this is hard for you. I'm a mess myself. But, honey, a long, long time ago your mother and I made a pact with each other that if one or the other of us died, we would look out for each other's children." Michelle's face went out of focus. Anastasia didn't seem to understand the words she uttered. "Now you're practically a woman and obviously you won't need much lookin' after. But, well, anyway your Mom and I exchanged life policy information and stuff like that. She took care of you, Anastasia; you won't have to worry about money."

"I'm trying to tell you that your mother loved you very, very much." She continued to speak to a dazed Anastasia. "I know you already know that, but she left something for me to give to you. I'm going to give it to you now. I'm not sure what it is." Michelle in slow motion, reached into her bag and handed Anastasia an envelope. Her mother's familiar handwriting leapt out at her. It simply read "Anastasia." Then the envelope floated away. She tried to chase it, but she had legs that didn't seem to want to move. Anastasia pumped her legs, kicking the blankets that covered her.

She mumbled an incoherent sentence and thrashed again, continuing her journey in the throes of cinematic slumber. Suddenly, Anastasia found herself lying full length across her mother's bed, taking deep breaths, inhaling her scent. Then, she began to cry. She cried for what seemed like hours. Finally spent, not having another tear left, she forced herself from the bed. The bathroom was decorated with dozens of mirrors, attached at odd angles and in strange places. Anastasia rinsed her face and as she raised her head, for the slightest moment she thought she saw Leslie. She quickly turned to see if her mother was there. She wasn't, yet she was. Anastasia saw her reflected in her very own face. Startled, but pleased, she studied her face in the mirrors, examining it from various angles. Never before had she realized how much she resembled her mother.

Ever so slowly she watched herself as she undressed and stepped into the shower. She lathered herself with her mother's favorite bath gel. She shaved her legs and underarms using her mother's favorite toiletries. Somehow this little ritual made her feel better. But something was nagging at her. As if by magic the envelope Michelle had given her appeared in her hand. At the same time, abruptly, she was no longer in the shower.

"Oh, that's what's bothering me. I should read this," she said as she eagerly opened it as if it were a wonderful surprise.

Dear Anastasia:

Love of my life–I know you must be feeling so much pain and sadness right now because I am no longer with you. I wish I were there to tell you where I've gone. Death is a mystery but life, your life, should continue on with joy. I will forever be with you, watching everything that you do. I am there stroking your face ever so lightly, holding your hand, always guiding you on your path of life and adventure. You will miss me, but I am with you. When you wake in the morning and hear birds chirping, that is me urging you to wake up, sleepy head. When the sun's rays stroke your face and warm you, that is me giving you a hug. When something funny makes you laugh, I am there. When music you hear makes you tap your foot and bop your head, as I know you do, I am there. You see, my dear, sweet daughter, I've never left you. My spirit will guide you. Please smile for me now. Your life is just beginning, live it to the full as you know I did. Learn from me and always, always listen quietly to your heart. It will never lead you wrong. I go in peace, my daughter. I love you always.

Anastasia read the letter, then floated weightlessly across the room, staring blankly at the day, still holding the letter in a tight-fisted grasp. A sudden gust of wind caused the curtain to flutter and gently stroke her face. She brushed it aside. A bird appeared, close enough to touch. It stared at her. Startled, she wondered what was going on, thinking, this is weird, birds never do this. Then, it started to sing its own beautiful bird song, head twitching from side to side, gazing at her. It flew away as the clouds shifted and the sun burst through. Everything happened in milliseconds. Was this a sign from her mother? she wondered. Then the horrible fact that her mother was gone struck her. Abruptly, she screamed, "No! No! Noooooooo!"

The confines of her dream finally released her as she fell to the floor. She screamed and moaned, "No, Mama, no, Mama, come back, Mama. Nooooooooo!" Wildly thrashing, her head snapping back and forth as her eyes frantically searched her room, finally registering where she was.

Leslie rushed into her daughter's room, heart pounding furiously, gripped with fear at not knowing what was going on, why her daughter was screaming her name. It was two-thirty in the morning. Leslie feared an intruder was in Anastasia's room.

"What, baby? What? I'm here, baby." Leslie rushed in to find Anastasia sitting on the floor in a dazed stupor.

"It's all right," Leslie crooned as she gathered Anastasia in her arms, stroking and smoothing her tangled hair. "I'm here, baby. I'm here."

Slowly Anastasia opened her eyes. Her mind began to register that it had all been a dream. The sight of her mother brought a fresh bout of tears.

"I'm sorry, Mama, for everything I've done. I almost lost you. I'm sorry. I'll be good, Mom. I'll be good. Don't go away. Please, Mom, don't go away."

"Shhh, baby, it's okay. I'm not going anywhere. You had a dream is all. It's okay." She rocked her and soothed her sweat-soaked brow.

"You left me!" she wailed. "You left me."

"I'm here. Okay. Sit up, Anastasia. Sit up," she coaxed. "Don't cry," Leslie crooned. "I'm here."

Once she had calmed down, Leslie continued to stroke her hair, speaking to her in a gentle voice. "I guess you just had one heck of a nightmare, huh?"

"Yes," Anastasia weakly answered through hiccups, sniffs and more tears that slid down her smooth brown, youthful cheeks.

"Do you want to talk about it?"

"I'm scared to tell you 'cause it might jinx us."

"Was it about you and me?"

"It was more about you and I feel so bad for what happened in it. Gawd, I hope it doesn't come true." She shuddered.

"Perils always come at midnight. Did you know that?"

"What?"

"That's what I call a sleepless night or a night filled with nightmares that scare you half to death. Most of the time, whatever we're dreaming about, whatever danger we're fleeing from, is all in our heads. And you can make it go away."

"How?"

"Well, think real hard about what has happened to make you have such a scary dream. Did you watch a horror movie tonight?"

"No."

"Have you done something to someone that deep inside you feel bad about?"

Anastasia searched her mother's face as tears welled up again.

"I've been terrible to you. I know I have. Half the time I don't even understand why I'm so mad all the time. I've even felt like running away to keep from hurting you anymore."

"Now that would break my heart," she said as she hugged her tighter. "You don't have to run away. You just need to face your feelings. And we—you and I—need to talk about them and maybe we can figure out what's going on with you. But that can't happen if you keep pushing me away."

"I don't even know what to say. I'm so confused. I know I love you, Mom, but why do I act like I hate you, too?" Anastasia said, clearly ashamed as she lowered her eyes.

"Because I'm the closest person to you and it's easy to take out your frustrations on someone you see all the time. I remember being a confused teenager myself, and I know there're a lot of things going on inside of you. I'm sure your hormones are a big part of the problem. I realize you're frustrated with yourself—with your feelings—but what I'm having a hard time dealing with is disrespect—disrespect of yourself and me."

"I'm sorry."

"Me too, baby. But I'll forgive you if you forgive me."

"What'd you do, Mom?"

"Too many mistakes to count right now. I know you probably think I don't miss your daddy, but I do."

"You do?"

"I think about him all the time."

"I do too. When he first died I'd talk to him and I'd actually hear his voice, like he was talking back to me. But now, I . . . can't . . . hear . . . him . . . anymore! I feel like I'm going crazy."

"Oh, Anastasia, I'm so sorry that's happening, but believe me, you're not going crazy. Memories sometimes do fade with time, but you are your father's child. You are a part of him and he will never ever leave your heart. Never!"

Leslie paused and looked at her daughter, seeing the upturned nose and small lips that were so much like Darryl's. She continued to hug her, a smile lingering on her face. She could feel Anastasia's body warmth and for reasons she didn't understand, that made memories of Darryl come to her mind then, stark and clear.

"Do you remember the time when you slammed your finger in the car door?"

"Yep." She smiled, then, "I was screaming my head off until I saw that Daddy was crying too." She could see her daddy then, tears in his eyes as he took her little hand inside his large one and inspected it for serious injury. After he asked her to wiggle it and she could, he knew it wasn't broken. Then he put her tiny finger to his lips and kissed it softly.

"Do you know that there are only two times that I ever saw your father cry?"

"Really?"

"When they placed you in his arms after you were born and that day, the day you hurt your tiny little finger. He loved you so much. He loved both of us with all his heart. Do you remember the time . . ."

And the two women talked for nearly an hour, sharing their memories of Darryl.

"Do you feel better now? Are you ready to try to go back to sleep?" Leslie said as she began to help Anastasia off the floor and into her bed.

"Mom?"

"Hmmm?"

"Will you please go to the doctor and find out why you keep having those headaches?"

"I already did. I didn't get a chance to tell you about it because you've been so angry and distant. My doctor said my blood pressure is high, so he put me on medication—a little tiny water pill—to help bring it down. And he also said I needed to do more to modify and alter my stress level. Now that I'm working on."

"So you're okay, you're not going to die from it?"

"No. I don't think so. I'll do as the doctor ordered and I

should be fine. Okay?"

"Okay."

"Goodnight, Anastasia."

"Goodnight, Mom. I love you."

"Me too," Leslie said as she planted a kiss on the tip of her nose, the exact duplicate of her father's.

CHAPTER XXV

The jazz club was crowded when Leslie and Robert arrived. Almost every table was taken. Leslie realized then that she'd probably made a mistake by wearing one of her most uncomfortable pairs of shoes simply because they matched her outfit. Although they were sexy, she was in for a long night if she had to stand. She caught her reflection in the smoky mirrors of the club and was startled at what she saw. It was amazing how that happened to her from time to time. It was as if she'd forget completely all about how she looked. Her posture was elegant, refined, even regal. Her choice of a forest green slinky dress with green satin, sling-back, strappy heels had a stunning effect. Her hair had recently been restyled in a flowing bob, which softly framed her face. She and Anastasia had had a lot of fun experimenting with new shades of makeup. Her eyes, heavily outlined in black, were very dark and intense, giving her a look of elegant sophistication. Robert, not for the first time, told her she was beautiful, causing her cheeks to burn as she shyly accepted the compliment.

A couple who looked as though they were arguing quickly left a table near where they were standing. Robert swiftly grabbed it before anyone else had the chance. Thank God, Leslie thought, as she settled comfortably in the cane back chair. The club boasted a number of exotic drinks with clever names. Leslie selected a fruity drink that came in an hourglass-shaped container, which displayed the name of the club on it. A take-home souvenir. She glanced around the room to take in the sights and sounds of fellow jazz enthusiasts, until her eyes softly alighted upon Robert's face. He seemed to be scanning the contours of her face—her hair—her eyes.

"What?" Leslie asked with a sudden feeling of self-consciousness. Too much makeup, something in my teeth, she thought, what!

"Oh, nothing. Just admiring the woman I adore is all."

Leslie simply smiled, feeling at a total loss for appropriate words to utter back to him. The smooth sound of a saxophone played softly in the background as he reached for her hand across the white linen tablecloth.

"You look beautiful tonight; did I already tell you that?"

"Yes, Robert, you did. I'm starting to feel like I've never looked beautiful as much as you're telling me that tonight."

"You are always, always beautiful to me. It's just that tonight I feel something different in the air, something special."

"Hmm, I wonder what that could be. Maybe a full moon."

"No, maybe a full heart."

The stage lights went up and everyone began to applaud. The emcee announced that this evening was going to begin with a special twist. Tonight they were proud to present Erica, a local poet who would share some of her work—her love poetry—with the audience.

"Good evening, ladies and gentlemen." She paused dramatically, bowing at the waist.

"Love," she began, "is a universal subject that never draws a color line, that transcends the span of time. I love love. I mean the idea of being in love propels me forward each day. And because of that love and trying desperately to define its many muses and angles, I create a type of poetry that is simplistic but oh-so-real. I hope you enjoy the words I will share with you tonight as much as I enjoyed writing them."

The lights softly dimmed and someone brought a stool for her to sit upon. She took a deep breath and began to read:

Gentle Love

I've found gentle love. *You know the kind of love that covers and blankets you in the kind of warmth you remember when you were a child snuggling, deep and peacefully with your favorite blanket, being rocked ever so tenderly upon your grandmother's lap.*

Yes, I've found gentle love. The kind of love that cascades and penetrates your body like a warm shower—touching you in secret places, refreshing and cleansing—sensually guiding me to heights of ecstasy, refreshment—of being replenished to begin another day anew.

I've found gentle love. The kind of love that tickles my ears, hearing your deep, baritone voice that always reflects patience and joy, elicits laughter and advice that delicately guides me to new beginnings, fresh thoughts, the masculine point of view.

Yes, I've found gentle love. When we daily do a synchronized dance with each other around the kitchen, while making our bed, splashing each other while we wash the cars —we dance well together—you and I.

Numerous empty words like I love yous, or silly endearments like sweetheart, darling, honey—they are not uttered. But the I love yous are evident every time that electrical current passes between us, when your hand brushes mine, when we sit so close together that we inhale and thoroughly enjoy the scent of one another. When I feel sorrow or pain but see it reflected in the pool of tears that forms in your eyes—no I love yous are needed.

My gentle love searches across a crowded room to find this chocolate face and when our eyes meet—the exact same light comes on, the exact same smile crosses our faces and the exact same wink is shared. And from across the room your gentle love envelopes me like a cocoon and I feel, I know, I am deeply blessed.

When I am in trouble you never scold me or rebuke me. Instead you reach for my hand and carefully guide me to understanding, to that sometimes narrow path of peace and

Vicki Andrews

you show me how to find a way out of my self-made maze of confusion.

My gentle love. My gentle lover. Every breath I take I enjoy because of you. And if God needs me and takes me away—I hope I'll be wrapped in your embrace. Without fear I will go.

My gentle love. My gentle lover. I love you so.

She stood then, gestured grandly, crossed her arms over her chest, then blew a kiss to the crowd.

The audience sat in stunned silence, and then the stillness was shattered by a crescendo of applause that seemed to threaten to bring the roof down.

Robert squeezed Leslie's hand even tighter; his facial expression echoed her words. She knew Robert was her gentle love, her gentle lover. And at that very moment her heart seemed to swell with pride and joy, a gentle mixture of pure, unconditional love. Leslie wondered, not for the first time, how she'd been so lucky to find a man like this one. To find passion.

Erica remained standing while she smiled and waited for the crowd to cease clapping. Once everyone was quiet she said, "A very good friend of mine is in the house and the poem I just read was requested by him. You see, he's a businessman and he's helped me earn some serious money by investing in businesses. He's the only Black man I know who handles mergers and acquisitions, buys and sells companies, and he's very knowledgeable about investments."

Leslie glanced at Robert who continued gazing at the stage. Leslie thought, well, then she doesn't know my baby; he's a mergers and acquisitions specialist.

"Anyway, my friend asked me to read this particular poem tonight because he's here with a special friend. I wanted to change the wording to reflect that this is a man speaking to a woman, but he wanted me to read it just the way it was. He knew she would understand the meaning. Can you turn up the lights, please?"

The house lights came on. Leslie, stunned by the sudden bright lights, had trouble adjusting to the brightness.

246

"Robert, are you here?" Erica said. Leslie's mouth dropped open. Robert stood. He did not look at Leslie.

"Ms. Leslie, could you please also stand?" Erica continued. "Robert's got something he wants to say to you."

Embarrassed and surprised, Leslie shakily stood. The house lights dimmed as a spotlight shined on the two of them. She mouthed to him, "What are you doing?" and he just smiled. He quickly came around to her side of the table and bent to his knees. Leslie whispered, "Oh my God."

"Leslie, you are my gentle love, my gentle lover. It seems that all my life I've searched for a woman like you. You see, I knew deep in my heart that you existed but it took a while to find you. But now that I have, I'm not lettin' you go. So, I'd like to know—" he paused as someone handed him a miniature but beautiful broom wrapped in cream colored silk, adorned with flowers, lace, and tiny pearls.

". . . Would you jump this broom with me? Be my mate for life?"

She shook her head and her whole body trembled as tears swelled in her eyes. She was speechless. Her throat caught and she gulped, almost unable to breath. She just kept shaking her head back and forth. The audience waited in anticipatory silence.

She finally found her voice. She held out her arms to him. With a slight tremor she said, "Yes, from this day forward . . ."

He replied, "In sickness and in health."

"For richer or poorer," she chimed in, as one tear slid down her cheek.

"In good times and bad," he said, stroking her cheek, brushing the tear away.

She grabbed his hand and tenderly kissed it. She smiled, "I will love you for the rest of my life."

The crowd cheered and clapped and stood to applaud them and their love. The music started and the two of them began to dance their now familiar dance full of love, desire and now, peace.